The Blood of Patriots

PS Cleary

Table Of Contents

Acknowledgments

et me start out by saying I've never done this before. Perhaps if I hadn't resigned from my position in 2023, I may never have.

This project started because of a weird dream, occurring on successive nights after returning from Bergen County, New Jersey, from my father's funeral. It's about two people I didn't know. After having the dream a second night, my wife had been up reading. She told me that I was thrashing in my sleep and asked if I was okay. I told her about the dream. My wife responded by saying I should write about it. "Start a book," she said, "lay out an outline, a timeline." It was 4:30 a.m. when we talked about this, so naturally, I rolled over to go back to sleep.

Over the next few days, I laid out themes and a timeline and started to take pen to paper, developing characters and what they looked like, starting with the main character. I defined situational aspects of the story. Some will find similarities to me within Bill only because I tried to insert what my mindset might have been if I were one of these characters. I wanted folks to appreciate that element as they read it or tried to infer which character is this person in real life. The entirety of the story and the characters are fictional.

In addition, I'd like to thank Mr. and Mrs. Roberts, aka the Scooters, our very good friends. They helped by reading, offering suggestions, and providing encouragement throughout this process. They also fact-checked the military and weaponry aspects. They've been instrumental in helping to develop and vet alternatives to what I had initially envisioned.

Next, I want to thank Patrick Trotti, a young man I've known since he was four. I remember he was a sports encyclopedia as a kid, and he has grown up to be an author himself. His mother, Sharon, is one of our dearest friends. We're proud of the individual that Patrick has become. It was Patrick who first offered to review the material. He agreed to give it its first real read-through. Honestly, I wasn't sure I had anything of value, but he was very encouraging, providing terrific insights. The foreword to the book was developed from the feedback he provided. He also gave me some sage advice on the publishing process.

I want to thank Barbara Seith, an author in her own right, for her candid feedback on the third draft. She offered insights into the plot, dialogue, and character definitions.

I'd like to thank Rob Scheinerman and Suzanne Reyes for their encouragement and review of the material when I asked for it. I'll always be grateful for their feedback, enthusiasm, and support.

Lastly, I can't thank my wife enough throughout this time. She's read this material several times and listened to me read it out loud from chapter to chapter. She was instrumental in helping me develop the timeline, peppering me with questions about the characters and situations. She wanted to understand each character's motivation and why I felt the character's reaction was appropriate in those situations. We didn't always agree, but she was helpful in keeping me balanced. Lastly, she has been my love and support since we met. I only hope that she feels the same way after 30+ years. Lord knows. I've made it challenging, to say the least.

Prologue - 1922

It was a cool, rainy November morning on the backroads of Kilmihill, County Clare, Ireland. Big Jack Quinn was leading his first mission to destroy a bridge used to supply the British forces in the area. Big Jack was planting the dynamite on the bridge's piers while Paddy O'Connell, his trusted confidant, was setting up the wires needed to attach to the trigger. As Big Jack placed the dynamite, Paddy handed down the wires, then ran the spools of wire to a spot just off the bridge. It was 5:30 a.m., with a light rain making it seem even darker on the road. Daybreak would be at 6:30. Paddy received notice from the local brigade commander that a large convoy of trucks was due to pass over this bridge at 6:30, so time was of the essence.

At 6:00, Big Jack finished placing the dynamite on the piers of the bridge. Paddy was connecting the spools of wire together; attaching them to the trigger would be his last step. In the distance, Paddy could see local brigade members taking up defensive positions along the large creek embankments, moving into position to provide cover as well as to eliminate as many of the British soldiers as they could.

At 6:15, Big Jack and Paddy weren't in position yet as they continued to inspect the connection of wires and leads to the dynamite on the bridge. They finished their examination; now, all there was to do was wait.

As they waited for the convoy, Big Jack recalled the prior evening's conversation with his wife, Maggie. The previous night, they had spoken about what Maggie should do if something happened to Big Jack. As they enjoyed a shepherd's pie for supper—a treat, as times had been tough for all of Ireland—Big Jack talked about the revolution, as well as the toll it was taking on his family. He felt the struggle was just, but being at war constantly was weighing on him.

Big Jack told Maggie, "We need to control our destiny in Ireland, providing for a better future for our children."

Maggie replied, "I don't give a shite about the cause. I need you to be safe. Your children need their father; I need my husband."

Big Jack smiled. "Maggie, my dear, it'll all be fine."

Big Jack was John Andrew Quinn—a farmer, a patriot, and a father. Big Jack was an imposing figure: 6'4", 250 pounds, with red hair, blue eyes, and a welcoming, soft smile. Big Jack was as strong as an ox, with broad shoulders. He was smart and hardworking, but he was committed to an Ireland free of British rule. Maggie, his wife, was Mary Margaret Dalton. She was a petite lady, standing 5'4" tall and weighing 120 pounds, with dark brown hair and deep, coffee-colored eyes. She was raised on a nearby sheep farm, not far from the schoolhouse where Big Jack and Maggie went. Maggie was determined to keep her family safe. She was smart, funny, and passionate about her family. Big Jack and Maggie had three children.

Their first child was John Andrew Quinn, Jr. He was known as Little Jack, eventually Uncle Jack to those who knew him. He was born in 1921. Little Jack was a fine boy with red hair and blue eyes, like his father.

Their second child was Michael Anthony Quinn, known as Mick, born in 1922. Mick was a little guy with light blonde hair.

Maggie was pregnant with her third when the mission was planned. She was six months into her third pregnancy in as many years. Their third child would be a son, William Patrick Quinn, known to the family as Paddy. He was born and died in 1923, two days after his birth. He died of a severe respiratory infection, which doctors didn't react fast enough to. Throughout Maggie's life, she always spoke of the day that she'd get to be with her baby boy.

Big Jack told Maggie, "Whatever happens to me, make sure our children are looked after, get them proper schooling, and never let them join this fight. I'm fighting for them so they'll be able to choose their own future in freedom."

Maggie nodded, rocking in her chair as they sat by the warm fire. These were the thoughts running through Big Jack's head as he lay in wait for the British convoy. It was his family that was the center of his mind, not the mission. It was 6:30, and still no convoy.

Suddenly, Johnny McFarland waved from the riverbed. *They're* coming down the long, winding road. The Clonderlaw bridge was curved, with roads leading to and from the bridge with multiple S-turns, aligned with rock walls on each side of the road. It was very difficult to see anyone coming until they were right upon you.

As Johnny got his men in position, Paddy and Big Jack took cover. Suddenly, Big Jack noticed one of the charges had come loose, so they frantically tried to reattach the last switch. The first truck was bearing down—quickly. They saw the headlights just over the bridge when Paddy yelled, "Got it!"

Paddy had connected the last wire. The first truck was now in the middle of the bridge, where Big Jack had his hand on the trigger.

He looked at Paddy. "Ready? Fire!"

BOOM, BOOM, BOOM, BOOM, BOOM! The charges went off almost simultaneously. The bridge was destroyed. The first three trucks that had made it onto the bridge were now lying at the bottom of the large creek bed, engulfed in flames. The brigade moved into place. Big Jack heard muffled gunshots down at the bottom of the creek. The brigade wasn't taking prisoners.

The fourth truck didn't make it to the bridge but was able to back up to a spot where they were able to regroup.

When the explosions occurred, Big Jack was blown back approximately 25 feet from his original position, with blood coming out of his ears as a result of the percussion blast. This was why the gunshot sounds were muffled.

By 7:00, the mission was complete, with all the boys heading back to their safe houses to celebrate their victory, as well as hide out from the British authorities.

Chapter 1
1922 – Ireland

It was 5:00 a.m. on the family farm in the village of Knock, County Clare, Ireland. It was the day after the Clonderlaw Bridge attack. Big Jack was up early, tending to the peat fire before heading out to the shed.

Maggie, Jack, and Mick were still asleep. Mick was only two months old and had a touch of colic, so Maggie wasn't getting much sleep. Big Jack decided he'd start his long day, making his way out to the shed and bringing in more peat to keep the fire going.

When he returned inside, Maggie had made her way into the kitchen, still sleepy, asking, "Would you like some breakfast, love?"

Big Jack smiled. "Please, love, something quick. I need to get out into the field early."

Maggie walked over to Big Jack and kissed him, then headed to the icebox to grab some cheese and milk for tea. She had put the kettle on before Big Jack returned with the peat, hearing it now whistling behind her. Maggie poured two cups of tea while Big Jack ate the cheese very quickly, along with the brown bread Maggie had made the day before.

When Big Jack finished, he said, "Thanks, love. I'm heading out now."

Maggie didn't say anything. She smiled, grabbing her husband's empty plate and heading over to the sink to wash them. Maggie heard the door behind her click as Big Jack left for the shed.

As Big Jack made his way back to the shed, he noticed a shadow near the tractor. Cautiously, he approached the tractor with his trusty hunting knife in his hand.

As he got closer, Paddy whispered, "Big Jack, it's me, Paddy."

Big Jack asked, "Why are you here so early?"

Paddy replied, "The Constabulary knows what happened on the bridge. They're coming for us."

Big Jack said, "How do you know that? Look, come into the shed. I need to get the feeders loaded up."

Paddy quietly followed him into the shed.

Once inside, Paddy said, "Our brigade commander says we have an informer."

Big Jack said, "Who?"

Paddy replied, "Billy Shaughnessy. One of our informants at the Constabulary saw Billy talking to their commander two days before the attack. He showed up yesterday afternoon, appearing to have been beaten. When asked what happened, Billy said, 'I'm fine. I just slipped in the shed, knocked over a rake, and it hit me in the head.' The bruising does not line up with his story."

Big Jack asked, "So now what?"

Paddy said, "We've gotten the order."

At first, Big Jack didn't say anything, mulling it over in his mind. It was hard to believe Billy was a traitor; it did not add up. Billy was also a friend; his dad passed away about five years ago, and now he was having a rough go of it on his farm.

Paddy, looking for a response, asked, "We need to take care of this quickly."

Big Jack replied, "Are you sure that it's Billy? He hates the English as much as we do."

Paddy nodded. "Yes. Our inside man confirmed it."

Big Jack asked, "When do we leave? Do you know where he is? I thought he was at one of the safe houses."

Paddy said, "The brigade commander approved him to go home, so he's alone, at home, right now."

Big Jack nodded, then headed into the tool room, removing a panel of wood and retrieving weapons for them both.

Handing a weapon to Paddy, Big Jack said, "Can't believe he betrayed us."

Paddy nodded. "Let's get going. Perhaps we can get there before daybreak."

Big Jack nodded, motioning toward the shed door. Before leaving, he placed the panel of wood back to cover up his weapons cache. Only Maggie knew of its existence in the shed, mainly for her protection. Paddy and Big Jack left the shed, taking the tractor to the northwest corner of the farm. Big Jack made a few stops along the way to lay some feed for the cattle.

Paddy asked, "Why are you stopping so much?"

Big Jack replied, "If we know about Billy, perhaps he knows we're coming. This looks like I'm laying feed, then just saying hello to a neighbor. Both sides of our conflict have more leaks than a sinking ship."

Paddy, not considering the stealth of it all, said, "Okay."

The next stop was the feeder station nearest Billy's farm, where both got off the tractor very close to the fence. Big Jack laid the feed, and then both proceeded over the fence. Once they were in Billy's field, they split up, where Paddy went up the right side of the path while Big Jack pushed up on the left side of the path, each having stone walls to provide cover. Billy's farmhouse was 100 meters from the fence line between the farms.

As they approached the main house, it was clear all the lights were out, strange as most farms were quite active this time of day. As they made their way to the front door, Paddy peered in the parlor window, noticing the house seemed empty; all the furniture was gone from the living room. They made their way inside, heading toward the kitchen. Big Jack took the lead spot while Paddy followed, covering them from the rear.

As Big Jack entered the kitchen, Billy was waiting at the kitchen table, his gun in his right hand. As Big Jack entered the kitchen, Billy shot him in the chest. Big Jack was dead instantly. Paddy attempted to enter the room, but Billy fired upon him twice, lodging two bullets in the doorway's trim. After the second shot, Paddy fled out the front door back to Big Jack's tractor.

As Paddy made his way out the door, Billy came to the front step, yelling, "You goddamn fuckers!"

Paddy made his way back to the tractor under the cover of darkness.

Chapter 2
1922 – Ireland

Paddy made it back to Big Jack's farmhouse, unfollowed by Billy. When Paddy pulled the tractor over to the covered shed, Maggie was outside, tending to some laundry. It was daybreak. The moment Maggie saw Paddy, she began to cry, knowing Big Jack wasn't coming home. Paddy turned off the motor and went to Maggie to comfort her, but she was inconsolable.

She screamed, "How did this happen?"

Paddy simply replied, "He died trying to eliminate a traitor."

Maggie sobbed momentarily, then began to think. She needed to see the local priest and set up Big Jack's funeral.

Maggie asked Paddy, "Can you stay with the children? I need to make the arrangements."

Paddy said, "The brotherhood will take care of all that. Be with your children. I'll manage it through the brigade commander."

Paddy then left, heading down the main driveway.

Maggie finished hanging the laundry before returning, now contemplating what to do next. Her instincts were to protect her children and make sure they didn't follow a similar path, honoring Big Jack's wishes. She thought maybe she'd sell the farm and move away to America. Perhaps it was time to leave Ireland. It wouldn't be an easy journey with three small children. She also thought this was her home. She would need to figure out how to run the place on her own. The children were little, so understanding the death of their father would be left to the stories they'd hear from Maggie or Big Jack's mates over the years.

Word spread quickly about Big Jack in the village. Neighbors came calling with food, something to help ease the suffering. Paddy returned to the IRA safe house to inform the brigade commander what had happened. When Paddy got there, the brigade commander was waiting on him anxiously, wanting his briefing. The brigade commander was a tall, slender fellow by the name of Seamus Corcoran, in his early 30s, having been fighting for the cause since 1915.

When Paddy got into his office, he offered this brief: "Commander, we couldn't carry out our mission. Billy laid in wait. We lost Big Jack. I barely made it out alive. Please, I'd like to go back and finish the job."

Seamus said, "Sorry to hear all that. Big Jack was a good man; he'll be missed, of course. Why didn't you stay to finish it? Billy's going to be on the run now."

As these words were floating in the air, the commander's aide came in. "Sir, we have a report that Billy has left town. He was spotted on the train to Dublin, riding with English soldiers."

The commander shouted, "Jesus, Mary, and Joseph! Get word to our friends in Dublin right away. Let them know we want him taken out immediately."

The aide nodded, leaving the room to deliver the commander's wishes to the Dublin brigade.

The commander asked, "Does Big Jack's family know?"

Paddy replied, "Yes, sir, they do. I told Maggie this morning. I also told her we'd handle the arrangements for his burial."

The commander replied, "All right, get it set up. Hopefully, we catch this bastard before he gets to Dublin. Anything else?"

Paddy replied, "No, sir."

Paddy turned and then left the room. He went over to the church to find Father McLoughlin, the parish leader—a fine man if there ever was one. He supported the cause, granting absolution accordingly. He was well-liked by the congregation, but his sermons were too long and exaggerated.

When Paddy got to the parish office, it was as if Father McLoughlin was waiting for him.

When Father McLoughlin closed the door behind them, he asked, "How's Maggie?"

Paddy replied, "Father, as well as can be expected. I told her we'd take care of the funeral arrangements."

Father replied, "I'll pay her a visit later to pay my respects. I'll have the parish office set up the church for the funeral services. I assume you've got security set for this?"

Paddy replied, "Yes, we'll cover that. Father, I must head over to the morgue to get his body ready. I'm sorry, but I need to run."

Father said, "I understand, my son. God bless you."

With that, Paddy left, walking across the street and into the mortician's place of business. Mr. O'Shea was the mortician.

When he saw the door close behind Paddy, he said, "Paddy, my boy, I'm terribly sorry to hear about Big Jack."

Paddy replied, "Aye, thanks, Mr. O'Shea. We need to get his body at the Shaughnessy farm. He should be in the hallway leading into the kitchen."

Mr. O'Shea said, "We'll send the truck up there to fetch him. We'll take good care of him, Paddy. I promise."

Paddy answered, "Thanks. I better start working on the security for this."

Paddy left. Mr. O'Shea went to his truck, heading for the Shaughnessy farm. Within two hours, Big Jack's body was retrieved. Upon returning, Mr. O'Shea began the process to make Big Jack presentable for an open-coffin viewing. Fortunately, the gunshot wounds were to the chest.

Within four hours, Paddy was back at the funeral parlor, picking out Big Jack's casket. He went upstairs with Mr. O'Shea to go over the viewing parlor. Everything was in order: Big Jack in the center of the back wall, a white and green shamrock flower arrangement on his left, a white and green cross flower arrangement on his right, and the Irish flag draped over his coffin. Both men stood quietly, not wanting to disturb the silence. After a few nods between them, Paddy left, heading out the front door of the funeral parlor. The service would be the next day.

The service started at 9:00 a.m. with a blessing at the funeral parlor then a full mass at the church. Then, back to Big Jack's farm for the burial. Paddy had arranged to have a grave dug on the farm the afternoon after the incident. As for the viewing, many of the local commanders came to pay their respects to the grieving widow. Promises were made that they'd get those responsible for this tragedy. Maggie said almost nothing to the guests.

All she could muster was, "Thank you for coming. Jack would have appreciated it."

Maggie was still in shock. Retribution for the cause did not interest her; she wanted her Big Jack back, wondering who she could see about that.

Father McLaughlin came in, and the place fell silent. He began with a reading, then a second reading, then the blessing.

As the father wrapped up, he said, "Now we'll make our way to the church."

The funeral viewers made their way out of the parlor while the pallbearers made their way to the casket. Mr. O'Shea closed the casket, then nodded at Paddy—the signal the casket was ready to be transported to the church. The pallbearers picked up the casket, placed it on their shoulders, and made their way to the church.

As they were walking over to the church, Kevin McFarland said, "I bet Big Jack could use a whiskey."

All the pallbearers smiled, even though they were carrying a friend to lay him to rest.

As the pallbearers entered the church, it was clear the church was packed. There were more people at the church than at the funeral parlor.

Father McLaughlin said the mass and thankfully gave a short homily.

Father finished the mass by stating, "To you, O Lord, we commend the soul of John Andrew Quinn, your servant: in the sight of this world, he is now dead; in your sight, may he live forever. Forgive whatever sins he committed through human weakness, and in your goodness, grant him everlasting peace. We ask this through Christ our Lord."

As Father McLaughlin wrapped up the service, the pallbearers returned to the sides of the coffin, picked it up, and then headed to the funeral car. Big Jack would be making his final trip home. Father McLaughlin followed out to the car.

He told the gathered congregation, "The burial services will be on the Quinn farm. The family will welcome guests after the burial."

From there, the congregation made its way up to the farm. It was only two miles, a good stretch of the legs. The pallbearers rode with the casket, making it to Big Jack's farm well ahead of those walking up from the village.

An hour later, Father McLaughlin committed Big Jack to the earth while they bowed their heads in deference to their fallen brother. *Big Jack would have been impressed with the turnout,* Paddy thought. So many came to pay their respects.

After the burial, folks gathered quietly in the parlor of Big Jack's house. Some shared fun stories about Big Jack over a pint. Maggie, for the most part, stayed in the kitchen, talking with her mum. No one recalled her coming out to speak with anyone. Who could blame her after all that had happened?

As the pallbearers were sharing a pint, the commander appeared at the front door. He strode into the house like a Viking and came right up to Paddy.

He said, "Boys, we got him on the train to Dublin."

They all took a deep breath. To be honest, it was bittersweet. It was great avenging their fallen comrade, but many knew Billy since he was a young lad. It was hard to reconcile what had happened.

Suffice it to say, it was a tough time in Ireland.

Chapter 3
January 1940 – Ireland

Big Jack's son, Little Jack, was now 19 years old, having been arguing with his mother most of the day about his decision. Little Jack was joining the IRA, even though Little Jack wasn't so little anymore. Jack wanted to follow in his father's footsteps and fight for Irish independence. His mother told him his father had been against any of his sons being involved in this cause. Big Jack wanted his children to be educated and have productive careers. But Uncle Paddy would tell a very different story to Jack, glamorizing him with fictional stories, romanticizing the struggle, and embellishing Big Jack's record to push his eldest into the cause. It seemed Paddy was intent on drawing him in, seemingly casting a spell on Jack, by Maggie's account. It was clear Jack had made up his mind to join.

At one point in the argument, Maggie grabbed a wooden spoon, smacking Little Jack in the head. "Your father never wanted this for you. Do you have shite for brains?"

Little Jack just smiled. "Mum, it'll be fine. Uncle Paddy said he'd look after me."

Maggie returned fire. "You're not listening. Your Da never wanted this for you. To be honest, your da never trusted Uncle Paddy, nor should you."

Jack was unfazed as he saw this as a rite of passage. Mick sat quiet, taking it all in. If he was going to choose sides, he would always side with his mother. He wasn't a fan of Uncle Paddy, either.

The arguing continued throughout breakfast, and then Jack said, "I'm heading outside to get the feeders stocked. I'm not sure there's much more to discuss."

As Jack's words hung in the air, there was a knock on the front door. Maggie went to the front door, sighing as she peered through the window. It was Paddy. She felt obliged to open the door.

When she opened the door, she said, "Paddy, what's brought you here? Little Jack's told me the news. I'm not happy. Big Jack never wanted this for any of the children. Both of you sat in my kitchen, speaking those very words, days before Jack was killed."

Paddy was a little taken aback by all this. "Jack's not little anymore. He chose this path of his own free will."

Maggie shot back, "You're full of shite. He's told me you've told him stories about how his da wanted him to join up. We both know Jack never wanted this for him."

Paddy smiled. "What do you want me to do, Maggie? He's a grown man who can make his own choices."

Maggie couldn't argue the point; Jack wasn't a little boy anymore.

She thought for a second. "Promise me you'll protect him. You don't have a family of your own. Look after him like he was your son."

Paddy nodded. "Aye. Will do. Have you considered my offer, Maggie?"

Paddy had risen in the ranks of the IRA, now the local brigade commander. He could keep the promise to Maggie. However, the real purpose of Paddy's visit has now been revealed, as two weeks earlier, Paddy proposed marriage.

Maggie had been alone with her two boys for 17 years since Jack's death. Paddy never married. Some considered him a good catch, but

Maggie was never sweet on him. She never encouraged him, either. She always remembered the night Big Jack told her, in their living room over a late-night whiskey, that he never trusted Paddy. While Paddy saw Big Jack as his brother, Big Jack thought of him as an IRA associate, never a true friend. Maggie sometimes wondered if Paddy was behind Jack's death, letting him lead the way at Shaughnessy's place that fateful day. The words hung in the air while Paddy became anxious at her silence.

Finally, Maggie replied, "Still mulling it over. Be patient. I won't be bullied into anything. I don't need a husband; the question is, do I *want* a husband."

Paddy, undeterred, asked, "Is there anything I can do to help you make a decision?"

Maggie turned to close the door. "No."

Paddy accepted this momentary defeat, heading toward the shed. Maggie wasn't a woman to be pushed into marriage. Little Jack was loading up the feeders, getting ready to head into the fields. However, when he saw Paddy, he stopped, hopped off the tractor, and made his way toward Paddy.

When they met, Jack said, "It's nice to see you. What are you doing here?"

Paddy replied, "Just checking on all of you."

Jack pointed at the tractor. "Was heading out to the fields. Need something?"

Paddy replied, "I've got your first mission."

Jack said, "What is it? Did you tell me, Mum?"

Paddy shook his head no. "Focus, lad. I'd never tell your mother about a mission. The mission is to blow up the Clonderlaw Bridge. The Black and Tans are loading up in town; as you know, that's the main road. We've got dynamite for the job. Just need a good man to get it done."

Jack nodded. "When?"

Paddy replied, "Next couple of days. We'll assemble the men tomorrow night at the pub."

Jack asked, "Anything else? I need to get the feeders out to the fields."

Paddy said, "No, tomorrow night. Meet me at the pub. We'll talk a little treason."

Jack smiled, heading back to the tractor. Before long, he disappeared into the fields. Only the puffs of smoke from the tractor could be seen from a distance.

Paddy turned, heading down the driveway toward the Shannon River. Paddy sat by the water, plotting the upcoming mission. Paddy knew they had dynamite, just waiting on the chargers to set it off. Then, he turned his attention to the men needed. Surprisingly, the Black and Tans never had a presence by this bridge. It made no sense to leave the bridge undefended. Paddy considered this an advantage, plotting how to attack the bridge. What he needed was a plan.

The Shannon River is vast, from the Grand Waterways all the way to County Limerick. It was a freshwater source and included good fishing, swimming, and even boating. The water is very clean, as it hasn't been used as a commercial waterway. Paddy always found it peaceful sitting near the edge—a good spot to clear one's head.

Paddy played out the game plan in his mind, concluding they'd need six men for the mission. Jack would be one of the men. Mick Donovan would lead the mission. Paddy sat by the river for an hour, taking in the peaceful sounds of the waterway. After the hour was up, he headed back to his office in the village.

When he walked in, the office personnel stood up and came to attention but said nothing. Paddy went directly to his office without saying anything to his staff, as he was deep in thought. Paddy closed the door behind him and took out a map. He outlined the plan from his head onto the map to have something for the team.

After 15 minutes of mapping it out, he opened his door, saying, "Run down to Mick Donovan. Tell him he should come straight away."

The runner nodded. "Yes, Commander."

And with that, he was off to find Mick. About 30 minutes later, the staffer showed up with Mick Donovan.

Mick entered the commander's office without knocking. "You sent for me?"

Paddy replied, "Got a mission. Clonderlaw Bridge must be destroyed."

Mick nodded. "Do you have a plan you want me to review?"

Paddy smiled. "Yes. Those British bastards have never protected the bridge, despite it being the main artery, since rebuilding it in the early 1920s. We are going to blow it to kingdom come. I outlined the areas where we can place the dynamite. It's close to how we did it back in 1921, but I wanted your opinion, as you're leading this."

Mick looked over the plan. "Would have planned it similarly. Need six men. I've got five, but I need one more. Ever since Terrence was killed, we've been short a man."

Paddy looked at Mick. "Jack Quinn's your sixth. I know he's new to all this, but he needs the training. He must cut his teeth now."

Mick replied, "Jack's a good lad. We'll get him schooled up."

Paddy smiled. "Thanks. We'll meet at the pub tomorrow night to outline the plan for the fellas. Will you get word to the five? I've already told Jack. That'll be all."

Mick replied, "Yes, sir."

Chapter 4
January 1940 - Ireland

The following evening was damp as it turned dark. A light rain began to fall in the village of Knock. It was 7:30 p.m., and all the men were assembled—time to unveil the plan.

Paddy arrived at 7:30 on the dot, heading to the back room in the pub. The men were commiserating when Paddy emerged through the door. As soon as Paddy was noticed, the room fell silent.

Paddy said with a slight smirk, "Fellas, we're going to talk a little treason. Mick's going to walk you through the plan. Save your questions till the end."

Everyone nodded and said, "Yes, sir."

Mick stood up next to Paddy, outlining the plan. He told them the target was the Clonderlaw Bridge and that he expected to hit it two nights from tonight. Then, he went into where the safe houses were when it was over. Mick went into excruciating detail, outlining every specific task for each participant.

Mick spoke for almost 30 minutes, ending with, "Okay, boys. That's the plan. Questions?"

At first, the group sat quietly, looking over the battle plan and contemplating their respective parts.

Mick asked again, "Questions? This is the time to ask, not when we're executing."

Jack was intently waiting for anyone to ask a question as he was trying to contain his excitement for the mission.

Finally, Joseph McTiernay asked, "Mick, this is the rally point? Why wouldn't it be here? Aren't we exposed to any return fire?"

Mick nodded. "We considered that. Perhaps we have that as our secondary rally point. At the time of the strike, the first rally point should have the cover of darkness."

Joseph replied, "Aye, sounds grand."

Finally feeling the release of the first question, Jack then asked, "What happens if we find they're surveilling the bridge?"

Paddy looked a little annoyed by the question, but Mick seemed to understand what he meant.

Mick said, "We're planning to recon the bridge before we strike. So far, the enemy hasn't paid any attention to the bridge since your da blew it up 20 years ago. We've got you covered, lad, don't worry."

Little Jack smiled. "Got it, thanks."

Paddy said, "Okay, fellas, that's the plan. Tomorrow night, we will meet here to review it one final time, and then we will get into positions for Friday morning. Anything else?"

The men at the table shook their heads no, while Jack was in awe, now knowing he was part of this brotherhood, doing his part to fight for the great struggle.

The next evening, the men assembled at 10:00 p.m., the planned meeting time in the same room. Mick outlined the battle plan. Paddy didn't come to the meeting, as he trusted Mick to finalize any adjustments to the plan. Mick took the fellas through the battle plan one last time. Nobody offered any questions.

When Mick finished, he said, "Okay, fellas. Let's get this done. Everyone back to the safe houses when it's done."

With that, the men stood up to begin supplying up for the mission—chargers, sticks of dynamite. Several men would be armed, providing covering fire if necessary. As such, these men tended to their weapons. At midnight, the men left the Fisherman's Hut pub through the back entrance, heading to the Clonderlaw Bridge. The bridge was seven miles away, which gave the boys an hour to get in position. Placing the dynamite would take a couple of hours, so the darkness would be critical to staging the bridge.

At 1:00 a.m., the men were at the bridge. Mick worked with Joseph, lining the bridge with dynamite, while their two runners were Jack and Seamus McTiernay. As the four men reached the farthest section of the bridge, two British soldiers were walking onto the bridge. At first, the British soldiers didn't see the four men until Seamus tripped over the curb of the bridge. At this point, their cover was blown.

The two British soldiers began to shout, "Stop! Who goes there?"

Mick whispered to the men, "Stay quiet. It'll draw them closer."

Jack was surprised at how calm he felt, then suddenly—a shot. The British soldier saw Seamus moving on the ground and shot at him. He missed, but the bullet ricocheted off the pavement, striking Jack in the leg. Mick and Joseph attempted to take firing positions. However, after hearing the first shot, the British had reinforced the two on the bridge. Soon, the fellas might be outgunned.

Mick gave the order to pull back. Joseph leaped off the bridge into the water below. Mick pulled back along the wall, even returning fire while he made his way back across the bridge. Jack attempted to crawl to the side of the bridge, but the British soldiers were upon him too quickly. Seamus attempted to fight back but was overmatched without a gun. He took out his hunting knife, but one of the British soldiers shot him in the head before Seamus could ever get close to him. The other British soldier, one of the original two, made his way toward Jack. Jack saw his comrade's fate, deciding it was easier to fight another day. His leg was wounded badly. Jack surrendered. The only good to come from his surrender was that the British soldiers stopped pursuing the other men.

Jack was put on a stretcher and had his hands tied to its wooden arms. Jack was placed in the ambulance and then taken to the British medical stand.

On the way over to the medical stand, a British officer named Montague asked, "So, who was with you on the bridge?"

Jack said nothing, prompting the British officer to begin punching him in the ribs.

He said, "Answer me, son, or we're going to make this rough on you."

Jack became defiant. "I've got nothing to say."

Montague continued the beating until they got to the roadside hospital.

A doctor greeted the truck, yelling, "Montague, hit the prisoner again, and I'll take it up with the colonel. Let me tend to his wounds, then you can interrogate him."

Montague, recognizing the doctor outranked him, backed off. The orderlies took Jack into the tent. The doctor wore a white coat with white linen scrubs. Jack couldn't tell what his name was.

When the doctor got him on the table, they cut off Jack's clothing to examine him. Jack had blood on his shirt, as well as his jacket, from wiping his hands on them after applying pressure to the wound in his leg. Despite the situation, the doctor was thorough in his examination. His compassion is something that has always stuck with Jack. After the examination, the doctor removed the bullet fragment from Jack's left leg.

The doctor asked, "Want the fragment as a souvenir?"

Jack moved his head no but said nothing.

Montague reappeared, asking the doctor, "So, when can I speak to him?"

The doctor said, "A couple of hours. Remember, he's just a kid."

Montague interrogated Jack for several hours, but Jack didn't crack under the pressure. When Jack went in front of the magistrate, he told the high court he had nothing to say. In the end, Jack was arrested, tried, and convicted, sentenced to a five-year stretch.

Chapter 5
September 1940 - Ireland

It was Easter 1940 when Mick Quinn went to Limerick Jail to visit his brother, Jack. Jack was serving his five-year sentence for his attempt to blow up the Clonderlaw Bridge. Mick made the trip every two weeks to visit him and see if he needed anything. However, this visit would be his last. Mick had received a work visa, so he was emigrating to the United States. His mother's brother, Anthony, had agreed to sponsor him as well. Anthony was working on a construction site, and Mick got a job.

Mick never spoke to Jack about his plans, so he figured the conversation with his brother wouldn't go well. When Jack appeared in the seating area, Mick greeted Little Jack with a hug.

Mick said, "Great to see you, big brother."

Jack smiled. "How was the trip down?"

Jack was always interested in the logistics, the planning, and the execution of just about everything.

Mick said, "Aye, fine. Hit some rain along the way, but it was nothing."

Jack asked, "How's Mum?"

Mick replied, "Fine, just worried about you. What's wrong? You look terrible."

Jack whispered, "Hunger strike. The inside brigade commander wants to protest the deplorable conditions here. We're treated like animals. There's only one guard who treats us like human beings."

Mick looked horrified. "How long will it be?"

Jack replied, "No idea. If anything happens, you'll need to look after Mum."

Mick peered over at him. "Aye, I'll take care of it. Got something else to tell you. It's something I've been thinking about over the past few months but never had the courage to bring it up to you while you're in here."

Jack interrupted. "America?"

Mick replied, "Yes. Uncle Anthony sponsored me, so I've got a job when I arrive."

Jack responded, "That's terrific, little brother."

Mick then asked, "Jack, if I sponsored you, would you come to live with us in America? I plan to sponsor Mum as soon as I can."

Jack calmly replied, "I would. Without you or Mum, nothing's left for me here. I could sell the land, perhaps buy a cottage in America."

Mick was relieved Jack was taking this very well.

Mick said, "Jack, please be careful in here. I know you think you can trust some of the other inmates, but be cautious. Remember, we need to have a pint as soon as you get to America."

Jack replied, "Appreciate your concern. I'll try my best. When are you leaving?"

Mick said, "Saturday. This will be my last visit here."

Jack nodded and smiled but didn't say anything at first. There was nothing else to say. Mick made his plans, good for him.

Jack finally said, "Thanks for coming to tell me. I wish you all the luck in the world."

What Mick hadn't appreciated was what time it was. Jack and Mick had two more minutes before the visit was over. Both got up, giving each other a long hug. Unbeknownst to Mick, Jack placed a package in Mick's pocket without the guards noticing.

One guard came over. "Knock off the grab ass. No touching of the inmates."

Mick responded, "I'm saying goodbye to my brother before heading to America."

The guard simply said, "Your visit is concluded."

With that, Jack was escorted back inside the prison. When Jack reached the gate, he turned, waving at Mick with a slight tear in his eye. Mick waved back, then headed out of the prison. Mick made his way to the train station and then boarded his train about an hour after leaving Limerick Jail.

After boarding the train, Mick reached into his pockets, looking for his pack of cigarettes. However, he found the package Jack had slipped into his pocket. The package was wrapped in brown paper, with twine tied over it. It looked like a Christmas present. Mick opened the package, revealing a bible. Mick began to wonder why Jack would give him a bible. Mick opened the cover, where he found a note from Jack.

The note said, "Mick, I knew you'd head to America sooner rather than later. Please take this as a reminder of your big brother. Also, spend the money in here wisely."

Mick was somewhat shocked. *But what money?* Mick flipped through the pages. When he got to page 24, he noticed the pages had been cut out to fit quid inside. Mick quickly closed the bible, as he didn't want to be waving quid about. Mick finally found his cigarettes, lighting one. He sat near the window of the train, blowing each puff upwards toward the window, staring out the window, contemplating his upcoming journey, as well as the money from Jack.

The trip home took two hours between waiting on trains and walking home from the station. When Mick arrived at the station, it was a five-mile walk home. Mick had placed the bible in his pocket. After getting up to the house, he came in the front door, but it appeared no one was home. Mick went to his room, shut the door, and opened the bible. He pulled out the money and then counted it. When he was done, there was $5,000, all in $100 USD notes. *How did Jack have this kind of money in Limerick Jail? Also, why not Irish pounds?*

Mick looked at the bible more closely, noticing the cover had a pocket over the back book binding. Inside the pocket was the next clue. It was a letter dated six months prior from Peter Carmody, writing from Brooklyn, NY, telling Jack he had a place for him in Brooklyn when he was out.

Peter wrote, "I admire your dedication, sitting in silence to protect your brothers. I've enclosed the following to make your stint easier. All the best, Peter."

Mick thought to himself, *Who the hell is Peter Carmody of Brooklyn, NY? Why would he be in contact with Jack?* After 30 minutes of dissecting all this new information, Maggie had come home.

Maggie called out, "Mick, love, you home?"

Mick replied, "Aye, got home 30 minutes ago. Where have you been?"

Maggie ignored his question. "How did it go with your brother? Pissed about America?"

Mick said, "No, he was supportive. Mum, do you know anyone named Peter Carmody from Brooklyn, NY?"

Maggie whipped around, shouting, "Don't you ever mention that name again!"

Mick, surprised by his mum's reaction, asked, "So you know a man named Peter Carmody? I don't understand why you're getting upset."

Maggie realized her reaction was a little hard for her son to process. It had been a long time since she'd heard Peter Carmody's name. Peter was sweet on her, in a two-man race for Maggie's hand between Big Jack and Peter. Maggie's parents liked Peter more than Big Jack, as Peter's family came from old money. Big Jack was a cattle farmer with what her parents felt were limited prospects. However, Maggie chooses Big Jack over Peter after Big Jack's proposal of marriage. He spoke about the life he wanted to build with Maggie. She was swept away in the romantic haze of it all. Peter, on the other hand, never seemed to be able to express how he felt about Maggie.

When Maggie told Peter, he was crushed, he shortly immigrated to America. Since Big Jack died, Mary received a condolence card from Peter each year on the anniversary of Big Jack's death. Maggie always found his cards thoughtful, but Peter never inquired about rekindling the relationship. Maggie might have welcomed that, especially a year or so after Big Jack's death. Maggie never forgave Peter for not fighting harder for her hand.

While Maggie was lost in the moment, Mick asked, "Mum, who's this Peter Carmody?"

Maggie replied, "He was sweet on me years ago. He and your father were vying for my hand. When your Da asked first, I said yes. I loved your father so very much. When Peter found out, he decided to immigrate to America. How did you come across his name?"

Mick pulled the bible from his pocket, showing the letter from Peter to Jack.

Maggie poured over the letter, then asked, "Where did you get this?"

Mick replied, "Jack put this in my pocket before I left. Didn't notice it until I was on the train. It was filled with $5,000, along with this letter."

Maggie said, "I wonder why Peter is in touch with Jack."

Mick said, "Would Uncle Anthony know him?"

Maggie replied, "Yes, he should. Just be careful around Peter. I have it on very good authority that he is working with the Italian Mafia, running guns for the cause. Promise me you'll stay clear of him."

Mick responded, "I'm not interested in getting into that. I need to pack my bag, so I'm going to head up to decide what I'm taking with me."

Maggie nodded as she turned toward the stove. *She needed a cup of tea after all this—no, wait—a whiskey.*

Mick went upstairs, beginning the arduous task of going through his closets and deciding what to take with him. He'd have limited space, bringing only one bag on the trip.

Over the coming days, Mick prepared for his departure, making a point to stop in at the pub to say goodbye to his mates. They toasted each other, wishing each other future success.

Before long, it was time to head home for his last night. When he arrived, Maggie had gone to sleep. She was an early riser, and she could be very testy without a good night's sleep. Mick poured himself a whiskey before heading to bed. After gulping down the whiskey, he laid his head on the pillow and fell asleep quickly. It was 1:00 a.m.; he'd be leaving to catch the train at 6:00.

At 5:00, Maggie came upstairs to wake Mick, but he was already awake, putting the straps on his bag for the journey. Maggie had arranged for Margaret Boyle, a friend, to drive them to the train station. Margaret was waiting outside for them as they emerged from the front door. The drive to the station was 30 minutes.

When arriving at the station, Margaret said, "Best of luck, Mick."

Mick nodded, then opened the car door for his mum. Maggie stood in front of her boy, welling up with tears. Mick, too, was welling up.

Mick said, "Mum, I'll send for you and Jack as soon as I can. I love you, Mum."

Maggie leaned in, kissing Mick on his cheek and putting her arms around his broad shoulders, fearful this might be the last time she saw her middle son. As she hugged him, tears were flowing from her eyes. Mick consoled her, rubbing her back with his left hand.

Finally, Maggie pulled away. "Safe travels. Do your best in America. I love you, too."

The train conductor shouted, "All aboard!"

Maggie smiled. "You better get on the train."

Mick said, "Yes, Mum."

Mick boarded the train for Dublin, sailing for America the next day.

As Mick waved from the train car window, Maggie reached into her pockets. What she hadn't noticed was that Mick slipped an envelope into her pocket while they embraced. Maggie returned to the car and opened the envelope. Inside was $2,500. Mick left her half of the money Jack had given him. Maggie began to cry at his thoughtfulness while Margaret put the car in drive to head home.

Chapter 6
October 1940 – Brooklyn, NY

Mick arrived in New York City on June 6, 1940, sailing into New York Harbor, met by Uncle Anthony. At the time, the sponsor needed to be present when an immigrant stepped onto U.S. soil.

As Mick came down the plank, Uncle Anthony was waiting under the pier, trying to stay out of the rain. When Mick saw him, he waved, making his way over to him.

Mick shook his uncle's hand. "Aye, great to finally be here. I can't thank you enough for sponsoring me."

Uncle Anthony smiled. "That's what families do. Is that all the luggage you've got? My car is parked around the block."

Mick replied, "Aye, this is it."

Uncle Anthony said, "We should get going. The ride is about 30 minutes. When you get there, we'll get you settled; then we'll get a bite to eat. You've got to be hungry. Is your mum well? How was the trip?"

Mick replied, "Aye, sounds grand. The trip over wasn't too bad. Hit some rough seas in the Atlantic on the second day, but it wasn't too bad. Mum sends her love."

Uncle Anthony responded, "That's grand. Also, I forgot to mention that you start work on Monday, so you'll have a few days to get settled and even take in a couple of sights. Did you drop your mum a note to let her know you arrived?"

Mick said, "Aye, I dropped the note in the mailbox as I came off the boat. Again, I can't thank you enough for all this."

Uncle Anthony didn't respond as he started toward the Brooklyn Battery Tunnel. He turned on the radio to listen to the World Series between the Cincinnati Reds and the Detroit Tigers. Red Barber was on the radio, calling game seven of the series.

Uncle Anthony looked over at Mick. "It's not the All-Ireland, however, baseball's king here. Everyone gets hooked. I'm a Dodger fan, just promise me you won't root for the New York Yankees—ever."

Mick smiled. "I'm not sure what you're talking about, but I'll give it a try. Perhaps we could take in a baseball game this week."

Uncle Anthony said, "This is the last game for the season. It'll have to wait until April."

Mick shrugged his shoulders, gazing at the horizon before heading into the tunnel. As they emerged from the tunnel, Mick saw signs for Red Hook. Uncle Anthony lived in the Bay Ridge section of Brooklyn.

Mick asked, "How much longer before we get to the flat?"

Uncle Anthony said, "We're 20 minutes away. Do you need to stop?"

Mick replied, "No, just curious. The city's amazing, very different than Knock."

Uncle Anthony chuckled. "That's for sure."

After 20 minutes, they pulled up in front of the apartment building where Mick would live for the next 10+ years. The apartment was on 3rd Avenue and 86th Street, above a local pub called The Three Aces Pub.

Uncle Anthony dropped Mick off in front of the pub. "The door to upstairs is on the left. I'll park the car and be right back."

Mick nodded, opening the car door to get out, then opened the door to the backseat, grabbing his suitcase. After the door closed, Uncle Anthony proceeded around the corner, finding a place to park.

Mick waited in front of the pub, taking in the sights. He was a farm boy at heart, so being in such a densely populated city seemed overwhelming. He was already homesick, missing his mother, as well as Jack. As all these thoughts were floating in his mind, Uncle Anthony came from around the corner.

As Uncle Anthony approached, he said, "Let's get you settled. I'll admit I'm hungry. The pub has good food, always fresh."

Mick nodded as both headed up the stairs into the apartment. The apartment was on the third floor.

When Uncle Anthony opened the door, he said, "This is it. The kitchen is on the left, your bedroom is down the hall, the last door is on the right, and the bathroom is across from your bedroom door."

Mick replied, "Aye, grand."

Mick headed to the bedroom. The apartment was smaller than Mick expected, but he had a room to sleep in, not needing much else. He unpacked, then sat on the edge of the bed for a few minutes, looking out the window. He noticed a streetlight close to the window, with the street having lots of traffic, too.

Uncle Anthony knocked on his door a few minutes later. "Ready to go?"

Mick emerged from the bedroom, nodding. "Aye, ready."

Mick and Uncle Anthony made their way downstairs into the pub. Uncle Anthony took a seat at the bar, motioning for Mick to do the same.

Within seconds, Mr. O'Sullivan appeared. "Anthony, this is your nephew, the one you've been telling us about."

Uncle Anthony nodded.

Mr. O'Sullivan extended his hand to Mick. "Welcome to America. It's certainly not anything you're used to, but it grows on you over time."

Mick replied, "Thanks, it's nice to meet you."

Mr. O'Sullivan asked, "Two pints of Guinness?"

Mick responded, "That'll be grand."

Uncle Anthony then said, "Danny, we need the menus too. Any specials?"

Mr. O'Sullivan replied, "Here's the menu. One special at the top."

Mick didn't say anything as Mr. O'Sullivan waited on another patron.

Finally, Mr. O'Sullivan came over. "So, what will it be?"

Anthony and Mick ordered the fish and chips. Mr. O'Sullivan placed the orders with the kitchen while Anthony and Mick took in the World Series game. Anthony tried to explain some of the finer points, but Mick was mainly confused, as it had little resemblance to proper football or even hurling. The two sat chatting about this and that over their meals.

After eating dinner, Mick asked, "Uncle Anthony, do you know Peter Carmody?"

Uncle Anthony turned his head slowly, somewhat stunned by the question.

Before Uncle Anthony could respond, Mr. O'Sullivan replied, "Lad, he's the owner of this place. Helps a lot of people in the neighborhood."

Mick replied, "Do either of you know why my brother would know him?"

Uncle Anthony shook his head and angrily said, "We'll talk about that at home. No one here knows who you are."

Mick, a little surprised by the turn of the conversation, said, "I didn't mean any disrespect."

Mr. O'Sullivan replied, "It's your first day, lad. Don't worry. If Mr. Carmody wants to meet you, he'll find you."

Mick felt anxious about Mr. O'Sullivan's last statement. He looked at Uncle Anthony, but all he did was shake his head from side to side. Mr. O'Sullivan gave them the bill, Anthony paid the bill, and then they left the pub to return to Mick's new home.

When they got inside the flat, Uncle Anthony said, "Do you have shite for brains, lad?"

Mick, a little confused by the insult, said, "I don't understand why this question is such a problem. I just wanted to know who he is. I've got nothing against him. I don't *know* him."

Uncle Anthony could now see Mick was genuinely inquiring.

Anthony said, "No one talks to or about Mr. Carmody in public. He's very good at what he does and keeps a low profile. He got you the job you've got."

Mick replied, "I appreciate that, but how does he know Jack?"

Uncle Anthony now understood the origin of his question. "With your brother's situation, Mr. Carmody's nephew was on the Clonderlaw Bridge with Jack. Carmody's nephew told his uncle what a hero Jack was. Mr. Carmody paid his respects to your brother for how he handled his imprisonment. Understand now?"

Mick responded, "I saw a letter Mr. Carmody sent to Jack, but I didn't know about Carmody's nephew. That's why Jack received all that money."

Uncle Anthony replied, "What money?"

Mick said, "Two days before leaving for America, I visited Jack in Limerick Jail. He slipped a package into my pocket before I left the jail. When I opened the bible, I found $5,000, along with a letter from Peter Carmody. When I asked my mum about him, she told me this story about Carmody being an old flame of hers."

Uncle Anthony cut Mick off. "He was very sweet on your mum, but she never once considered him, as he didn't tell her about his feelings. While his family came from old money, he always planned on leaving for America. That bastard talked of nothing else when we were kids."

Mick was a little confused by Uncle Anthony's laying out of the events, so instead of asking more questions, he decided to head to bed.

Mick said, "Uncle Anthony, I'm a little tired. I'm heading to bed."

Uncle Anthony smiled. "Aye, goodnight, lad."

With that, Mick was off to bed, wondering how Peter Carmody was connected to this situation.

Chapter 7
December 1941

It was December 7, 1941. Mick has been in America almost a year. At work with his mates, as well as those at the pub, everyone had an opinion about whether America would end up in a war. On this early afternoon, it was clear war was inevitable. Working down on the docks and spending time at the pub—patriotism for his new country had grown over his short stay in America. Even Mick felt a sense of duty as each day progressed.

Listening to the afternoon radio reports was chilling. Many people were angry about the attack. Others espoused revenge for Pearl Harbor, while many sat quietly, absorbing the first punch, wondering what it meant for our servicemen, now heading to war.

Sitting at the pub with Mick was Jimmy Ryan, who was raised in Brooklyn, but his people were from Galway. Jimmy was angry, with two pints in him already, contributing to his anger.

Jimmy looked at Mick. "We need to join up, do our bit."

Mick replied, "Can I do that? I've only been here 10 months."

Jimmy replied, "Go to the recruiting office to ask. What branch do you want to serve in?"

Mick said, "Honestly, I don't know."

Jimmy and Mick bantered about what was involved, then decided to head to the recruitment office. When they arrived, the line was out the door and down around the block. Many had the same ideas. Jimmy was running his mouth a mile a minute, with several of the other men wanting him to shut up, seemingly an expert on all that had happened today. What Mick was listening for was what branch was best.

After two hours of waiting, they stood in front of the recruiting officer, Captain Michael Byrne.

He started out slow. "This is my hundredth recruit of the day. What branch are you interested in?"

Jimmy responded, "Which branch has the best food?"

Another man shouted, "Navy!"

However, Captain Byrne wasn't amused at all.

The captain said, "Son, do you know what happened today? Men died on our watch. It's possible half the Pacific Fleet is in ruins. Are you concerned about which branch has the best food? Are you fucking kidding me?"

Jimmy simply said, "I'm sorry, sir."

Then Captain Byrne asked Mick, "So, what branch of the service?"

Mick replied, "Where I can be most useful."

Mick's Irish brogue was apparent to the captain, who asked, "How long have you been in America, son?"

Mick replied, "Ten months, but I want to serve my new country."

The captain replied, "We need you in the Marines."

Mick nodded but said nothing. The captain got Mick's paperwork completed.

The captain said, "Welcome to the Corps. You'll get your orders soon for boot camp. Hey, for you—Huckleberry or Ryan, whatever your name is—it's probably safest if you're in the Navy. They love wiseasses in the Navy."

Jimmy quickly realized it was best to say nothing, and then they left the recruiting office. Jimmy and Mick headed back to the pub. It was nearly half-past six, and the radio reports were worse later in the day. The pub was a somber, sullen place on most nights, but this was probably the most sullen Mick had seen it. No one spoke; the bartenders were passing pints around without anyone asking. After finding a seat at the bar, the radio was the only thing anyone could hear.

The next day, was the first time pictures were available in the newspaper. President Roosevelt spoke from the Capitol to the U.S. Congress.

FDR stated, "Yesterday, December 7, 1941—a date which will live in infamy—the United States of America was suddenly and deliberately attacked by naval and air forces of the Empire of Japan." He spoke defiantly, asking Congress for a declaration of war on Japan. During FDR's speech, Mick began soaring with pride for his adopted country, drawn closer to it by signing up to defend her.

Over the next few weeks, there was inaction of things when war was declared while people tried to get on with life. There were all sorts of wardens—bomb shelters, black-lined sheets to protect from naval or aerial attacks, and siren drills. On the docks, they continued to load ships bound for England, part of FDR's Lend-Lease program, while each day Mick came home from work, expecting to hear where he'd be assigned.

On December 24, 1941, Mick's orders arrived. It was a letter from the president of the United States of America, saying to report for USMC military training no later than January 2, 1942, in Parris Island, South Carolina. A transport train would leave NYC on December 30, 1941.

Mick called out, "Uncle Anthony, got my orders."

Uncle Anthony replied, "I saw them. When do you report?"

Mick said, "I board a train for Parris Island, South Carolina, on December 30th."

Uncle Anthony stood up, putting his arm around Mick like a father would. The gesture was strange to Mick; Uncle Anthony never embraced Mick before.

Uncle Anthony got choked up. "Remember, war's sheer bloody murder. Protect your mates, and make it home. Don't ever hesitate; always shoot to kill. They'll teach you that at boot camp. Just remember, it takes nerve, as well as skill, to fire under pressure. Remember to slow your breathing when you are under fire; it will calm you down."

Mick chuckled. "I've got six days before I leave."

Uncle Anthony put his left hand on Mick's shoulder. "Don't forget what I told you. This is life and death, my boy. You need to be prepared to do whatever it takes to come home. I learned that in the IRA. It's sheer bloody murder. You'll see it's not about glory. It's about the preservation of our way of life and then living with the consequences of those actions. I've done some terrible things for my beloved Ireland, all of it in defense of her, but I must live with the faces of the comrades that didn't make it, even the ones I sent to their maker. Never underestimate the power of the gun in your hands, lad."

Mick was starting to understand what his uncle was saying, but as a combat Marine deployed in a forward area, you never could appreciate Uncle Anthony's words until he was in the thick of it.

On the morning of December 30, 1941, Uncle Anthony drove Mick to Penn Station. The traffic around the station was terrible, with shaking hands in the car the best sendoff they'd have. Mick found his way down to the track, then boarded the train, beginning the slow journey south toward South Carolina.

At first, many men were quiet, not knowing what to say or who might be listening. The train was packed, most of whom were smoking cigarettes. It was bitterly cold outside, so having the windows open was not a luxury to release any smoke from the smoke-filled car. The only relief was when the porters came through for announcements.

When they opened the car doors, it was like the smoke enveloped them.

They were about an hour into the trip, just outside Philadelphia. The man sitting across from Mick in the four-man seats facing each other said, "Hello, I'm Bill Baker from Long Island, NY."

Mick replied, "Pleasure. Mick Quinn. Grew up in Ireland, but I live in Brooklyn now."

The man on his left chimed in, "Hey, fellas, can I join in? Dominic Righetti, from the Bronx. Nice to meet you."

The man sitting next to Mick chimed in, "Hey, boys, nice to meet you. Jack Morris from Brighton Beach."

They all nodded, politely smiling at each other. Bill was complaining about the cigarette smoke, so Mick and Dominic put out their butts. Baker was not a smoker.

Baker asked, "So, what do you think boot camp's going to be like?"

Dominic chimed in, "My brother Guido went last summer. When he came home, he lost 25 pounds. He said the food was awful, and the training was intense."

Baker asked, "Dominic, is your brother deployed?"

Dominic responded, "He got his orders just before I left. 3rd Marine Division."

Jack looked at Mick. "Mick, you said you were from Ireland. Did I hear you right?"

Mick replied, "Aye, that's right."

Jack asked, "Why did you come to the United States?"

Mick replied, "Better opportunities."

After breaking the ice and passing through Philadelphia, the four strangers who met on the train that cold December morning would become lifelong friends.

None of them knew what fate held for them. They'd fight on Guadalcanal, Gloucester, Peleliu, then Okinawa, in the 1st Marine Division, losing many comrades along the way, but the bonds between these four men lasted until the day they died, forever intertwined in each other's lives.

They called Bill Baker simply Baker; any other nickname didn't seem to fit. Baker was wounded on Peleliu, surviving a grenade blast, taking shrapnel in his right leg, badly wounded. It was Mick who got to Baker first, dressing his wound and carrying him to safety while continuing to engage the enemy. After the war, Baker lived in Long Island, New York, working for the NYC Transit Authority as a motorman.

Dominic Righetti, they called Paisano, given his Italian heritage. Paisano had a dangerous weapon—a flamethrower. While the weapon was great against an enemy, it was equally dangerous having a bomb strapped to your back. Paisano always seemed to be in the right place at the right time; he was the only one who wasn't physically wounded. After the war, Dominic moved back to the Bronx, working in the NYC electrician's union for 40 years, ending his career as a highly touted labor leader.

Jack Morris, they called Momo. Momo's special skill was recognizing enemy patterns. He was extremely observant, always looking for a tactical advantage. Momo saved his entire squad one late night, seeing a nighttime enemy patrol attempting to break the line. It was his two-hour stint on watch while the other three slept. It was a dark, rainy night, and it was very difficult to hear the enemy patrol, especially with their rubber-soled shoes, coupled with the rain. Mick slept closest to Momo when Mick was awoken by Momo pointing in the direction of the enemy, as well as seeing another patrol attempting to outflank them. As it turned out, there were 50 Japanese men coming to their four-man unit. Momo was cool under pressure, positioning the other three to maximize their effect. His quick assessment of the situation saved his entire unit, including the captain. After the war, Momo was probably the best known, becoming a prosecutor in the Southern District of Manhattan, securing convictions against some of the most notorious criminals.

Mick didn't have a nickname like Baker; nothing else seemed to fit other than Mick. Mick was wounded on Guadalcanal in fierce hand-to-hand combat, being slashed with a sword across his left cheek, but not before killing his attacker with the blunt end of his rifle. In Okinawa, he survived another hand-to-hand combat fight with a Japanese soldier. This soldier emerged from a tunnel as Mick passed by its opening. The soldier was caked in mud, making it very difficult to see him until Mick was upon him. The soldier grabbed Mick, pulling him into the cave while stabbing him in the belly on his right side. As the Japanese soldier removed his bayonet, Mick lunged at him, knocking his helmet off. After a brief struggle, Mick ended the fight, beating the soldier to death with his helmet. After the war, Mick went back to his construction job, becoming a family man. However, Mick never really recovered from the scars of war. While he went to work each day, he truly was a functional alcoholic. Mick drank to sleep and to forget; however, it would have an immeasurable impact on his family.

When it was all over, it was a miracle they made it home alive, seeing some of the worst fighting ever in the history of warfare.

Chapter 8
June 1945

It was 5:00 a.m. on June 12, 1945. Jack was being released from Limerick Jail today. As he packed up his few possessions, a few lads said goodbye from their cell doors.

On the inside, Martin Flynn was his best mate, knowing each other from the village. His family was always well respected. Martin was 6' tall and weighed 175 pounds, with dark brown hair. Martin was a good soldier and was great at executing. Martin's cell was next to Jack's. However, Martin was not in a good place. He was extremely nervous, seemingly punch-drunk with the monotony of prison life.

Martin came to the gate. "Jack, I need you to get me out of here."

Jack knew Martin had five more years left on his sentence, being convicted of not just participation in a mission but also involvement in the making of firebombs. Jack had to intercede on Martin's behalf at least two times over the past six months in some jailhouse squabbles over disagreements regarding the treatment of prisoners.

Jack said reassuringly, "I'll do everything I can to help."

This provided the comfort Martin was looking for.

Jack continued, "Be careful, stick with our people. We'll formulate a plan."

Martin replied, "Thanks, Jack. I knew you'd come through."

At this point in the morning, the guard appeared at Jack's cell door.

John Davies, the guard, said, "All packed?"

Jack replied, "Yes, Gov., I'm ready to go home."

John Davies smiled. "Let's get you processed, then."

John Davies escorted Jack to the processing center, completing the paperwork, and then out the door. The process took 30 minutes, but to a man who's been locked up for five years, it was an eternity. Finally, with all the paperwork processed, John Davies opened the final door that went out to the streets of Limerick.

John Davies said, "Best of luck, Jack. I hope we never meet again in here. I've never shared your politics, but you're a good man, especially the way you looked after your friends."

Jack smiled. "Thanks. You're one of the few guards I respected. You treated us with respect. Thanks for that. I agree; I hope we never meet again in here."

Jack stepped through the door and out onto the early morning street, walking toward the bus stop on the opposite side of the street. This would take him to the train station, a step closer to home. Jack spoke to nobody on his return home, soaking in the sights. Seemingly, not much had changed in the last five years, so Jack wondered how Mick was. Mick was still in the Pacific—Okinawa, according to the last account. Mum followed the papers closely, surmising in her most recent letter to Jack that she thought Mick was in Okinawa. Jack's mum never visited him in Limerick Jail, telling Jack in her letters she was worried about retribution. Jack understood her concerns, never making an issue of it.

As Jack got off the bus, he made his way to the train station a mile down the road. Fortunately, he had a small bag, so it was easy enough to make it to the train. When he arrived at the station, Jack went inside to purchase a ticket.

Jack told the attendant, "Can I get a ticket to Knock?"

The attendant said, "That'll be one pound."

Jack removed the quid from his pocket, paying the attendant.

The attendant grabbed the pound, handing Jack the ticket. "Track 2."

Jack nodded, making his way onto the track 2 platform. His wait for the train was long—almost two hours before it rolled into the station. The train was packed, and it took almost an hour to offload the passengers and cargo. It was now half-past 11. The train loaded up at noon, shoving off just before 12:30. *The train ride wasn't too long. Perhaps I'll be back for tea,* he thought.

Once the train was rolling, everything seemed to be new and exciting as Jack looked out the window of the train car. Jack saw a new brewery that had been built just outside of Limerick, which wasn't there when Jack went to prison. Most of the ride went through farmland, so it was beautiful to see the majesty of the landscape. Also, Jack thought of his cattle ranch, thinking about what he'd do next. Mick and Jack talked about reuniting in America with Mum before Mick left for America. However, Jack wasn't sure if Mum wanted to go to America.

As these thoughts weighed on Jack's mind, his stop was approaching. Jack gathered his things, making his way to the train car door. As the train pulled in, the station appeared to be empty as Jack stepped off the train. In the distance, Jack saw a man standing in the vestibule of the station. As Jack moved closer, he noticed it was Paddy coming to pick him up. Paddy and Jack greeted each other with a handshake.

Paddy said, "Damn, glad to see you, lad. You look good."

Jack replied, "Aye, it's good to be home."

Paddy smiled. "My car's just down there."

Jack smiled. "Thanks for the lift."

After getting situated in the car, Jack asked, "Paddy, I know I've been back five minutes, but can we do anything about getting Martin Flynn released?"

Paddy replied, "Getting him out isn't the problem; the English finding him is."

Jack, a little confused, said, "He's not handling this well. We need to do something."

Paddy changed the subject. "So what about you going to America? Your mum told me Mick had told her you'd all reunite in America after selling the farm."

Jack glanced over. "It was a lot of talk at the time."

Paddy replied, "If you stay, I'll have work for you."

Jack smiled. "I need to see Mum so we can talk. Did she ever accept your proposal?"

Paddy coldly looked at him. "Told me no two years ago."

Jack, not sure what to say, replied, "Thanks for the lift home. I'll see you at the pub later."

Paddy nodded as Jack got out of Paddy's car, looking around and taking in the front yard landscape, which appeared to have not been cut in six months. There were weeds taller than Jack as he made his way up the driveway. As he got to the top of the driveway, he could see the old cottage looking a little run-down. It hadn't been painted since Jack did it some ten years ago. Jack thought that with Mick gone, keeping the place up must have been hard for his mum.

As Jack made his way toward the peat shed, he could smell something awful—a burning smell coupled with rotting meat in the sun too long. As Jack moved past the peat shed toward the main gate to the pasture, he saw over 30 head of cattle dead in the field. As he made his way over to the first steer, he could tell it was shot. The blood by the exit wounds appeared to be a couple of days old, as the blood on the outside of the cattle was sticky to the touch.

Suddenly, in the distance, he heard a woman crying. It was Jack's mum.

When she saw Jack, she yelled, "Look at what they did! I was told this was payback for your stunts. One of the British soldiers said it to me."

Jack looked around. "Mum, I don't know what to say. I'm sorry."

Jack's mum said nothing, shocked at the carnage.

Jack walked back to the tool shed and started the tractor. He spent the rest of the day herding the cattle together and building a fire to destroy the dead animals. "So much for being home," he thought. His mum tried to stay in the field but couldn't muster much strength after this tragic loss. Jack had just finished assembling the carcasses as twilight descended upon the field. With his mum standing on the back porch of the cottage, Jack doused the animals in petrol.

Before setting fire to the pile, he made sure to have a water hose nearby to control the flames. Jack dropped a match; with a whoosh, the fire ignited brilliantly. Over the next few minutes, thick black smoke poured into the sky from the burning heifers.

It was a sight Jack would never forget, a memory he would take with him from Ireland to America. That evening, they decided to sell the family land and leave Ireland altogether.

But before leaving, Jack needed to resolve Martin's situation.

Chapter 9
June 1945

It was June 13th, 1945, the morning after Jack returned home from Limerick Jail. He woke early, heading into the village to find some breakfast and to find Paddy. He made his way to the pub and ordered breakfast—the traditional Irish breakfast, including the blood sausage Jack had looked forward to. He hadn't had anything of the sort since going into Limerick Jail.

Jack sat at the bar, sipping his tea while he waited for breakfast. The pub was quiet. Jack kept an eye out for Paddy, as he'd been plotting since he awoke that morning regarding Martin's situation.

Ten minutes later, Mr. Fahey arrived with Jack's breakfast, placing it in front of him and asking, "Welcome home. Anything else I can get you?"

Jack replied, "Aye, this is grand, thanks."

Jack proceeded to eat his breakfast, listening to the radio Mr. Fahey had on. The war in Europe was over, so the focus shifted to the Pacific. The reports on the battle for Okinawa were brutal: fierce fighting and lots of casualties. Jack asked his mum the evening before if she'd heard from Mick. Maggie told him she hadn't received a letter in over a month. However, Mick told her there could be gaps in communication, so not to worry. Mick always ends his letters with, "Love you, Mum, see you in America soon." Last evening's conversation was playing on his mind as he finished his first breakfast at home. As he took his last bite, Paddy walked into the pub. Jack turned toward Paddy, but Paddy started to pass him.

Paddy said as he walked by, "I know, Martin, but I can't talk about it right now."

Jack was undeterred, following Paddy into his office and then shutting the door.

Once the door was closed, Paddy said, "What are you doing here? I really don't have the time for this."

Jack replied, "I've got a plan, just need to review it with you."

Paddy responded, "OK, Jack. Lay the plan on me."

Jack started, "I've got a friend that's a medic at Limerick Jail. He owes me a favor from our time inside. I helped him out with a problem he was having, but that's not important."

Paddy interrupted, "Get to it then."

Jack replied, "I can get word to him. I'll pay a visit to see a sick friend. He'll need to get Martin into the infirmary. The infirmary has an exterior door to a small courtyard. The guards don't patrol the area very well. Escape would be easy from the infirmary."

Paddy thought for a moment. "OK, how do you get in and out?"

Jack said, "Ambulances go in and out regularly. I'll go into the jail, then take him out to a waiting ambulance. From there, we'll exit the jail as we come in."

Paddy thought for a moment. "What happens when you are outside the walls of the jail?"

Jack replied, "After coming home to what I did yesterday evening, I've decided to sell the farm and go to America. I'll purchase three tickets so Martin can come. We'll be ready to sail within the week."

Paddy thought for a moment. "I'm sorry about the cattle. I hoped it wouldn't happen, or we could've stopped it. Are you really going to sell?"

Jack replied, "Nothing else to keep us here. The next stop is to the realtor to let them know we're interested in selling. The land is good land, fertile, and great for cattle, even raising hay. It should sell for a good price. Also, we've got no outstanding debts, so it will all be a profit, much-needed cash to move to America."

Paddy said, "Sounds like a good plan. Seamus Walsh is looking for land. Might want to stop over at his shop."

Jack nodded. "Thanks. I'll stop over. Once the deal is done, we'll pick a firm date to get Martin, then head for America."

Jack left Paddy's office, heading for Seamus Walsh's shop. He was a local blacksmith, having left the business from his father ten years prior. When Jack arrived at the blacksmith, Seamus greeted him at the front counter.

Seamus said, "Jack, good to see you. Welcome home."

Jack replied, "Thanks, glad to be home. Look, I stopped by to talk about selling our land. Paddy mentioned you're in the market."

Seamus replied, "Aye, want a farm and the blacksmith shop together. How many acres?"

Jack replied, "I'm looking to sell the whole farm, 500 acres."

Seamus said, "So that's approximately 20,000 pounds."

Jack responded, "21,000 pounds, but for you, how about 20,500 pounds."

Seamus responded, "How long do I have to come up with the money?"

Jack replied, "We're planning on leaving soon. Can you make this happen?"

Seamus said, "Yes, I can get situated within two weeks. Does the furniture come with it?"

Jack responded, "Other than the clothes, it's all included. We can't take anything else."

Seamus walked over and shook Jack's hand. "Deal."

Jack replied, "Deal. Within two weeks, we'll need the money."

Seamus then said, "Heard about the cattle. I'm sorry to hear about that."

Jack smiled but said nothing as he left, heading for home to let his mum know he'd just sold the farm. When Jack returned from the village, his mum was outside doing laundry.

Jack snuck up behind her. "Hey, Mum. I sold the farm."

Maggie turned. "That was quick. To whom?"

Jack said, "Seamus Walsh agreed on 20,500 pounds, furniture included."

Maggie started to cry. "That's a good price. Can't believe this won't be our land."

Jack put his arms around his mum, trying to console her, but it had little effect. Other than her boys, the family farm was the last thing of Big Jack she had.

After a moment of holding his mum, Jack said, "Mum. We've got something else to talk about."

Maggie stepped back. "What else?"

Jack said, "Martin. I've got a plan to get him out so he can come with us to America. Martin's not doing well. I walked Paddy through the plan. He agrees it'll work. After Seamus pays us the money, I will give you 80% of the proceeds to take with us to America. I'm going to keep 20% for my use. We're going to sail from Liverpool to America. You'll go a day before us, buy three tickets. Martin and I will follow the next morning after we get him out of Limerick Jail."

Maggie responded, "Jack, this sounds dangerous."

Jack replied, "Mum, the plan is sound. Paddy and I went over it this morning. After getting the quid, we'll get word to Martin. We'll be shoving off within the next two weeks."

Maggie asked, "What is the plan to get Martin out?"

Jack replied, "Mum, it's probably best you don't know the details. Just know Martin, and I will meet you at the hotel in Liverpool the next morning."

Maggie nodded. "Aye. My little Jack is little no more."

Jack smiled, then headed inside to lay out the plan in a bit more detail. Also, he needed to get word to his contact inside, as well as Martin. This required someone to go for a visit to Limerick Jail— someone who might have a reason. Then, thinking of Fiona Flynn, Martin's sister, Jack was always a little sweet on her, hoping he could get her help bringing the message. Jack wrote on a piece of paper what was needed inside, as well as the specific date. Jack paid Fiona a visit before walking over to the Flynn farm.

Fiona Alish Flynn was a petite young lady, 18 years of age, with long, curly dark brown hair and dark brown eyes, standing at 5'5". Her eyes held a softness accentuated by her wonderful smile. Fiona was funny, very polite, courteous, and a natural caregiver. She had nursed her mother through failing health, and as the oldest of her siblings, she tended to her only brother, Martin, after their mother passed away. Fiona protected him from their father's wrath, though, at the time, nobody knew about the trouble in their house.

Jack headed up the main driveway, noticing Fiona was in the garden picking fresh vegetables. She wore work pants with muddy boots and a light brown shirt. Though her attire wasn't overly attractive, she looked pretty, at least to Jack. Fiona noticed him coming up the driveway, standing up and waving at Jack.

When Jack got to the garden, Fiona said, "Welcome home, Jack! It's very nice to see you. What are you doing all the way up here?"

Jack smiled. "Thanks. Look, I came about, Martin."

Fiona interrupted. "Is he ok?"

Jack replied, "For the moment, yes. But he's not doing well. Jail is really getting to him."

Fiona asked, "Is there anything we could do to help?"

Jack said, "Yes. I've got a plan to get Martin out. I need you to go visit him to give him this message. You'll need to slip it to him somehow. This could be a wee bit dangerous."

Fiona thought for a moment, then said, "What's the plan?"

Jack replied, "I'm not sure you want all the details. All I'll say is, when you see Martin, say goodbye for a long while."

Fiona asked, "Going to America?"

Jack smiled. "Yes. Was planning on taking him with me."

Fiona asked, "When?"

Jack replied, "You should go visit Martin tomorrow. I'll set things up on my side."

Fiona smiled. "No, when do you go to America?"

Jack took a deep breath. "Within the next two weeks. Sold my land already."

Fiona sighed. "Can I come?"

Jack, sensing her desperation, said, "Not sure I want you involved too deeply. When we've reached America, we'll sponsor you to come over. I'm not sure we can pull all this off. My mum's going a day in advance to Liverpool to get the tickets."

Fiona replied, "I could go with your mum to get a fourth ticket. I've got to get out of this place. Since Mum died, me Da hasn't been right."

Jack looked a little surprised. "What do you mean? Has he hurt you?"

Fiona had known Jack since they were children. Jack and Martin have been friends since primary school. Jack was also pretty good at reading situations, sensing something was very wrong.

Fiona started to get choked up. "He's tried a couple of times to hurt me. You know what I mean, don't you?"

Jack looked at her. "I think so. Did he put himself upon you?"

Fiona asked, "What do you mean?"

Jack sighed. "Force you to have relations. Is that how he hurt you?"

Fiona replied, "Yes, he's tried, but I've fought him off. Happens whenever he's drunk."

Jack nodded. "I'll let my mum know we'll be four. Come stay with us until we go."

Fiona had tears streaming down her face. "I can't thank you enough."

Jack smiled. "Better head home. I'll let Mum know we'll be four. It won't be a problem after I tell her what has happened. Come by this afternoon, around tea."

Fiona said, "Thanks. I'll be down before supper. We can make plans this evening."

Jack replied, "Aye, that'll be grand. I better run."

Jack left Fiona in the garden, then headed down the driveway toward home. It was 13:00 and Jack thought of how quickly his life was changing.

Chapter 10
June 1945

It was 16:00 on June 13th, 1945. Jack was on the front porch having tea when he saw Fiona coming up the drive. She had one suitcase, a hat on, and her gray wool coat. When she reached the porch, she was sweating from the long walk carrying her things.

Jack asked, "Why'd you wear the coat?"

Fiona said, "Easier than carrying it."

Jack asked, "Tea?"

Fiona nodded as she sat in the empty chair next to Jack. Jack was expecting Fiona; as such, he had a cup for her ready to go.

Jack asked, "Milk?"

Fiona replied, "Please."

Jack handed her the cup of tea; then both sat on the porch staring at the horizon over the Shannon River. Jack thought to himself this might be the last time he'd see such beauty.

After a few minutes of silence, Fiona asked, "When did you want me to go to Limerick?"

Jack replied, "Tomorrow. I ran into Seamus on the way back from your place. He told me he'd have the money as early as next week."

Fiona asked, "What money?"

Jack responded, "Sold the land. We're going to set up in Brooklyn, near Uncle Anthony, as well as Mick when he comes home from the Pacific."

Fiona smiled, seeming relaxed by his answer. At 17:30, Maggie emerged from the house.

Maggie said, "Supper in 15 minutes."

Fiona asked, "Can I help with anything?"

Maggie replied, "No, dear, sit and relax."

What Fiona wasn't aware of: before arriving, Jack had shared Fiona's difficulties with his mum. Maggie was sympathetic to the situation, asking no questions. Besides, they were preparing for the trip to America, so change would be inevitable.

At 17:45, Seamus McDermott arrived in the driveway.

Seamus approached the porch. "Jack, can we talk?"

Jack looked at him anxiously. "Sure, something wrong?"

Seamus replied, "Nothing's wrong. I've got the money for the farm."

Jack said, "You've got it here, now?"

Seamus said, "Yes. Stay until the mission is complete. Talked with Paddy. I know you've got a plan."

Jack thought to himself, *who the hell else knows about this?*

Finally, Jack replied, "Thanks. We'll be executing sometime next week. You can check in with Paddy periodically; he'll keep you updated."

Seamus replied, "Here's the money. Leave the keys with Paddy."

Jack nodded. "Seamus, thanks for all this."

Seamus responded, "Best of luck to you."

With that, Seamus left, heading back down the driveway. Jack walked into the house, heading for the parlor. He opened the bankroll, counting the money. As expected, 20,500 pounds. Jack separated the quid into piles: 16,400 pounds into one pile, the remainder into a second pile.

As Jack was finishing, Maggie came into the parlor. "What's all that?"

Jack replied, "Seamus brought the quid for the farm and said stay until we get Martin out. Here's 80%, as we agreed. Please put it somewhere safe."

Maggie replied, "I don't believe I've ever seen this much money before. Supper's ready."

Jack said, "I'll let Fiona know."

Maggie responded, "I feel terrible for what she's been through since her mum passed."

Jack replied, "Mum, let's focus on the game plan. I'll take Fiona to Limerick tomorrow."

Maggie nodded, heading back to the kitchen.

Jack went outside. "Supper's ready. Also, we'll go to Limerick tomorrow morning."

Fiona rose from her chair, and both went inside to eat. The supper was uneventful. By 19:30, everyone had made their way to the parlor. Maggie turned on the radio, hoping to hear about the Pacific Theater, concerned for her son, Mick. Jack poured a whiskey, but neither Maggie nor Fiona was interested in one.

At 20:30, Maggie announced, "I'm heading to bed."

Fiona replied, "I'll do the same. Thanks so much for this."

Maggie smiled. "Goodnight, love."

With that, Maggie and Fiona headed off to bed. Jack poured a second whiskey, continuing to listen to the radio. As he listened, he continued to cycle the plan in his head. At 22:00, Jack turned off the radio, heading to bed himself.

At 05:00, Jack woke up like a shot, his heart racing and sweating heavily. He was having a nightmare about his early times in Limerick Jail. Suffice it to say many guards were unkind. It was 05:15 when Jack headed into the kitchen. When he arrived in the kitchen, Fiona and Maggie were already there, sipping tea and chatting. Noticing tissues on the table, Fiona's eyes seemed puffy, like she'd been crying.

When Maggie noticed Jack, she popped up, saying, "Morning, sleepyhead."

Jack nodded, heading to the cupboard for a cup, then to the stove to pour himself a cup of tea.

Jack sat down at the table. "What's going on?"

Fiona didn't say anything. What Jack didn't realize was Fiona was in love with him. Fiona felt Jack would think less of her if he knew the truth about what happened to her at the hands of her father. After a long silence, Fiona got up from the table heading into the bedroom to get changed.

After Fiona left the kitchen, Maggie said, "Jack, love. Fiona's had it far rougher than I imagined. She's embarrassed. Thinks you'll think less of her."

Jack replied, "Mum, what happened? I care for Fiona deeply. There were times in Limerick Jail, just the thought of her kept me going and gave me hope for our future."

Maggie said, "OK, love. You know she's very much in love with you. Told me over tea."

Jack smiled. "I suspected, but we've never spoken of it."

Maggie said, "You'll need to brace yourself; this isn't going to be easy to hear."

Jack nodded. "Please, continue."

Maggie replied, "After Fiona's mum passed, her father took to the drink heavily. When he was drunk, which was most of the time, he was abusive to Fiona, especially. She was the oldest. Fiona was expected to fill in for her mum."

Jack said, "So what happened?"

Maggie replied, "Please don't interrupt, let me finish. Fiona's dad was very abusive, both mentally and physically. When I say that Fiona was expected to take over for her mother, I mean in every way. Do you understand what I'm saying?"

Jack sat quietly for a moment, then said, "You mean physically, as man and wife?"

Maggie didn't say anything; she just nodded her head yes.

Jack replied, "What can I do to help her?"

Maggie said, "Be gentle, understanding. She shouldn't be judged; it's not her fault. She's going to need that. Believe me, I know from my own experiences."

Jack looked up at Maggie. "What do you mean?"

Maggie replied, "It happened a long time ago, but I don't want to dredge up the past. You needed to know about this as it will help you understand Fiona better, as well as how she may react to things differently than you'd expect."

Jack said, "Thanks, Mum. Let me go get dressed. I've got one or two errands to run in town before we head to Limerick. We're going to leave a little later the next day."

Maggie smiled at her son. "Please don't do anything stupid. We're leaving tomorrow."

Maggie knew her son well enough to know that while he didn't say he loved Fiona, it was written all over his face, as evidenced by his actions toward her.

Jack made his way to his bedroom, got changed, and headed out the front door without saying a word. Jack headed to the shed before leaving, retrieving his revolver. Before placing it into his coat, Jack made sure the revolver was loaded. As Jack emerged from the shed, he headed down the driveway. When Jack reached the bottom of the driveway, he turned right, heading toward Flynn's farm. Jack had unfinished business there.

Jack entered the main gate of the Flynn farm, which was unmaintained. The grass in the front yard was over a foot high; the driveway appeared to be neglected, too. It was down to the bare dirt; stones weren't even visible, which made it almost impossible to get equipment up to the shed.

As Jack made his way up the driveway, there was no activity on the farm. Nobody was out tending to the cattle nor in the shed working on the tractor, appearing not to have been running for months. As Jack reached the shed door, he heard someone snoring. Jack peeked inside. It was Fiona's father, sleeping it off as it was. The smell of alcohol was burning the hairs in Jack's nose, oozing from his pores.

Jack kicked him in the leg. "Wake up, you drunk bastard."

Fiona's father opened his eyes very narrowly. "What the hell do you want?"

Jack said, "Stand up, you drunken bastard."

Fiona's father attempted to stand but fell just as quickly. Jack noticed a rake close by, which Fiona's father was reaching for.

Jack stepped on his hand. "You know why I'm here?"

Fiona's father again started to stand but went down again. As he reached for Jack's leg, Jack kicked him in the mouth. Within seconds, the old drunkard was out cold. Jack saw the water trough, grabbed a small bucket, filled it, walked over to Fiona's father, and dumped the water over his head.

Startled by the cold water, he said, "What the hell do you want?"

Jack replied, "Get up, you bastard. Take off your clothes."

Fiona's father said, "You want me to do what?"

Jack responded, "You heard me. Do what you're told!"

Fiona's father complied, standing up and then removing his clothes.

Jack then said, "Take off the undergarments too."

Fiona's father asked, "What for?"

Jack then placed his revolver on Fiona's father's head. "You're going to find out, you drunk bastard. I'm doing this so you feel the humiliation Fiona felt."

Fiona's father said, "I didn't do anything to Fiona but love her."

Jack angrily said, "Liar."

Jack grabbed his belt, whipping the man all over his body, inflicting all the pain in the world on him, beating him senselessly to the point where Jack was winded when it was over. After the humiliation, Fiona's father lay face down in the peat in the barn, moaning in pain. He turned over, now face to face with Jack. Jack thought how pathetic he was, feeling satisfaction in humiliating him while avenging Fiona.

Jack recalled the prior evening, Fiona had hidden her arms with a sweater. However, after supper, she pulled up her sleeves while washing dishes, where Jack noticed bruises that seemed only a few days old. The thought of Fiona suffering at his hands overwhelmed Jack. He ended everyone's misery by removing his pistol and shooting him in the temple.

Jack defended Fiona and avenged her in his own way, believing this outcome was just after what her father had done to her. No man should ever put their hands on a woman. Jack grabbed a shovel that was nearby, then headed out behind the shed, where he found a mound of dirt. He dug a four-foot hole in front of the mound, dusted it with lime, then buried Fiona's father. After covering him, he pushed the mound forward a little to conceal the gravesite. As it would be told, Fiona's father disappeared into thin air.

Then Jack thought it was time to get ready for the journey to America. The next day, Fiona entered Limerick Jail to visit her brother. She visited with him for an hour. When she emerged from jail, Jack was waiting for her at the bus stop. She gave Jack a thumbs up as she headed across the street, signaling Martin had gotten the message.

Chapter 11
June 28th, 1945

Jack made his way to Limerick this morning to get Martin. Paddy gave him a truck with a medical insignia to get into the infirmary. So far, things were going off without a hitch. Jack drove to Limerick early the morning of the escape, taking precautions and heading straight into Limerick Jail.

Jack circled the prison the morning of the escape, scoping out different escape routes for himself if needed. At 08:30, Jack pulled up to the prison gate, where ambulances and deliveries came into the prison. The guards at the gate seemed preoccupied as Jack entered, quickly realizing he didn't recognize any of the guards.

The guard stopped Jack. "State your purpose."

Jack replied, "Dropping off medical supplies."

The guard asked, "Identification?"

Jack handed him fake identification to look over.

The guard said, "Here, pull up over there."

Jack complied, pulling his truck next to the infirmary door. Jack knocked on the door. His inside friend, Kevin Nealy, opened the door. Kevin didn't say a word, just ushered Jack into the infirmary. Other than Martin, the infirmary was empty. Martin was transferred to the infirmary two days before the escape attempt. Kevin had set up an IV for Martin with the pretense Martin needed medicine. As it turned out, it was a simple saline solution. Kevin had removed the IV five minutes before Jack made it to the door. He saw Jack from the window when he arrived.

Martin was excited to see Jack, asking, "So what's the plan when we're out of here?"

Jack replied, "Martin, focus. Let's get to the van first!"

Martin nodded while Kevin supplied a white lab coat like the one Jack was wearing. In addition, Jack got identification for Martin as well, figuring that if the guards didn't recognize either of them, he could be Jack's assistant if the situation presented itself.

Jack said, "Martin, study the ID quickly. They didn't search the inside of the truck, so I think if I can get you inside the van, they might not check on the way out. If they do, you're Michael O'Hara, my assistant, got it?"

Martin replied, "Got it."

Martin looked over the card quickly, and then both headed for the door. Jack went out first, opening one door on the back of the truck and using it to shield the infirmary door from the guards. Once Jack opened the door, he stood back from it to see if the guards had noticed. Jack thought it was clear; they didn't. After 30 seconds, Jack motioned to Martin to come out of the infirmary, quickly loading him into the van, then placing two bags of laundry over the top of him, at the very least obstructing the view in the van. With Martin secured, Jack closed the doors while Kevin waved at Jack, closing the infirmary door.

Jack got in the van and headed to the exit. There was a delivery truck entering as well, and the guards seemed very intent on checking its contents. As Jack pulled up to the gate, only one security guard was there. Jack noticed the other guards were taking things off the other truck, placing them in what appeared to be a vehicle parked on the street. Jack pulled up to the guard.

The guard said, "Get everything taken care of?"

Jack replied, "Yes."

The guard replied, "I'll be back."

Jack sat waiting as the guard circled the van. When the guard got to the back door, he peered in the windows, seeing the laundry bags. The guard tried to open the back door, but Jack had locked it. The guard went to the left side of the vehicle, checking underneath the van. Finally, he made his way back to the driver's side window.

Jack asked, "Everything ok?"

The guard said, "Small load today?"

Jack replied, "Took what they gave me."

The guard handed Jack his ID, responding, "Here, have a nice day."

Jack took the ID, then put the truck in drive as the guard signaled to open the gate. As the gate opened, Jack drove through, heading back to Main Street, carefully maintaining speed so as to not draw any unwanted attention.

Martin asked from the back, "We out?"

Jack replied, "We're out. Stay where you are until we're closer to the coast."

As Jack got onto the coastal highway, nothing. No alarms, no Garda. Could it be this easy? After an hour of lying under the laundry, Martin joined Jack in the front seat. After getting seated, Martin yammered a mile a minute about what happened after Jack's release. Then, the two talked about leaving for America.

Martin asked, "Where are we going?"

Jack replied, "Brooklyn, NY. Remember, Mr. Carmody sponsored us, and we got jobs waiting."

Martin replied, "What kind of jobs?"

Jack responded, "Good jobs, working for Mr. Carmody, raising capital and munitions. Mr. Carmody wants to keep the pressure on things and sway American opinion for our cause."

Martin nodded, then returned to take in the landscape as they made their way to Dublin before pushing off for Liverpool. From Liverpool, they'd sail to America.

The journey from Limerick to Dublin took several hours. Jack stopped to refuel once, stopping on the side of the road twice so they could relieve themselves. As Jack drove, his mind transitioned between Fiona and the trip, deciding to remain focused on putting out to sea before celebrating any freedom. Regarding Fiona, he played over what he did in her honor. It was the first time Jack killed a man. Jack replayed her father's reaction to what happened, finding him drunk at that time of day. Jack concluded he was a despicable creature, forcing himself upon his daughter like that.

After the long drive, Jack disposed of the van at the location Paddy had provided. It was a car shop just off a busy street in Dublin. Jack took a rag, wiping down the steering wheel to remove any fingerprints, then locked the van, leaving the keys in the mail slot, as he was instructed to do.

After leaving the garage, Jack and Martin headed over to the hotel where the ladies were staying.

After arriving in the lobby, Jack asked, "Quinn party, what room?"

The clerk said, "Quinn, yes, here it is, 705."

Jack nodded while Martin waited near the lift. After Jack had gotten the room number, they got on the lift and headed for the room. When Jack got to the room, he knocked.

Fiona said, "Who's there?"

Jack replied, "Jack and Martin."

Fiona quickly opened the door, ushering them into the room. When the door clicked behind them, Fiona grabbed Jack, hugging him as if he had just come home from two years of combat. Maggie was in the background, smiling at Jack, giving him a mother's look of approval over the future wife he'd chosen. Quickly, Fiona then hugged her brother, thankful he was doing well.

Jack looked at Maggie. "Get the tickets? Any problems?"

Maggie said, "Got four tickets, we're set."

Jack smiled, then lay down on the bed in the room, falling asleep quickly. It was 17:00 when they arrived at the room. Fiona caught up with her brother while Maggie listened to the radio. Jack, on the other hand, was snoring loudly, having lain down on his back. The others were quite amused at this. Finally, Maggie walked over to Jack, touching his leg.

Jack startled. "What's going on?"

Maggie laughed, asking, "Would you like to get some supper?"

Jack replied, "Aye, I could eat."

So, the four went down for dinner. At the table, they were quiet, whispering about the day's events as well as the trip to America. Jack explained it would take several days by boat.

Martin asked, "Am I traveling as myself?"

Jack said, "No, not until you reach America. I've got the same issue. Once we put in at Ellis Island, we'll revert to our original identification. Paddy and I made sure to do the paperwork properly. I've got paperwork for everyone."

Maggie asked, "So, we don't know each other on the boat?"

Jack replied, "Once we're out to sea, we can do whatever we'd like. It's best if we look like strangers at first. Eliminates suspicion."

All agreed with Jack's assessment. Now, they needed to get to Liverpool.

Arriving at the Dublin waterfront, they went through customs. Standing in line, there seemed to be thousands of people looking to make the trip to America. The noise leading through the customs area was loud, raucous even. As they got closer to the guard station, Jack thought he recognized one of the guards, but he couldn't remember from where.

As he got up to the guard, the guard said, "Jack, good to see you."

When Jack heard the voice, he knew it was Paddy McFarland. After his father passed away ten years ago, he moved to Dublin. Jack winked when he took out the paperwork.

Paddy said, "Mr. O'Brien. Where are you headed?"

Jack said, "Liverpool, then America."

Paddy smiled. "Your papers are in order. Safe journey."

Jack smiled as Paddy repeated the process with Maggie, Fiona, and then Martin. Same questions along with the same responses. The four headed for the boat to second class. Maggie had used some of the proceeds so they'd be comfortable on the journey. After arriving in the second-class area, the four sat with each other, not following Jack's original counsel. Jack stared out over Dublin harbor.

Jack said, "This may be the last time we see Ireland."

Fiona replied, "Perhaps, but we get to start a new life together."

Maggie chimed in, "It's about a new start. We're the American dream now."

Martin sat silent, taking in the views of the harbor. Fiona sat next to Jack, quite close, holding his left hand, squeezing it gently. Jack was a little taken aback, as Fiona had never done this before. Maggie looked over at Jack, smiling, seeing they were both in love.

After an hour, they set sail for Liverpool. Jack looked at his watch, surmising they'd make it in time to catch the first ship in Liverpool the next morning. Fiona continued to hold Jack's hand; however, she fell asleep on his left shoulder. Maggie brought a book, so she was reading. Jack found a newspaper stand on the boat, grabbing one before heading for their seats. Martin was also fast asleep, secure, and out of prison, heading for America.

Jack tried concentrating on the newspaper, but his mind was racing with a variety of thoughts. The first was to stay focused on setting sail for America. Nothing else would matter if they were detained. Second, Jack hadn't told Maggie that Peter Carmody had helped them. Jack was convinced if she knew, she never would've left Ireland. He planned on telling Maggie while they were sailing for America. His last thought was Fiona; he needed to protect her, keep her safe, and love her despite what she's been through. These thoughts seesawed in his head for the remainder of the trip. Jack was the only one of the four that didn't sleep from Dublin to Liverpool.

When they docked in Liverpool, it was very early the next morning, around 05:00. The terminal where they docked was a five-minute walk to the ship for America. As the four disembarked, they maneuvered the crowds to get close to the ship. As fate would have it, they were taking passengers when they arrived despite the boat not putting out until 06:30. The porters assisted with the luggage as they made it to the second-class seating area. By 05:45, all four had their seats. By a lucky twist of fate, they weren't required to go through customs again, as the boat they were sailing on was in the same section of boat slips.

The boat sailed at 06:30 on the dot. Before long, they'd start the weeklong journey from Liverpool to NY. Before sailing, Jack got some tea for the four of them, as well as some biscuits to nibble on for breakfast.

As Jack returned to the seats, Maggie asked, "Two weeks, then we'll be in America."

Fiona smiled her beautiful, contagious smile. "I can't wait. I can't thank you enough for taking me away from all that."

Jack whispered to Fiona, "I'll always look after you."

Fiona smiled, sipping at her tea.

Martin asked, "Fiona, what are you talking about?"

Fiona shrugged her shoulders but didn't say a word. Martin grabbed the paper from Jack, beginning to thumb through it.

Martin peered over the paper. "No news from Limerick, aye?"

Jack glared at his friend as if to say, *have you got shite for brains?*

Maggie tapped Martin on his left shoulder, then whispered, "We're not there yet, so shut up, you."

This prompted laughter from them all. Martin went back to reading the paper while Jack stared out the window, watching the coastline disappear. Jack thought it was best to get the missing information into Maggie's hands.

Jack asked, "Mum, can we talk on the deck?"

Maggie replied, "Sure, what's wrong?"

Jack responded, "Nothing's wrong. I just need to tell you something."

Maggie and Jack headed out to the rear observation deck; it was an open area where part of it was uncovered from the elements. Thankfully, it was a sunny morning, warm and inviting.

Maggie asked, "So what have you got to tell me? You're in love?"

Jack said, "Well, I am, but that's not it. I didn't mention this to you because if you knew, you might not have come."

Maggie looked perplexed. "Go on!"

Jack said, "Peter Carmody, through Uncle Anthony, was our sponsor. He's arranged it."

Jack was surprised at Maggie's reaction, as she had none. She seemed to take it all in, staring at her son.

Finally, Maggie said, "After the cattle, I figured he had to be involved somehow. Any time Anthony wrote, he talked about his friendship with Peter."

Jack replied, "You're not mad?"

Maggie responded, "I'm disappointed you didn't tell me, but I understand why. Let's rejoin the others. Enjoy the journey."

Soon, they'd be well into the Atlantic Ocean. It took almost two weeks to make the journey. When they finally arrived, Maggie's brother was there to meet them at the dock, like he did when Mick came four years prior. When Maggie saw her brother, she began to cry.

Anthony smiled. "Maggie, it's been a long while. Hope the crossing went well."

Maggie replied, "It's been almost 20 years since I last saw you. You look well."

Anthony responded, "Thanks, the years have been good to you as well."

Maggie replied, "Thanks."

Anthony said, "This everyone? If so, we should head over to my car. The ride to Brooklyn should take us 40 minutes."

The group made it to Uncle Anthony's car and then headed through the Brooklyn Battery Tunnel. The trip took an hour, given the city traffic. When they arrived at 3rd Avenue and 68th Street, Uncle Anthony left them at the curb in front of the apartment. Jack and Martin would stay in the same apartment Mick lived in with Anthony. Anthony had bought a house in Brooklyn but kept the apartment for Mick, awaiting his return. Across the hall was another apartment where Fiona and Maggie would be staying. Jack was already scheming about purchasing his first business. Given what they'd gotten for the farm, he expected that would go a long way in America.

Anthony took them upstairs to the apartments and then sat with his sister as the group got settled.

Then Anthony suggested, "The pub downstairs is quite nice. Anyone hungry?"

Maggie replied, "I could eat."

Jack, Martin, and Fiona all nodded, so the group went downstairs for an early supper. As they went into the Three Aces Pub, they were seated by a hostess at a table for six. After ordering a couple of pints, a wine for Fiona and a sherry for Maggie, the waitress took their dinner order. As she went into the kitchen, a man came out of the basement office at the end of the bar. That man was Peter Carmody.

Instantly recognizing Maggie, he came to the table immediately. Maggie hadn't seen Peter at the bar.

Peter came to the table. "Excuse me…"

Maggie interrupted him. "Oh shite, Peter?"

Peter smiled. "Maggie, it's good to see you. Welcome to America."

Maggie replied, "Thanks for all your help setting this up. Let me introduce everyone. You know Anthony, but this is Jack, my son."

Peter smiled, extending his right hand. "Jack, it's nice to finally meet you."

Maggie then turned to Fiona. "This is Fiona, a family friend; she's a Flynn."

Peter smiled. "Nice to meet you, Fiona. I went to school with your dad. I was sorry to hear about your mum."

Fiona smiled politely but said nothing.

Then Maggie turned to Martin. "This is Martin Flynn, Fiona's brother, a friend of Jack."

Peter smiled, saying, "Martin, welcome. You're the lad who just left Limerick, right?"

Martin said, "Aye. It's grand to be here."

Peter said, "Enjoy the food. Jack, let's talk tomorrow, say 08:30. Talk about our plans."

Jack responded, "Aye, see you in the morning."

With that, Peter left the table just as the food arrived. The five sat at the table, talking about old family friends enjoying their meals, especially the Shepherd's pie. It was 18:30 when the meal was over. They went back to the apartments while Anthony drove to his house. By 19:30, the four were exhausted, all lying down on the bed, fast asleep.

Chapter 12
July 1945

Jack made his way to Peter Carmody's office promptly at 08:30. Peter was on the telephone when Jack arrived, wrapping up his call. Peter noticed Jack at the door, waved him into his office, and gestured toward the chair in front of his desk.

Peter said, "That's grand. I've got the right man for the job; he just arrived. Ok, we'll talk soon."

Peter hung up the phone and then headed to the coffee pot for a refill.

Peter asked, "Jack, some coffee?"

Jack said, "Sure, black, please."

Peter nodded as he grabbed a second mug, filling both cups. He then returned to his desk, placing the coffee in front of Jack.

Jack said, "Thanks."

Peter replied, "Jack, let's get down to brass tacks. You overheard my phone call, right?"

Jack replied, "I overheard your side of the conversation, but I wasn't eavesdropping."

Peter responded, "I know. Look, I've got a deal set to move some weapons back to Ireland. With the war almost over, stockpiles of weapons are for sale."

Jack said, "Makes sense. What do you need me to do?"

Peter smiled, "I want you and your friend Martin to deliver the weapons to the waterfront and get them onboard so they can sail to Ireland tonight. This is a quick turnaround. Your end will be $5,000."

The amount, of course, got Jack's attention.

Jack paused momentarily, then said, "Sounds grand. This will have to be today, I take it."

Peter nodded, "Yes. Also, Anthony is going to be with you. He's a good soldier to have."

Jack asked, "Any security problems we need to be aware of?"

Peter replied, "Little, we control this dock. We mostly use it for imports of whiskey, but for these purposes, too. You and Martin will pick up the truck at the Brooklyn Naval Yard. Go to Slip 30 and ask for Michael O'Hare. He'll be at the gate and will escort you to the ship. Should be easy."

Jack replied, "Does Martin need to be involved in this? He's still jittery after the escape."

Peter said, "You lead this; take whoever you want."

Jack replied, "Where's the package? When can I pick it up?"

Peter smiled, sensing Jack's enthusiasm, "Pick them up around the corner. We've got a vacant shipping building where the weapons are being loaded as we speak."

Jack said, "Grand. I'll head down. Inspect the situation."

Peter replied, "Grand. Report back to me here after the delivery is done. Don't use the phones. Just come to my door, give me a thumbs up."

Jack stood up, smiling at Peter, then exited his office. As Jack emerged from the pub, it was a hot summer day, well above 90 degrees. Jack thought he might never get used to the heat in Brooklyn. In Ireland, there were very few days of this kind of extreme heat. Jack made his way to the factory, where he found the door closed. He knocked on the door, and Uncle Anthony opened it for him.

Jack said, "Thanks, all set?"

Anthony replied, "Almost, loading up the last couple of crates."

Jack replied, "Grand, you're coming with me, right?"

Anthony responded, "Yes, that's the plan. I'll drive us down to the Naval Yard."

Jack nodded but said nothing. Instead, he walked over to the truck as the final crates were loaded. The two men noticed him immediately, appearing to be nervous at first.

Jack asked, "Need a hand?"

Both men shook their heads, no, continuing to load the last crate. When they wrapped up, under Jack's supervision, they closed the doors.

Jack said, "Anthony, let's get going."

Anthony got into the truck as Jack climbed into the passenger seat. Soon, they were off to the Brooklyn Naval Yard. The trip was only ten minutes.

On the ride over, Jack said, "Anthony, we're to ask for Michael O'Hare when we get to the gate."

Anthony said, "I know Michael, good lad."

They made their way over to the Brooklyn Naval Yard, and within fifteen minutes, they arrived at the gate.

As Anthony pulled up, he opened the window. As it turns out, Michael O'Hare was the guard at the gate.

Michael said, "Anthony, you know where you're going?"

Anthony nodded, "Michael, this is my nephew, Jack; he's joining the crew. Arrived yesterday."

Michael asked, "This is the nephew that was in Limerick Jail?"

Jack nodded yes.

Michael reached his hand in the window to shake his hand, saying, "My brother was Peter O'Hare. He told me you saved his life in that shithole."

Jack said, "Aye, Peter O'Hare. Remember him well, good lad. I didn't do much; I just had his back in a scrape. That's what friends do."

Michael smiled. "He's told me it was a little more than that. He'll be coming over soon."

Jack replied, "Grand."

Anthony chimed in, "Best we get going."

With that, Peter opened the gate to allow the truck to head toward slip 30. As the truck pulled down to the slip, several longshoremen were loading cargo onto the ship. When Anthony pulled up, he waved the foreman over to the truck. Within thirty seconds, the longshoremen were unloading the weapons, placing them on pallets to be lifted into the cargo storage. Jack watched, amazed at how quickly the longshoremen loaded up the pallets. Within three minutes, the pallets were being hoisted onto the vessel with a large crane.

Jack was standing by the water when Anthony came over to him. "Better get moving."

Jack replied, "Aye, grand."

With that, they both returned to the empty truck, heading for the exit. As they got to the gate, Michael was standing post, so when Anthony waved his hand from the car window, Michael opened the gate, allowing Anthony to leave the naval yard quickly.

As they pulled out onto the highway, Jack said, "That was too easy."

Anthony replied, "Not when you control the dock as well as a couple of guards. Then it's all about timing."

Jack nodded but said nothing. As Anthony drove the truck back to the warehouse, Jack thought this was way too easy, but it was also an easy payday for him. When they returned to the pub, Peter was sitting behind his desk with two envelopes in front of him. Jack stood at the door, giving Peter a thumbs up.

Peter said, "Come in, glad it went well. These are for you."

Peter handed one envelope to Jack, then the other to Anthony. Both men placed the envelope in their respective pockets. Peter nodded at them, indicating he had other business where both men should leave. Anthony and Jack got up from the chair, left the office, and headed out to the pub. Both men would sit in a booth, ordering breakfast.

Jack asked, "While this was a good payday, is there more that we can be doing?"

Anthony smiled. "This was a test for you, I think. See if you can execute it. Be patient, and I could tell he was impressed."

As the breakfast arrived, both men sat quietly eating, listening to the news on the radio. They spoke of the fighting on Okinawa. Jack listened intently as he knew Mick was fighting there. The reports were grim, resulting in heavy casualties; however, the commentator was very positive this would lead the Allies to ultimate victory. Jack was only concerned with Mick's return.

Chapter 13
November 1945

With World War II over, men were returning home in droves. Jack hoped each day that he'd see his dopey brother walking on the street toward the pub. Maggie had received a letter dated September 1st, 1945, in which Mick wanted to drop her a note to let her know he was okay. The relief for a worried mother was palpable; she thought perhaps Mick would survive this ordeal.

It had been a few months since their arrival. Things with Peter Carmody were going well; Jack was earning a nice living for a recently arrived Irish immigrant. It afforded him the opportunity to treat his mum and Fiona to several new dresses, even taking in the picture shows three times a week.

Maggie asked Jack, "When will you pop the question to Fiona? I know she's hoping for that soon."

Jack replied, "Was thinking about doing it at Christmas."

Maggie smiled at the thought of adding a new daughter to the family. Maggie and Fiona had gotten close since their arrival, already developing a mother-daughter bond. Fiona worked as a waitress in the Three Aces Pub. Maggie was still looking for some form of work. Jack was providing for all of them anyway, so Maggie's urgency wasn't too high.

On the morning of November 2nd, Fiona had a meeting at the immigration office. She wanted to get the ball rolling, sponsoring a friend. Peter Carmody told Jack about his contact there. His contact would help with all the red tape; her name was Aine O'Neill.

Early this morning, Fiona got dressed in her best new dark red dress. She had a cup of tea with Maggie before leaving. Jack asked her if she needed a lift, but she declined.

Fiona said, "It's only a couple of blocks; I'll be fine walking over."

Jack nodded, acknowledging she was right. The office was only a couple of blocks away, in a safe neighborhood. At 08:30, Fiona left for the immigration office, having folded the paperwork to fit into her purse.

About thirty minutes later, there was a knock on their apartment door. It was the police.

Jack answered the door. "What can I do for you, sir?"

The policeman said, "Do you know Fiona Flynn?"

Jack replied, "Aye, I do. Is she ok?"

The policeman replied, "She was taken to the hospital. It's serious. She was struck by a car as she went across the street. She was conscious at the scene, but her injuries were quite bad. She asked for Jack Quinn specifically to come to meet her. We can ride you over."

Jack replied, "OK, let's go."

The policeman drove Jack to the hospital. When Jack arrived, he went to the front desk in the emergency room.

Jack asked the nurse, "My name is Jack Quinn. I'm looking for Fiona Flynn."

The nurse turned ashen.

Jack asked, "Where is she? Is something wrong?"

At this point, a doctor came to the desk, and the nurse replied, "Doctor, this is Jack Quinn, a friend of Fiona Flynn."

Jack replied, "Nice to meet you all, but can you take me to Fiona?"

The doctor replied, "I'm sorry, she didn't make it. Her injuries were extensive, given the rate of speed the vehicle was going."

Jack stood in shock, not knowing what to say.

The doctor said, "They haven't moved her yet; you can sit with her if you like, but you can't touch her. I'll tell you, the injuries are severe, so prepare yourself."

The doctor put his hand on Jack's shoulder, escorting him to the room Fiona was in. When Jack arrived, the doctor pulled back the sheet from over Fiona's head, pulling it down to her chest, covering her breasts. Jack stood silent, saying a prayer for his beloved Fiona. The doctor left Jack alone with Fiona as he began to cry over her.

Ten minutes later, the doctor came back in. "I'm sorry, but we need to move her downstairs to the morgue. If you head down, they can tell you when she'll be released so you can plan the arrangements." Jack, still in shock, nodded, then followed the orderly downstairs.

After arriving downstairs, Jack was asked to sit in the waiting room and told that the coroner would come out shortly. Jack waited for two hours before the coroner came out to see him.

When the coroner arrived, he said, "I'm very sorry for your loss. Were you close?"

Jack replied, "Yes."

The coroner said, "Again, I'm sorry for your loss. We can release her remains to a funeral home once you've made arrangements. Here's the number to call. You'll need to provide them with your address so we can coordinate pickup."

Jack nodded, not knowing what else to say. Jack stood up, saying nothing, heading for the elevator door. He emerged outside the hospital, still in shock over what had happened. Jack began to wonder who the driver was and how he could do this to Fiona. Jack's shock started to turn into anger. Instead of heading home directly, he went to see Peter Carmody.

Jack made his way to the pub, heading to the back office where Peter was. Peter was alone in his office, sipping coffee, seemingly contemplating a plan. When Jack came to the door, Peter stood up.

Peter said, "Jack, how's it going?"

Jack replied, "Not good. Fiona was killed today, hit by a car at a high rate of speed."

Peter responded, "That's terrible. I know how much you cared for her."

Jack nodded. "The police didn't indicate if an arrest was made. Is there a way to find out what happened and who this clown is?"

Peter replied, "I've got a few contacts on the NYPD; let me make some calls. Look, don't do anything rash; we need to be very sure about what happened."

Jack responded, "Oh, I'll wait, but when we have the facts, I'm taking care of this personally."

Peter nodded, understanding Jack's anger; however, more words weren't going to be productive. Instead, he picked up his phone to make his first call to the precinct commander. Jack listened intently as Peter laid out what Jack had shared. Jack listened to a lot of "uh-huh"s on Peter's part.

Then Peter said, "I know that guy. Where's he living?"

Jack asked, "What's going on?"

Peter waved him off, signaling not to interrupt him, while Peter grabbed a pen, scribbling the address on a blank sheet of paper.

Peter said, "Bill, thanks for the information. I'll let you know how we're going to deal with him."

With that, Peter hung up the phone.

Jack said, "Can I have the address? I'll take care of this right now."

Peter replied, "Hang on a second. Let's do this smart. Let me handle this. Go make the arrangements for Fiona's service. We're friends; let me take care of this. He'll feel your pain, I promise."

Jack realized, at this moment, that Peter was right. *I've got a friend who can take care of this.* Peter admired Jack's desire to seek revenge but felt it was best if he tended to burying Fiona. Jack was part of a team, so Peter was using this to teach Jack how to deal with these situations and not lose his temper. *Be methodical when planning revenge.*

Jack accepted Peter's offer. Then Jack headed home to inform Martin and Maggie about what had happened. When Jack came home, Maggie could see her son was very upset.

Jack said, "Mum, Martin, sit down at the table."

Maggie replied, "What's happened?"

Jack replied, "Fiona was struck by a car. The police came by earlier to take me to the hospital. When I got to the hospital, I was told she had passed. Her injuries were too severe. She died in the ambulance; there was nothing they could do for her."

Maggie sat silent, in shock, starting to cry. She got up from the table to put her arms around her son, knowing this was a devastating blow. Martin sat in shock, saying nothing. The room fell silent, other than the quiet sobbing from each of them.

Finally, Martin broke the silence, asking, "Do we know who hit her?"

Jack replied, "We do. Peter's offered to take care of it so we can focus on Fiona's funeral."

Martin replied, "She's my sister; nobody else should be handling this but us."

Martin had transitioned into a full rage at this point, banging his hand on the table and shouting revenge for his sister. His reaction was understandable; Jack felt the same way, but Peter reiterated that sense of belonging to something greater, as well as what friends do for one another. However, Martin wasn't hearing it at all.

Martin said, "I'm going to see Peter. *I* want to take care of this."

Jack replied, "I tried that already; he said he'll take care of it."

Maggie chimed in, "Martin, if Peter says he'll handle it, he will."

Martin responded, "Not good enough. I'm going to see him now."

With that, Martin got up to leave the apartment, but not before hearing someone rustling with a key outside the door. Suddenly, the door swung open. It was a man with a scar over the left side of his face, dressed in a marine uniform with sergeant stripes.

Maggie yelled, "Mick! Is it really you?"

Mick replied, "Mum, it's great to see you all. What's going on?"

Jack replied, "Fiona was killed this morning, struck by a car."

Mick knew how sweet Jack was on Fiona, even before he went to prison. Mick recalled that they were the boy-girl tandem that chased each other on the playground. As Mick dropped his duffel bag, Maggie went to her son, hugging the stuffing out of him, so much so that Maggie was pinched by Mick's medals.

Jack said, "Mick, glad to see you. Welcome home."

Mick replied, "Sorry about Fiona. I know how much you loved her."

Jack nodded but didn't say another word.

Mick looked at Martin. "Sorry about your sister."

Martin blew past Mick, saying, "I'm heading to Carmody now."

Jack replied, "Martin, I know you're upset, but that's a mistake. What are you going to do, yell at him to let you have this?"

Martin replied, "Well, we've got to do something."

Jack responded, "Peter will handle this. Better to have someone, not family."

Martin yelled, "I don't care."

With that, Martin made his way out of the apartment down to the pub to confront Peter. What no one realized was that Martin had put his pistol in his right pocket before he left. Martin stormed into the pub with a full head of steam, moving toward Peter's office. When he arrived at the office, Peter's bodyguard stopped him.

The bodyguard said, "State your business."

Martin said, "Need to talk to Peter about what happened to my sister."

The bodyguard replied, "We know what happened. Jack was told it would be dealt with. That's all you need to know."

Martin attempted to get past the bodyguard, pulling his gun out and aiming it at the bodyguard. What Martin didn't realize was that a second bodyguard came up from behind him. The second bodyguard placed a revolver on the back of Martin's head.

The second bodyguard said, "Put your weapon down. We know you're upset, but this isn't the way things are done here."

Martin attempted to turn around to face the second bodyguard when he heard Peter say, "I know you're upset, but I'm taking care of it. Focus on your family. We've got this."

Martin replied, "Unacceptable…"

Peter cut him off, yelling, "I'll tell you what's unacceptable: you come in here this way, ordering me around, threatening my men. You're on thin ice right now. I'm trying to be sympathetic, but you're making it difficult."

The second bodyguard still had his weapon drawn, as did Martin. Martin suddenly turned in Peter's direction. Peter put his hand out, attempting to grab Martin's right wrist. Before he could grab Martin, the second bodyguard fired his pistol into the back of Martin's head. Martin was dead.

Peter said to the second bodyguard, "Why'd you do that?"

The second bodyguard replied, "He had a gun in his hand and turned right at you. What choice did I have?"

Peter thought for a second, "Understood, get rid of the body. If anyone asks, he stopped by here looking for revenge, but we threw him out. Take him up by the bridge, the construction site, you know where. Let me know when it's done."

On the same day, despite the joy of having Mick home, Jack would mourn his first love, as well as the loss of a great friend. Jack inquired with Peter about when Martin came to visit him.

Peter said, "He came in here very angry, waving a gun. We told him to leave. Haven't seen him since."

Jack never knew exactly what had happened to Martin, but he knew Martin had put Peter in a bad spot—a spot Jack had hoped he'd never be in with Peter.

Chapter 14
February 1950

Things had gone well since moving over from Ireland. Jack was thriving in his work with Peter Carmody, who kept him busy and took him under his wing. Peter involved Jack in matters that, in the past, only he would handle: negotiations with his mafia associates and Irish patriots. Jack managed deals, securing significant concessions and generating a steady cash flow. With an entrepreneurial spirit, Jack convinced Peter to reinvest their proceeds into local businesses. They got involved with taxi companies, local grocery stores, and even a motor car shop. Jack believed these businesses would bring in healthy returns—legitimately. To Jack, diversification was essential.

Peter and Jack also discussed a succession plan. Peter wanted to slow down, feeling confident he could, given Jack's strong performance. Besides, Peter knew Jack was sweet on his daughter, Kick.

Margaret Kathleen Carmody was a tall woman, standing 5'8", with dark auburn hair and hazel green eyes. Kick was a firecracker, a woman who knew her own mind and would speak freely for a woman of that time. She noticed Jack in the Three Aces Pub at a gathering Peter had one Friday evening.

Kick approached Jack that evening. "Hey, handsome, you look like trouble."

Jack took her first comments as an insult. "You don't know me from a hole in the wall, miss."

Kick laughed. "Miss? Let's start again. Hello, my name is Margaret Kathleen Carmody, but everyone calls me Kick."

Jack replied, "It's nice to meet you. Can I get you something to drink?"

Kick smiled. "I'd like a white wine, please."

Jack smiled. "Coming up."

Jack headed for the bar to get Kick a white wine, as well as topped off his whiskey. Peter was at the bar when Jack arrived.

Peter said, "You know the girl you just met?"

Jack said, "Assuming she's related, based on her last name."

Peter replied, "That's my only daughter. I love her, but she's a firecracker. You better understand what you're getting yourself into."

Jack responded, "Are you telling me she's crazy?"

Peter laughed. "No. She's opinionated and not afraid of expressing those opinions either. Some men might have a problem with that."

Jack smiled. "Mr. Carmody, I've got the best of intentions for Kick."

Peter smiled, turning back to the bar and looking for his whiskey glass. After Jack retrieved the cocktails, he headed back to Kick.

When Jack returned, Kick asked, "What was that all about with my father? You do know he's my dad?"

Jack smiled. "He told me. I told him my intentions were honorable."

Kick smiled, cracking, "You better."

Kick continued to be smitten with him. She was American-born and raised by her father to be an American woman. Kick was also very different from Fiona, especially in her forwardness, which took Jack back a little.

Jack asked, "Kick, would you like to go to dinner tomorrow evening?"

Kick replied, "Sure, just not here."

Jack smiled. "I'll make reservations. Pick you up at 18:30?"

Kick smiled, pleased with Jack asking about dinner. They went out to dinner the next evening, really hitting it off and talking about the future. Jack indicated he was looking to start a family; to his surprise, Kick did want a family, but not immediately. They enjoyed the dinner very much, finishing each other's sentences throughout the conversation.

This is how it was for nearly nine months: dinner out a few times a week, talk of their future together. It had been a long time since Jack felt this way about a woman like he did with Fiona.

One evening, after a date, Jack returned to the apartment to find his mum and Mick chatting. Mick was telling her about something that happened at work while both sipped tea.

When Jack arrived, Maggie asked, "So, how did the date go?"

Jack smiled. "Aye, grand. You know, tonight we talked about marriage?"

Mick replied, "Really? Who brought it up first?"

Jack said, "Kick did. Look, I'd really like you to meet her. I think you'll love her. She's so much fun and energetic."

Maggie said, "Marrying a Carmody, how ironic."

Jack replied, "You won't like her because she's a Carmody?"

Maggie replied, "I think it's funny how this happened. I have nothing against the girl. When are you asking her for supper, or do you have different plans?"

Jack responded, "I'd like to bring her Sunday; is that ok?"

Maggie smiled. "Sure, I'll get something nice."

Jack replied, "Thanks, I'm heading in. Talk with you in the morning."

All three said goodnight as Jack went to his bedroom. He started to think about asking Peter for Kick's hand. He thought Peter would be pleased. Jack then needed to find a jeweler to pick out a ring. Jack had an early meeting with Peter, so he thought it was best to talk about marrying his daughter after the business was finished. As these thoughts danced in his head, he lay down, quickly falling asleep.

The next morning, Jack was up early. Maggie was making breakfast for her boys before they headed to work. Jack ate quickly, heading out early to meet Peter, hoping to catch him in a good mood early this morning.

As he entered the pub, Jack headed to Peter's office. Peter was sitting behind his desk, yelling at someone on the telephone. When Peter saw Jack, he waved him into the office, placing his hand over the receiver.

Peter said, "This idiot from the Bronx. He's short again."

Jack replied, "I had a feeling. Want someone to pay him a visit?"

Peter yelled back into the receiver, "You're a goddamn deadbeat! Have what you owe me by 15:00 today! No more extensions, no more excuses!"

The man on the other end of the phone was yelling back as Peter hung up the phone.

Peter looked at Jack. "What's our topic today?"

Jack replied, "I've got two topics."

Peter said, "Go on."

Jack replied, "First—the man from the Bronx. I was planning on visiting him this morning, but now I'll wait until 15:00. I'll have Mickey with me. Assuming you want us to lay on a beating if he doesn't have the money?"

Peter said, "Ok, remember it's $15 grand."

Jack replied, "Understood. Be prepared to lay a beating on him."

Peter said, "Second item?"

Jack replied, "We had a problem down at the docks yesterday evening. Someone broke into our stash. We had a lookout on the place, but he was alone against five guys. He said they were *paisans*, Vinnie's crew."

Peter smiled. "Thought you were going to ask for Kick's hand?"

Jack said, "That can be our third topic."

Peter replied, "Go on."

Jack said, "This situation needs to be dealt with delicately. We own that dock; I've put ten of our men down there in the evening, starting today. I can pay Vinnie a visit, but I'm not sure if that's better coming from you. How do you want to handle that?"

Peter laughed. "You go talk to Vinnie; I'll call him after you meet him. So, topic three?"

Jack sat up nervously. "Mr. Carmody, I love Kick with all my heart. I promise to keep her, be faithful to her, and to always have her best interests in mind."

Peter, stone-faced, said, "Children?"

Jack replied, "Yes, we'd like to have children."

Peter stood up, heading to his private stash of premium Irish whiskey, the stuff you could get only in Ireland. He poured two glasses, then sat down in the chair next to Jack. This was something that Peter did only on rare occasions.

When Peter sat, he said, "You two are a good match. She'll push you, and you'll rein her in. She reminds me very much of my wife when we met. You remind me of myself in my youth. You know I was sweet on Maggie before I left Ireland."

Jack said, "I've heard that."

Peter replied, "Your father was a good man; they were well suited for each other. He died too young. But with that said, Maggie's rejection made me consider what was important. That's why I came to America. It allowed me to start over again. It took a while before I got close to anyone, but when I met Kick's mother, believe you me, I was arse over teakettle with her. If you've got half of what I have with my wife, you'll both be very happy. Have you picked out a ring?"

Jack smiled, sipping his whiskey. "I wanted to ask for Kick's hand first."

Peter smiled, sipping his whiskey. "You have our blessing."

Peter wiped a tear from his eye, sensing the satisfaction of having a new son. Jack was beaming from ear to ear. He almost levitated out of the chair.

Jack said, "I'll take care of these things first, then I'll talk with Kick."

Peter nodded as Jack headed out of the office. He had a couple of hours to search for engagement rings. Jack found a beautiful ring at Kelsey Jewelers: a round, 2-carat diamond with a gold band that had emerald chips in it. Later that evening, Jack stopped at the pub, looking for Peter.

When he found Peter, Peter said, "So how'd it go?"

Jack replied as they were in mixed company, "With the first guy, it was a long way to Tipperary. With the *paisano*, he was taken aback by the whole thing. Looked shocked; it seemed genuine. Promised me an explanation tomorrow."

Peter replied, "It wasn't a rainy night in Dublin with the first guy?"

Jack said, "No, we made it clear he's on that path if he doesn't refund us. Also, can we talk in the back for a minute?"

Peter nodded, then headed for his office, with Jack following. As they entered the office, Jack closed the door behind them.

Peter asked, "What's up?"

Jack said, "I wanted to show you the engagement ring I got for Kick."

Jack opened the case with the ring.

Peter said, "It's beautiful; she'll love it. Good luck."

Jack smiled, then headed for the door; his day was done. That Saturday evening, Jack would ask Kick for her hand in marriage.

Chapter 15
March 1955

It was the morning of March 17th, a Saturday, when Bridget Fiona Brennan, better known as Bridie, was marrying Mick. They decided on a brunch service. Mick was home getting ready himself before heading over to the church. Jack and Kick, along with their first child, Fiona, went to pick up Mick. Mick was alone in the apartment now that his mother had passed away. She was a heavy smoker, as well as being exposed to cobalt in the Brooklyn Naval Yard during World War II. As Mick got dressed, he thought of his mother and how much he missed her, wishing she could be at the events.

At 07:30, Mick emerged from the apartment building just as Jack pulled up. Little Fiona was in the backseat, hollering up a storm and driving Kick a little crazy. Jack and Kick were married in 1951. Little Fiona was born on January 12th, 1953. She was suffering from the terrible twos. When Jack parked, Kick got out of the car.

Kick said, "You clean up nice. I'll sit in the backseat with Fiona. I warn you, she's having a bad day so far."

Mick smiled. "Want me to sit with her? She's my favorite niece."

Kick smiled, heading for the backseat. Jack never got out of the car.

As Mick climbed in, he said, "Morning, Jack. Everything ok?"

Jack replied, "Not much sleep with the little one. Also, we need to talk after the ceremony."

Mick responded, "About?"

Jack replied, "After, it can wait."

As Jack drove off toward the church, Mick was taking in the sights as Jack drove.

From the backseat, Kick asked, "Mick, are you sure about this?"

Mick, a little surprised, said, "What do you mean?"

Kick replied, "I'm sorry, but I don't see the attraction. I love you. I'm not saying this to be mean, but Bridie is a little bit off."

Mick asked, "Why don't you like her?"

Kick said, "She's very possessive of your time. She doesn't really talk to anyone in the family. Anytime we've been around her, it's like she thinks she's better than the rest of us."

Mick responded, "Why are you telling me this now?"

Kick replied, "Because we love you. Don't want you to make a mistake. I'm not sure you'll be happy with her."

Mick sat quietly for a moment, taking in what Kick was saying. Surprisingly, Jack sat silent on the topic; then again, he would be the next one to be heard from.

Jack replied, "Mick, Kick brings up some good points. I checked into her family—not a good lot. Say they're for the cause, but their support has been all talk. Anytime I've asked her father to do something, he's always got an excuse. Also, her father gave them Jimmy O'Leary a couple of months ago. Apparently, Jimmy cheated him at a card game. Rather than call him out, he went to the police, informing them about an illegal card game. You know how much our take is from that operation."

Mick answered, "What's that got to do with Bridie? Guilt by association?"

Jack replied, "Mick, where there's smoke, there's fire."

Mick shut down, saying nothing more. Any attempt to address him more on the subject was met with stern looks. From the rearview mirror, Jack smiled at Kick, giving her *the look. They said what they had to say; he's a man. Let him make his own decisions.*

When they arrived at the church, the street was buzzing with those coming to the wedding. Mick made his way to the vestibule to assess if all was fine for Bridie's day. After Mick did his initial assessment, Jack made his way into the vestibule with Kick and Little Fiona. Mick held the door to the church open for Kick as Kick made her way to the front pew. Jack escorted her to the pew, making sure his family was situated, then returned to the vestibule to greet the guests. Mick's only family was Jack's family of three. He had a few friends who came from work, but for many, it was a long trek to come to Brooklyn, as many were moving to Long Island with all the postwar housing expansion.

As for Bridie's side of the family, she was one of twelve, the youngest of their clan. Her father was a foreman for the longshoremen. Mick had met Bridie at an American Legion Hall dance sponsored by the union. Mick was swept away with Bridie. Bridie was a slim young lady with a mix of blonde and red hair, very fair-skinned with freckles, and standing about 5'4" tall. Many considered Bridie shy and reserved and did not share very much of herself or her opinions. Once she let Mick in, Mick saw a more caring side of her, a woman of faith, family, and decency.

Bridie didn't like Jack due to his involvement in the IRA. She despised the IRA, but when questioned, she never seemed to have an answer, always responding evasively. While others saw this as a flaw, Mick viewed it as a sign that she had character. Mick's opinion on the IRA was shaped by the death of his father at a young age. Additionally, after his years of service in the USMC, Mick's code for life had changed. He would fight to defend his family or adopted country; however, he had earned the right to live as he wanted, in peace, not in fear of jail, as he saw it. In Jack's opinion, Mick was moving to a moral high ground, treating his only brother as the black sheep of the family. In Mick's eyes, Jack never measured up to what he thought

Jack should be. This created a lot of friction between them, but they always remembered that they were brothers, no matter what.

Kick, on the other hand, was very disappointed in Mick's attitude toward Jack. Kick was proud of Jack, all that he had accomplished, all that he held dear, learning from Kick's father. Kick thought Jack was a self-made man, rising from the ashes of his father's death. Kick was very protective of her family, not liking when even blood spoke of her husband in demeaning ways. Also, Kick knew Bridie from the neighborhood. Kick clearly wasn't a fan. Bridie could be a bit of a bully when they were growing up, always wanting her own way. Being that Bridie was the youngest, her parents spoiled their twelfth child. Bridie took full advantage of this. Bridie attempted to bully Kick once on a street corner after school, but Kick wouldn't back down to Bridie that day or any other day.

As the guests were seated, Mick made his way to the altar with his brother by his side. As they waited for Bridie to show up, Mick leaned over to Jack, "What did you want to talk about? Got to admit, I'm curious."

Jack said, "We can do this later."

Mick replied, "Seriously, what is it?"

Jack responded, "I don't want to steal your thunder. It's your day, not mine."

Mick looked at Jack, smiling, "Kick's pregnant again?"

Jack smiled, "Yes, she's three months along. Look, I wanted to wait until after. I don't want to take anything away from your wedding day."

Mick winked at Jack, "Adding to your clan will never take anything away from this day."

As they wrapped up the conversation, the organ started to play. Within seconds, Bridie was entering the church with her father. As they made their way down the aisle, Mick thought how beautiful she looked—sweet, innocent, his.

Once Bridie made it to Mick, she smiled her loving smile. However, Bridie's father had the look of a stone-cold killer. Suffice it to say, Mick didn't like his new father-in-law, with the feeling being reciprocal. When Mick came to ask for Bridie's hand, he wouldn't give an answer, forcing the conversation to Bridie's mother, who was a very sweet lady. She saw the good in Mick, as well as how he handled coming back from the war, not dwelling on the past but focusing on making a better future. When Bridie's mother gave him the go-ahead, her father reluctantly went along. With that said, Bridie's parents didn't contribute to the wedding other than helping Bridie with her gown. Beyond that, they offered nothing. Mick would pay for the wedding out of his own pocket, with a nice gift from Jack that helped immensely.

Soon, the priest started going through the Mass, talking about marriage like he was an expert. Mick never understood how a priest could talk about being married or understanding the demands of marriage. While Mick understood that priests were married to God, he always thought it wasn't the same. *God may be listening, but they don't talk back to you. God wasn't there to put his arm around you when you were having a bad day.* Mick was also tarnished by his war experiences. Mick would say to his comrades, *"How can any God allow this to happen?"*

The priest finished his homily, which was long intended to be inspirational, but it was a more flowery language that Mick felt wasn't in the spirit of the day. However, Bridie loved Father Selbst; she thought the sun rose and set on him, an opinion shared by her parents as well. Mick wasn't his biggest fan. Mick felt the father tried to shake him down for money. It's customary to offer a gift for the use of the church, essentially a donation. Mick was prepared to make an offering of $25, but the father seemed offended by the amount.

The father asked Mick at the rehearsal, "Do you think that's enough?"

Not only was Mick offended, but so was Jack. Mick even needed to step between the father and his brother after the father's question. Here, they were at the altar rehearsing while the priest was shaking

Mick down for more tithing. For someone who knew the family all his life, he certainly seemed to have his own agenda.

Mick replied, "I'm comfortable with the amount."

Then Mick looked at Bridie, asking, "Can we talk over there?"

Bridie was a little surprised, as they were in the middle of the rehearsal; however, Mick didn't care. Mick escorted his future bride to a remote corner so they could talk. As he escorted her to the corner, the priest followed them.

Mick said, "Father, this is a private conversation."

The father said, "Nothing is private in my church."

Mick looked at Bridie, replying, "I'm about 30 seconds from walking out of here. Let's do this at the justice of the peace, then have this blessed party."

Before Bridie could respond, the father said, "I can't marry you if you're going to be like that. Shake your finger at God like that."

Mick was now angry, yelling, "You're not God! You're a shakedown artist! I don't give a rat's ass what you think! Leave us the fuck alone!"

Bridie was crying. "You don't want to get married now?"

Again, the priest attempted to respond, but Mick cut him off. "Father, I said leave us, now. If you don't, I'll leave here with your Adam's apple in my pocket and serve it up for breakfast. I was a Marine; believe me, I can do that before you even got close to me."

Bridie was hysterical now, thinking Mick was calling off the wedding. The priest was so offended he left the church, heading for the rectory, but not before turning out the lights in the church, leaving it lit only by a few candles that were burning.

Mick said, "Bridie, I'm not canceling the wedding, but I can't be married by Joe Shakedown Artist. I don't give a shite if he's your family priest or not. How can you be married by a man like that, with no morals whatsoever?"

Bridie was crying but also relieved that Mick didn't want to cancel the wedding.

Bridie asked, "So where do you think we'll get married?"

Mick said, "We can do it at City Hall. Who the hell needs a priest for this?"

Bridie replied, "But our marriage won't be valid in the church."

Mick sarcastically said, "Who cares what they think? Our marriage is about us, nobody else. Not a family member, not your fucking priest. We're not doing this to appease anyone. I won't do it. I fought for my life for four years and saw many friends killed in some of the most grotesque manners. I owe it to them to live a good life, be true to their memories, and have my family's best interests at heart. Nowhere in that is it right to take shite from a priest. One that never served a day in his life."

Bridie was taken aback. It was the first time Mick really talked about his military service. It was impactful on her to see the intensity he felt after ten years. At this point, Bridie's mother came up to them.

Bridie's mother said, "I'm not here to interfere; I want to help. I'll talk to the father and get him to see some reason. Mick, I agree with you. The father was way out of line; however, you didn't do yourselves any favors treating him like that either."

Mick replied, "Mum, I hear what you're saying. Perhaps I made a mistake not letting it roll off my back. On the other hand, I treated him the way he treated me. I expect to be treated the way I want to be treated; when others don't reciprocate, I treat them the way they treated me. You may think that's a flaw in my character. I won't be put upon by anyone."

Bridie's mum saw that she wasn't going to convince her new son-in-law to walk things back. It was her mum who visited the priest the following morning, not apologizing for what happened at the rehearsal but tearing into the father, defending her new son-in-law's attitude.

During the visit, she told the father, "If you don't get off this high horse, we'll be finding a new parish to attend."

She was just as indignant with the father as Mick was. All of this was running through Mick's head as they got to the most important part: the vows. The father read through the vows, having Mick repeat the words while he faced his blushing bride. The father then did the same with Bridie, gazing into Mick's eyes. From the corner of Mick's eyes, he saw her mum wiping a tear from her eye.

Finally, the father asked, "You may kiss the bride."

It was the one and only instruction from the father that he obliged. Soon the new couple would be walking down the aisle, stopping to greet Bridie's parents first.

Bridie's mum said, "Welcome to the family."

Mick smiled but didn't say a word as he saw the grim look on Bridie's father's face. He never said a word to Mick nor shook his new son-in-law's hand. The new couple then turned, walking over to Jack and his family.

When Mick got close to them, Jack shook his hand. Kick kissed Mick's cheek, offering congratulations.

Jack kissed his new sister-in-law on the cheek, which Bridie allowed, surprisingly. Then Bridie came face to face with Kick.

Kick said, "Welcome to the family! We're an exclusive sister-in-law club. We'll need to keep our boys in line."

Mick laughed, thinking Kick's comments were amusing—true, but amusing. Bridie, however, thought differently.

Bridie replied, "Thanks for the welcome. I'm one of eleven, so I've got family to support me."

Mick, Jack, and Kick were surprised by Bridie's reaction; however, they let the whole thing go for the moment. It was Bridie's day; they were along for the ride.

Chapter 16
August 1968

It was August 1st. Bridie had her fourth son in the wee hours of the morning. William Patrick Quinn was born at 04:00, entering this world hollering like an Irish tenor, cue-ball head, flailing his arms.

Bill was the last of their four children. In 1956, Bridie gave birth to a son, John Andrew Quinn II; however, he died two days after birth. Little Jack, as the family called him, was born with a congenital heart defect. He went into cardiac arrest, dying shortly thereafter.

Their second son was Michael Seamus Quinn, known as Roger. He was born in 1960. He was a cute boy, a very curious fellow for eight years of age. Why he was nicknamed Roger was a mystery. Bridie said Mick had called him that from day one, but Mick thought Bridie had started with it. To this day, the family still cannot get a satisfactory answer. However, "Roger" stuck.

Their third child was a girl, Margaret Rose Quinn, born in 1963. She had thin red hair and was very precocious for five years of age. She was smart, picked things up well, and was very much looking forward to having a baby brother.

This morning was about Bill and Bridie. Bridie slept while Bill was being looked over in the nursery. Mick came to the hospital after getting his other children off to school, reaching the hospital room at 09:30. When he arrived, Bridie was asleep. Mick decided to walk down to the nursery to see his new son. Mick wasn't at the birth, as he needed to take care of his other two children. By 1968, Bridie and Kick had fallen out. Kick accused Bridie of making an offhanded comment about her daughter, Diedre—something about her being stupid.

When Kick heard what Bridie said, she said, "You're not welcome here! How do you talk about a child like that?"

Bridie attempted to say something, but Kick went to the front door, throwing her out of Jack's house. Neither Jack nor Mick knew what happened until they came home from work.

Uncle Jack and Aunt Kick had five children. Fiona Lynn Quinn, born in 1953, was now a stunning brown-haired beauty with rich chocolate eyes and slight freckles on her face. At 15, she was coming of age—funny, pretty, and engaging to everyone she met. She had Aunt Kick's passion but lacked her edginess.

Aunt Kick's second child was Diedre Rose Quinn, sometimes called "Rosey," a nickname she hated. Born in 1955, she was, as they joked, sent by the gods to help the Brooklyn Dodgers win the World Series. Aunt Kick has a picture of Uncle Jack holding his newborn daughter in one hand, a beer in the other, standing in front of the TV, watching Johnny Podres pitch the game of his life against the NY Yankees to clinch the series. Suffice it to say, there's never been a louder roar from a city than there was the day Brooklyn won. Uncle Jack would talk about that day like it happened yesterday.

Aunt Kick's third child was Alanna Nora Quinn, known to the family as Nora. She was born in 1958. She was a very funny girl with brown curly hair and hazel green eyes. Uncle Jack joked with her all the time; it was her that forced the Dodgers to move out of Brooklyn. She liked baseball, sitting on her dad's lap watching a game. She was eight, a bit of a tomboy in the neighborhood. She had no problem playing baseball against the boys. She was good at it and not intimidated either.

Aunt Kick's fourth child was Cara Maeve Quinn, known to the family as May. She was born in 1960 with auburn hair, deep freckles on her face, and a sweet smile. She was looking forward to having a little brother like her cousin, Rosy. They would joke with their mums that they'd have someone to boss around.

Aunt Kick was pregnant in the summer of 1968, due in early November with her last child. Uncle Jack and Aunt Kick had already chosen his name. It would be Ciaran Joseph Quinn.

As the families grew, they started to drift apart over the feud between Aunt Kick and Aunt Bridie. Bridie told Kick that she never said anything like that, but Kick had a close friend she trusted who told her Bridie shot her mouth off in the coffee shop. Jack and Mick tried to stay clear of the feud, telling their wives, for the sake of the family, that they needed to let it go. Uncle Jack's thinking was *blood is blood*. Mick felt similarly to Jack, but he also felt the need to stick up for his wife. This made the holidays quite a lot of fun as a kid, seeing their parents acting like children.

One holiday, things got so out of hand that Jack and Mick ended up in a bit of a scuffle. They'd been talking about something said about Diedre, who sat at the dinner table, growing visibly upset. By then, Jack had downed a couple of whiskeys, and his temper flared. He slammed his hand on the dining room table, causing the plates to jump and knocking over a full gravy boat.

Mick stood up and looked at Bridie, saying, "I'm done. We're leaving."

Jack stood up. "Good! Get the hell out of here! I'm tired of listening to the same old shite. Look at how you've pushed it! Totally unacceptable."

Mick said nothing as Bridie got up from the table. Mick and Bridie were collecting the coats for their children.

Bridie turned to Kick. "Thanks for a lovely dinner. Sorry, it was ruined."

Kick stood up, then started to take the food and their plates off the table. All the while, baby Bill was in the crib, hollering because all the commotion scared him.

Mick packed his family in the car, heading away from Jack's house at a high rate of speed, screeching the tires as he turned the corner. As he drove home, he continued to rant about what was said and what wasn't said—all the family beefs. Mick yelled about how his mum passed away and that Jack didn't come to visit her often. In 25 minutes, the family was home. After getting the children situated, Mick poured drinks for him and Bridie. Bridie rubbed his back, trying to get Mick to relax. After a couple of sips of whiskey, they both calmed down.

That would be the last collective family gathering. They would not sit for another meal together until Jack's daughter, Fiona, was getting married. Even at those family events, the families sat at separate tables.

Despite the family feuding, business was going well for Jack. Peter Carmody retired, heading back to Ireland for six-month stretches. Jack had come up through the ranks; Peter trained him well. Jack was respected not only by his business partners but also by the community. Jack was always a hard negotiator; he could also be ruthless to those who became his enemy. However, there was a softer side to Jack. He was very generous and always knew how to pay back a favor in a big way, too. Even with all the drama between Kick and Bridie, Jack always made time to be with Mick, whether it was Friday night boxing cards, baseball games at Shea Stadium, or even hockey games at Madison Square Garden. Uncle Jack was a big NY Rangers fan. As the children got older, Jack and Mick would bring them along to these events, even once taking all the children, without the wives, to Jones Beach, taking them for a day of fun and sun.

The kids all thought Uncle Jack walked on water. He was always there to offer support, stick a quarter in their pocket without anyone knowing, and then they'd see his large belly laugh when he suggested that the child reach deep into their pocket, never knowing what would be in there.

As for Uncle Mick, the kids were not as much of a fan. Mick had an edge to him, probably related to the horrors of war that he carried with him. Even in 1968, with the Vietnam War just engulfing his adoptive country, he would get very angry watching the news, seeing how soldiers were being treated when they got home. Mick once saw a young man dressed like the hippies of the time spit on a soldier who had just come off the subway. Mick lost his mind.

Mick yelled, "Hey! What the hell do you think you're doing? This soldier put his life on the line so you can stay home dressing like that and doing drugs!"

The young hippie said, "He's a baby killer."

Mick screamed in his face, "You don't know what you're talking about! Have you ever stood the post?"

The young hippie said, "No, I'd never do that."

Mick screamed in his face, "Piece of shit! You won't honor his commitment! You've got no idea what it's like to stand the post and watch your best friends killed in ways you can't imagine! You stand there with a smug look on your face like you're morally superior because you're afraid to do your duty!"

The young hippie shouted back, "Get out of my face, old man!"

Mick punched the young hippie, knocking him to the ground with one punch. Blood poured out of the young hippie's mouth. When he opened his mouth, Mick saw he had knocked four of his teeth out.

Mick stood over him. "Got anything to say now?"

The hippie replied, "No, sir."

Mick said, "The next time you see a soldier, thank him for his service. You owe them that debt of gratitude."

With that, Mick disappeared down the street, even before the soldier could thank him. Mick always lived by a code. *Provide financially for your family. Never lay your hands on a woman; treat them the way you'd treat your own mother. Treat people the way you want to be treated; if they don't reciprocate, then treat them like they treat you. Last, always have your family's back; blood was blood.* Mick had drilled this into his first two children; as such, he'd drill it into his second son.

Chapter 17
September 1975

It was fan appreciation day at Shea Stadium, where the NY Mets took on the Philadelphia Phillies. Uncle Jack had gotten tickets for his brother Mick, as well as Jack and his son Joseph. Joseph and Bill were only a couple of months apart, both born in 1968.

At age 7, this was their first time seeing a game at the ballpark. Uncle Jack was more of a Yankees fan, but Mick was a Mets fan, having transferred his allegiance from the Brooklyn Dodgers when they stunningly moved to Los Angeles. Uncle Mick was a NY Giants fan, never transferring his allegiance to San Francisco. While Uncle Jack remained a huge Willie Mays fan, he switched to being a NY Yankees fan.

At 7 years of age, the park was majestic—the sights, the sounds, the smells. The field looked like a green carpet interwoven with brown dirt. The base paths were chalked up. The roar of the crowd with each pitch, the silent anticipation of the next pitch to come, holding your breath each time Rusty Staub came to the plate. This was a very good year for Rusty, driving in 100 RBIs, the first Met to do so since Don Clendenon. The sounds were incredible, as each pitch seemed to have the game hanging in the balance. The smells were also new to the two young boys: the smell of hotdogs, stale beer, and popcorn.

On this day, the game kept the boys entertained; however, the great thing was that Uncle Jack and Mick, two brothers, were speaking again. It had been two years since they had last spoken to each other, as the feuding between Aunt Kick and Bridie continued, neither giving an inch to the other.

A week before the game, Uncle Jack called to talk to Mick before making the invitation.

Uncle Jack rang Mick, "Mick, it's Jack. It's been a while. We need to talk. You're my only brother, regardless of whether the wives can't get along."

Mick thought for a minute, wondering what Jack's angle might be, "It's been two years; why now?"

Jack replied, "I could give you some flowery answers, but simply put, I miss my brother."

Mick responded, "I miss seeing you as well, but the wives are like cats and dogs."

Jack said, "Let's leave them out of this. I told Kick I was reaching out and that I didn't care if they could patch this up. I told her I'm not alienating my only brother."

Mick replied, "I agree; let's leave them to sort out their differences."

Jack asked, "I've got tickets to the game for fan appreciation day. I got four. I was thinking we could take Bill and Joseph with us."

Mick replied, "Aye, sounds grand. We'll come over to pick you up for the game."

Jack responded, "Great, see you then."

When Mick hung up with his brother, he noticed Bridie in the hallway of their Brooklyn home.

Bridie asked, "Going out with Jack?"

Mick replied, "He invited Bill and me to a ballgame. Haven't seen him in two years."

Bridie responded, "I don't want you hanging out with him."

Mick waved his hand dismissively, "Look, if you and Kick want to be at each other's throats, so be it. He's my only brother, we're going to a ballgame. Get over it."

Bridie wasn't happy, storming off to the kitchen and refusing to speak to Mick even through dinner that evening. Bridie could be possessive of her family, particularly Mick. She felt Jack was using this as an opportunity to sway Mick to bury the hatchet or to admit to something Bridie had never said. Always suspicious of people, Bridie saw the worst in them and was protective of herself, then Mick, and lastly, her family. Knowing the nature of Jack's business, she did not want Mick or, worse, her children involved; her way to ensure her family stayed clear of Jack's dealings was to cut ties completely.

For years, Jack tried to involve Mick in his business, tempting him with potential financial windfalls. Mick had been careful to stay out of it, fending off Jack's attempts. Mick was a foreman in the construction union; Jack had influenced the vote to go in Mick's favor, hoping this would strengthen their relationship and also open doors for Jack into labor unions. While today was about the boys spending time together, Uncle Jack intended to pick Mick's brain a little about some things he'd been hearing.

Mick picked up Jack at 10:30 for the 1:00 PM first pitch. As the young boys settled in the back seat, Mick and Jack began to talk about the day's matchup—whose pitching, whether one player would play today or not. The 1975 Mets were a .500 club, finishing 82-80. None of that seemed to matter for today's game. Mick and Jack kept the conversation light, never once talking about the dispute between the wives. Bill and Joseph asked a hundred times if they were there yet.

When they parked at Shea Stadium, the four walked toward the turnstiles, then down to the box seats Uncle Jack had procured. Positioned just off home plate toward the Mets dugout, the seats made it easy to see into the dugout, as well as the on-deck circle as a player was coming to bat.

When they sat down, Mick said, "Nice seats; must have set you back a little."

Jack smiled, "Yeah, the seats are nicer than I thought. Boys, want a hot dog and a soda?"

Both boys excitedly said, "Yes, please."

Jack raised his hand as the concession guy came by.

Jack said, "Four dogs, two Cokes, and two Schaeffers."

The concession worker replied, "That'll be $15."

Jack pulled out a $20 bill, handed it to the concession worker, and said, "This is for you. Come back in an inning or two."

With that, food and drinks were situated. They got to the ballpark just as batting practice was over. Not long after, the Mets would take infield and outfield practice before returning to the locker room before the first pitch. As the boys watched in awe at seeing their childhood heroes play the game they love, Uncle Jack pivoted his conversation with Mick.

Jack asked, "Hey, I've been hearing a lot of rumbling from the union hall the past week or so."

Mick curiously looked at Jack, "What have you been hearing?"

Jack replied, "Heard some of the old guard is not happy with some of the changes you're trying to make."

Mick smiled, "I didn't take this post to win a popularity contest. They want to act as if nothing needs to change. It can't stay this way; we need to work closer with the other side so we can maintain pay rates and benefits. This isn't 1952 where we can be like the Teamsters."

Jack smiled, "I got a call from Tim Reardon the other day asking me to help out."

Mick got stiff, "Look, I appreciate you helped me attain this post, but we agreed I'd run it the way I saw fit, come what may."

Jack replied, "I'm offering to help if you want it. I'd hate to see you lose this post so quickly. I'm just letting you know what I've heard."

Mick asked, "How can you help?"

Jack said, "I can talk to Tim and a few other old-timers. Let them know you're doing the right thing and that they can trust your judgment."

Mick replied, "How are you going to do that? I'm not for sale, Jack—you, of all people, know that well."

Jack responded, "I'll calm him down. We're brothers. I'm not looking for anything other than to help protect you in the post."

Mick changed the subject, "Game's about to start. Thanks for offering to help. Let me think on it."

All returned to enjoying the game. It was a close game, but the Mets would lose 4–2 on a two-run homer by Mike Schmidt in the top of the ninth inning. The boys were thrilled to be at the large stadium, bragging to each other about what a wonderful time they had. Mick took Jack and Joseph back to their place, afterward returning home.

When they returned home, Bridie was sitting on the front porch waiting on them. Bridie looked very angry.

When Mick got to the porch, he asked, "Love, what's wrong?"

Bridie replied, "Kick called me today."

Mick said, "Really, how'd that go."

Bridie returned, "She called to say how nice it was that you were able to get the boys to the game."

Mick replied, "That's got you mad, why?"

Bridie responded, "Then she brought it up again, just egging me on!"

Mick said, "Why didn't you tell her you had to go? Why go over it all again?"

Bridie curtly responded, "It figures you took her side."

Mick replied, "I did no such thing. Did she have a conciliatory tone, or was it the same old shite?"

Bridie said, "Started out conciliatory, but ended in the same place it always does. I'm to blame for saying something that I didn't say."

Mick calmly said, "Let it go. She's not worth all this."

Bridie then said, "She also called to tell me something. Tim Reardon is dead."

Mick shouted, "What?"

Bridie said, "Kick knew we're close with the family. Said he was shot in the back of the head down on the docks at the Brooklyn Naval Yard."

Mick turned around, saying, "I'll be back."

Mick got into his car, heading toward Jack's house. When he arrived, Jack's car was gone, so Mick figured he had gone to the pub. While it was nice to take the day off, his business didn't wait either. Mick arrived at the pub fifteen minutes later, heading inside to find Jack at the bar with a whiskey.

Mick came up from behind him, "Hear about Tim Reardon?"

Jack turned, "Mick, let's have a drink in my office."

Without allowing Mick to respond, both went to Uncle Jack's office. Jack went to his private bar, pouring Middleton Irish Whiskey into two glasses. Mick closed the door behind them, not wanting anyone to interrupt them.

Mick asked, "Heard about Tim Reardon?"

Jack replied, "I did when I got to the pub."

Mick said, "Did you have a hand in this?"

Jack angrily replied, "I didn't. Tim was a loudmouth, shooting it off to whoever would listen. That's why I didn't want him in that post. He wasn't practical. I didn't like him, but kill him over this? No way. He's small potatoes."

Mick replied, "Then who?"

Jack said, "Thought you didn't want me involved in this?"

Mick shot back, "This was a friend. I need to know."

Jack replied, "This goes no further. Old man Montouri wanted him out of the picture. He owed some people a lot of money. Liked to gamble money he didn't have. Those he owed grew tired of waiting. From what I heard, it was close to $50,000."

Mick replied, "I didn't know he liked to gamble."

Jack said, "Ponies mostly."

Mick asked, "What do I tell my people when they ask?"

Jack replied, "I know he's a friend, but why tell them anything? He got himself wrapped up in something sinister and paid for it with his life."

Mick replied, "My people will want some answers."

Jack said, "Tell them the truth. Turns out Tim was a degenerative gambler who didn't pay his debts."

Mick said, "I guess I could use that with those on the inside, but we need to show that we're willing to protect our union members."

Jack replied, "Agreed. Put some boys down on the docks and make it look like you're building a presence. It will die down in a couple of days, especially once it gets out about the gambling. They'll know, but not *sure* what they know. Make sense?"

Mick nodded, gulped his last bit of whiskey, then headed out the door with only a wave to his brother. The ride back would take twenty-five minutes, where Mick contemplated: did Jack tell him the truth? Was the ball game today a ruse? Was Tim a degenerative gambler? Mick saw no evidence to that effect. This situation posed more questions than answers.

Chapter 18
December 1975

The situation with Tim Reardon didn't die down; in fact, it escalated over the past two months. There was picketing at the dock, and fights broke out several times, with police making arrests. The story is about Tim being hooked on gambling, and the Montouris wasn't holding. With all this going on, Mick was caught in the middle, torn by his friendship with Tim versus the gambling accusations.

Mick knew Tim's wife, Aileen, so one evening, he paid her a visit.

Mick said as Aileen came to the door, "Aileen, I stopped by to check on you and the girls."

Aileen Reardon, née Aileen O'Toole, was a tired woman dealing with all the accusations about her beloved Tim. Aileen stood 5'7", close to 185 pounds, with blonde hair and blue eyes. She was warm and inviting under the best of circumstances. She was a homemaker and appeared to be a babe in the woods. However, Tim confided in Mick and said that he had told his wife everything.

Mick asked, "How are you and the children doing?"

Aileen said, "Aye, as well as can be expected. Many of our friends have been kind, checking in on us, sending food."

Mick replied, "That's grand. Is there something I can do to help? Benefits, compensation. That's what the union is there for."

Aileen replied, "Those people have been very helpful and sympathetic. But these rumors of Tim's gambling—they aren't true at all. Tim never placed a bet with anyone. Something else is going on. Can you help with that?"

Mick said, "I'll do my best. I must ask, are you sure about the gambling? As this story has been getting around, many folks close to him at work have verified he liked to play the ponies."

Aileen retorted, "He liked to *watch* the racing forms, but he never placed a bet. I can account for every dollar of his wages, as well as where the money was being spent. All of it!"

Mick said, "Okay, I'll see what I can do, ask around. Look, I've got to run. Call the house if you need anything, please."

Aileen said, "Thanks, Mick."

Then Aileen walked Mick to the door. Mick decided to pay Jack a visit. When Mick got to the pub, he walked in, heading straight for Jack's office. When Mick got to the office, one of Jack's boys was guarding the door.

When they recognized Mick, one said, "He's wrapping up a call. I'll let him know you're here."

Mick was undeterred, pushing past the men. When Jack heard the ruckus at the door, he hung up his phone after finishing the conversation.

One of the guards said, "Uncle Jack, sorry, but he wouldn't wait."

Jack said, "Boys, this is my brother; he's got privileges with me."

Mick said, "Fellas, can you excuse us?"

Jack nodded as his guards left the room.

Once the door was closed, Mick asked, "This Tim Reardon story isn't holding. I just spoke with Aileen. She told me she could account for every penny of his wages, as well as where the money's been spent. If she starts telling folks this, we're going to have a problem."

Jack said, "Who's she going to tell? She's not close with anyone other than Bridie. You can manage that."

Mick replied, "What really happened here, Jack?"

Jack replied, "It's involved. I'll tell you, but it goes no further than this room."

Mick said, "Okay."

Jack continued, "Tim was involved with the cause. He cheated a buyer not just once but three times. Shortchanged them a little more each time. He then sold the merchandise to his Italian connection. They always want an arsenal."

Mick replied, "He was running guns with you?"

Jack shot back, "He's an associate who works for me from time to time. I found out he had another supplier, so he was double-dipping, so to speak."

Mick fired back, "So you whacked him over this?"

Jack replied, "No, the other partner did it. They shot him because he wouldn't pay them back. They wanted a pro-rata portion of the missing merchandise plus a tax of fifteen percent on the whole deal. They made the terms impossible. He'd never be able to pay that back."

Mick asked, "Nobody would listen to reason?"

Jack replied, "When I was approached, they asked if we had fair dealings with Tim. I told them yes, but I used him sparingly. When I inquired why, I got the whole story."

Mick asked, "So the ball game, that was a ruse then?"

Jack replied, "No, it wasn't. Just a coincidence it happened that night. I had no knowledge of his plans. When I heard about what happened, I chalked it up to them dealing with a cheater."

Mick said, "I get it now."

Jack came back with, "They wanted me to handle this, but I told them it was their mess to clean up. I suspected Tim was in danger, but I couldn't have told you about their plans, even if I knew them."

Mick asked, "Why tell me now?"

Jack replied, "Enough time has passed; we needed to dial down the emotions here. Look, Tim may have been your friend, but he was a shady guy with us in this business. Simply put, he put himself in this position."

Mick responded, "Understood. His family?"

Jack said, "They'll get his benefits and pension. I'm assuming she doesn't have a clue about any additional bank accounts."

Mick said, "Not according to her. Look, let me go. I need to get home."

Jack nodded, escorting Mick to the door. Jack was relieved Mick knew the truth. While Mick wanted no part of Jack's world, he understood there were always consequences for someone's actions.

What Mick wasn't made aware of, in addition to Tim holding back, was that Tim was trying to outflank Mick in the union. He was attempting to quietly push Mick out of his post, causing problems for Mick on every front while pretending to be Mick's friend. While Jack couldn't buy Mick, he had a couple of inside informers. While Jack didn't take Tim out, he sanctioned it with the other investor. Jack was interested in protecting Mick. As fate would have it, Mick and Jack would be intertwined with the union business.

Chapter 19
April 1980

Mick had come up in the ranks of the union; he was now being asked to be its president. He had done well with the rank and file, even weathering the Tim Reardon affair. Mick never shared with anyone what Jack had confided in him.

This morning was the day of the vote. Jack called Mick to wish him well in the upcoming election; however, Mick was melancholy on the phone.

Jack asked, "This is a great post for you. Think how you can impact the men."

Mick said, "I'm getting older now. Maybe I need to step aside for a younger generation."

Jack replied, "Bullshit, you're the best guy for the job. If you want to retire soon, then bring some of the younger lads along. You've been talking about Michael McMullen and Bill McDermott. Those are strong young lads; show them the ropes."

Mick responded, "Aye. I've thought of it. I'm just not sure I want all the bother anymore. That last contract negotiation was rough."

Jack replied, "But it was you who got what the union wanted, forcefully too, I recall."

Mick said, "Thanks for the call. Let me go."

What Mick suspected, but Jack would never have admitted to, was that it was Jack who had a hand in getting the worker concessions. When the management came back with its final proposal, they agreed to the 6% wage increase, but Mick had to agree to at least fifty additional no-show jobs. These jobs were fake jobs for mafioso figures, even a couple in Jack's crew. Jack wielded this sparingly, using three for elderly men who couldn't make ends meet, men who lived alone in crummy apartments in the neighborhood. Besides, Mick wasn't stupid; it was a small price to pay. He could tell his membership, you wanted 6%, we got you 6%. Many of the other union members wouldn't read the fine print of the contracts.

Mick was fifty-eight years old now, an accomplished labor leader, who did his best to keep his membership employed, as well as get them the best contract, including pay and benefits. But the toll it was taking on his state of mind and physical features was mounting. Mick was constantly worried about the union's safety, keeping members employed, and minimizing trouble. His state of mind was fragile, he felt. However, the physical toll was starting to show itself, too. Mick had been in the hospital for an enlarged heart in January 1980. The doctors told him he was getting a serious heart condition. Also, he was diagnosed with diabetes; the years of eating sweets, as well as his love of Kentucky bourbon, were pushing him closer to a heart attack each day. Bridie wasn't making it easier, as she was on Mick's case to retire almost every waking moment. The pressure was unrelenting.

Jack also noticed a difference in Mick. The once strong rock of his family—ten years prior, Mick would have welcomed this post. Now, he seemingly couldn't care less.

On the day of the vote, votes were tallied at various union halls, with results available by 17:00 that day. Early returns had the race a dead heat, but Brooklyn hadn't been counted. When it was, Mick won with a fifteen percent margin. Michael "Lefty" McMullen was the other candidate. Mick knew him and his people well. Michael worked on the dock as a carpenter; he was a short man with a round frame, 5'6", close to 250 pounds. Michael was a gregarious fellow, funny, sharp, always ready with a story to tell. He was close to forty-five years of age, with a carrot top head, as well as deep hazel-green eyes. He could have been the flag of Ireland, folks would say.

Lefty called Mick to congratulate him on his victory.

After exchanging pleasantries, Mick said, "Lefty, tomorrow I'd like you to stop by my office. I'd like to talk about the future of the union and also to ask for your help. When I say help, I don't mean unifying after a loss, but a real post to help the union."

Lefty responded, "Mick, I'm flattered, a little surprised, but flattered nonetheless. I'll stop by in the morning."

With that, they hung up the phone. Mick outlined his plan to bring Lefty into the fold, helping him to run certain aspects of the union, namely the pension fund. Other than pay, it was the single largest thing to manage. Mick thought of the benefits of cultivating new leaders, leaving his strong legacy for the union, not for himself.

After the call with Michael, Jack called to congratulate Mick.

Jack said, "Congratulations. I'm glad this worked out."

Mick replied, "Aye. Look, I just spoke with Lefty. I asked him to stop by tomorrow to talk about what I'd like to do, as well as have him play a part in helping. I'm trying to bring new blood in and prepare them for the future. Any additional advice?"

Jack thought for a minute, "Lefty's good to bring inside the tent, but I would suggest you also bring in Bill McDermott; he's a whiz at finances. Could help a lot with the pension fund, as well as keeping union dues up. Lefty's a good cheerleader, but having both under the tent will solidify your position. Also, it lets the younger members see you're not just the old guard; you're showing them you're looking to the future."

Mick replied, "Good idea. I'll factor it into my plans."

Jack asked, "Fancy a drink, celebrate your victory?"

Mick said, "Thanks, but another time. I've got some planning to do."

With that, they hung up their phones. Mick continued to sit behind his desk, taking out a new piece of paper outlining different options on how to use Lefty and Mack. Jack's advice was sage; Mick knew Lefty's abilities, as well as Mack's. What Mick hoped for was that both men saw this as an opportunity, not a chance to create a rivalry. Mick needed to stress that point with both men. He wanted to shape a new vision for the future, garnering their help in strengthening the union across generations. Mick contacted Mack.

Mick said, "Mack, it's Mick Quinn. Was hoping you'd come to meet me in my office tomorrow morning. Lefty's coming over, too. I want to lay out the vision for the union going forward. I'd like both of you to play an active part. What do you think?"

Mack replied, "I'd be happy to help. What time tomorrow?"

Mick said, "09:00, my office. Just you, nobody else. This is a strategy session."

Mack responded, "Right. See you in the morning."

With that, they hung up. Now, Mick needed to reach back to Lefty, as he didn't want to blindside him at the meeting.

Lefty answered his phone, "Hello."

Mick said, "Lefty, Mick Quinn again. Just wanted you to be aware I invited Mack to our meeting tomorrow morning. I'd like all three of us to work together on shaping a future vision. I think if we pool our resources, we'll be able to reach across the factions in the union."

Lefty paused for a moment, "Bill, how do you think he'll help the cause?"

Mick replied, "He's a finance whiz. Perhaps we'll have him run the investments while you focus on your strengths, drawing the union tighter and looking out for future work. I think together we can set up a solid foundation for the future."

Lefty paused again, "I'll be honest, I'm skeptical, but I do appreciate what you're trying to do. I'll think more on it. See you in the morning."

With that, Lefty hung up the phone somewhat abruptly, Mick felt. Mick spent the next few hours contemplating the call with Lefty. *Mick* saw this as strengthening the future, playing to everyone's strengths— why didn't *he* share that opinion? Was it all his ego?

The next morning at 09:00, both men were promptly at Mick's office. He welcomed them and then asked if they'd like coffee before they started. Both men declined the offer. Mick jumped into his vision, outlining for them a role for each of them, as well as Mick's intentions in his role as president of the union. Mick spoke for fifteen minutes without interruption from either of them.

Mick wrapped up by asking, "So, fellas, what do you think?"

Both glanced at each other, then glanced at Mick. Lefty said, "Interesting broad strokes. I must say I think it's got a lot of promise."

Mack said, "Agreed, has lots of promise. One question, though: how do we improve on each other's areas? Meaning, how do I learn about Lefty's world, not a strength for me. Conversely, how does he learn about the finances?"

Lefty replied, "Great question. It was something I'd thought of last night."

Mick said, "That's where the partnership comes in. What I'm offering to you both is that you'll have input into just about every major decision. I'm not saying we're voting—ultimately, I'll have the final say—but I promise you'll get input on every major decision. Complete transparency; this way, you'll be able to see how all sides are done. Also, it leaves a future partnership as the union moves forward once my term is up. It's my plan to fulfill my term, then leave it to you two."

Both were shocked, never expecting to hear Mick essentially say he was going to do this for two years, then step aside. Mick watched to see the reaction of the two. Mack nodded, thinking to himself, but what was he thinking? Lefty was the better politician, great at assembling the troops, someone the union would stand behind. Mack similarly sat quietly, appearing to be running this through his head like figures.

Finally, Lefty broke the silence, "I'm surprised you'll only serve two years."

Mack chimed in, "Yeah, I'm surprised by that as well."

Mick replied, "Look, I'm fifty-eight years old; in two years, who knows if I'll want to continue? I'm looking to leave this in capable hands, teach you both how this works, leaving it better than I found it."

Both men nodded. With that, the meeting wrapped up, with the three agreeing to meet next week to take the broad strokes down into the weeds. After the meeting, Lefty and Mack quickly made their way in separate directions. McDermott headed to see Jack Quinn while McMullen went back to his office.

When McDermott reached the Three Aces Pub, he made his way to Jack's office. When he arrived, one of Jack's bodyguards motioned for Mack to head in, almost as if Jack was waiting on him. Jack was on the phone, seemingly wrapping up his call. Jack pointed at the chair where Mack then sat.

Jack said, "Right, sounds like it went well. Glad to hear that."

Jack sat listening intently, nodding as Mick spoke, but Mack only heard Jack's side of the conversation.

Then Jack said, "Mick, I've got to run. My next appointment is here. If either of them reaches out, I'll let you know."

With that, Jack hung up the phone.

Jack said to Mack, "He seems to think the meeting went well."

Mack said, "It did. He surprised us about what his plans were. Playing to our strengths. It was a side I'd never seen from him before."

Jack replied, "My brother's a good man, a little pious, but a good man overall. While we've got business to do, make sure you've got his back. Let's do this as aboveboard as we can. I'll make sure the loans are legitimate and see the union get their return on investment. What I'll need is for you to make sure Mick goes along."

Mack replied, "I'll do that."

Jack smiled, "Anything else to discuss?"

Mack said, "The one concern I've got is this creates a rivalry between me and McMullen."

Jack said, "Well, that's up to you both. It only happens if you let it."

Mack nodded, taking in Jack's thoughts.

Jack continued, "Why don't you guys go for a drink, talk things over—what you both want out of this? Look, I could see him becoming the next president, with you as the director of finance. You're a bit younger than Lefty; it could be a great succession plan, especially if you discuss it in advance."

Mack replied, "Yeah, I think I'll reach out."

Jack replied, "Let me know how that goes; I can reach out to him as well."

Mack said, "Thanks. Let me get out of here."

With that, the meeting was over. About an hour later, Lefty showed up at Jack's office.

Jack said, "Fancy seeing you today."

Lefty smiled, "Mack came to see you already."

Jack smiled, "Yep, spoke with Mick, too. Sounds like the meeting went well."

Lefty replied, "I'm not so sure."

Jack, concerned, said, "Really? Mack thought it was a good plan."

Lefty said, "It is *if* Mick's sincere."

Jack replied, "I can tell you one thing about my brother for sure. When he outlines a strategy, he sticks to it. He can be pious, but he honestly believes he's in this for the men. No different than his Marines. His legacy is not about himself."

Lefty said, "I appreciate the insight, but . . ."

Jack interrupted, "Look, I'll give you the same counsel that I gave the other guy. You two meet and talk about what the future looks like. I told him that I saw you as the next president, that he'll be the director of finance. He's a little younger than you, so set up the succession from Mick to yourself and Mack. It's a great way forward."

Lefty thought for a moment, then asked, "Do you think Mick will last the two years?"

Jack replied, "When Mick sets his mind to something, he'll do it. Why do you ask?"

Lefty said, "When I headed back to the office, I ran into some members who weren't happy with Mick's victory. One of the guys is Anthony McTiernay—you know that guy, he's nuts. He was talking real tough talk."

Jack responded, "I know that guy. You think he's a real threat or just talking bad about Mick?"

Lefty replied, "I'm honestly not sure. Let me go see Mack so we can talk. Let me get out of here. Thanks for the advice."

Jack smiled as Lefty now left. As the door closed behind him, Jack thought to himself, *Mick* hadn't had the job for twenty-four hours, and guys were already scheming against him. Jack called Mick.

Jack rang him, "Mick, Jack. Got a minute?"

Mick replied, "Sure, what's going on?"

Jack said, "Both of them swung by here. I wanted you to know that."

Mick responded, "Not surprised. What's the *real* reason for your call?"

Jack replied, "I told them you shared your vision with me. Told them it was solid, and they needed to work together to make this work."

Mick interrupted, "Thanks, but I figured this would happen."

Jack jumped in, "Yes, but Lefty was telling me there were a couple of guys at his office really upset about your victory."

Mick replied, "I'm not everyone's cup of tea."

Jack said, "He told me Anthony McTiernay was taking it real hard. Spewing how he needed to take you out of the picture. Or at least that's what Lefty inferred. Do you want me to set up some protection for you?"

Mick thought for a minute, knowing the reputation of Anthony McTiernay, a malcontent of biblical proportions. As Anthony would have anyone believe, the whole world conspired against him and his whole family. Anytime something didn't break his way, it was a conspiracy. Mick also knew this fed Anthony's paranoia, too; coupled with his threats of violence, this was a serious threat.

Mick said, "How would the security work? I don't want bodyguards 24/7."

Jack said, "You might if he's serious. Lefty thought it was serious enough to talk to me."

Mick replied, "Let me think about it. Anything else?"

Jack laughed, "That's it on the business front. Want to catch a game this weekend?"

Mick said, "Love that."

Jack said, "I'll get four tickets so we can take Joseph and Bill, like old times."

Mick replied, "Sounds good. Talk soon."

With that, Mick hung up the phone, reached into his desk drawer, and then removed the weapon he stored in it. While Mick hated violence, he wouldn't be put upon either. Mick took the gun holster out, placing it on his belt behind his back. It was lunchtime, so Mick went across the street for a sandwich at the shop. He stepped off the curb and then noticed a man heading toward him. As the man got closer, he saw it was Anthony McTiernay. Mick stopped between two parked cars, placing his weapon in his right hand as McTiernay continued toward him.

When McTiernay reached him, Mick said, "Anthony, I don't want any trouble."

McTiernay said, "Don't tell *me* what to do. I can't believe you won this thing. I bet Jack fixed the whole thing for you."

Mick replied, "Jack had nothing to do with this. Go back to your hall, Anthony."

McTiernay pushed closer to him, "You know why I'm angry?"

Mick replied, "No."

McTiernay said, "You fucked me on that job in Bensonhurst last year."

Mick said, "What job in Bensonhurst? I wasn't aware of a job down there."

McTiernay replied, "I was out of work for six months because of you."

Mick replied, "Again, I've got no idea what you're talking about. What I can say is that many of the members don't want to work with you. I've heard it time after time about how difficult it is to work with you—the paranoia, the conspiracy theories, not to mention that temper of yours."

McTiernay was getting very angry; he pulled out a knife he had on his belt. As Mick saw him reach for the knife, he put the weapon in his face. However, McTiernay was indifferent to the gun, having a crazed look in his eye.

Mick said, "Stand down, or I'll blow your head off."

McTiernay replied, "No different than your brother."

Mick said, "Stand down."

McTiernay didn't, lunging toward Mick. Mick pulled the trigger to defend himself, one shot to the forehead. McTiernay was dead in the street. The owner of the shop had come outside, seeing the whole thing unfold.

Mick asked the shop owner, "Please call the police."

The owner went inside, calling the police. However, a squad car showed up seconds after the owner went in to make the call. Someone else had reported a man with a gun on the street.

When the police arrived, the policeman said, "Hands up."

Mick said, "I'm going to place the gun on the street with the butt facing you first. Is that okay?"

The policeman was a little confused, "You still have the gun?"

Mick said, "It's in my holster. I'll keep my hands up if you'd rather take it from me."

The second policeman had drawn his weapon, advancing toward Mick.

Mick said, "Officer, I'm not looking for any more trouble. This man attacked me with a knife, so I defended myself."

As Mick was speaking, the second officer continued to advance toward Mick, then reached around Mick, securing the weapon.

The policeman said, "Sir, I'm placing you under arrest."

The shopkeeper came outside, "Officer, I saw the whole thing. Look, this man was defending himself. The other man was acting crazy. He didn't have a choice."

The policeman said, "I'll be in to get your statement. Harry, put him in the squad car."

The partner put Mick into the backseat of the squad car; however, he didn't handcuff Mick.

When the patrolman got him to the car, he said, "I know who you are. You're Jack's brother. Stay here while we get this sorted out."

Mick nodded but said nothing. The police got the statement from the shop owner, as well as a waitress from across the street, claiming she heard the man threaten Mick. When the police wrapped up gathering statements, they went back to the squad car.

The policeman said, "Mr. Quinn, we need to take you down to the station to make a statement. From all those interviewed, this was clearly self-defense. Do you have a permit for the weapon?"

Mick replied, "I do. Should be in my wallet."

The policeman said, "We'll review that at the station."

With that, Mick was off to the police station. Mick provided his statement while the policeman spoke with the detectives assigned to the case. Mick was escorted to an interview room while the patrolman ran it by the detectives. After stepping through the statements, the detectives went into the interview room with Mick.

Detective Fredricks said, "I'm Detective Fredricks. This is Detective Kelly. Why don't you run down your day so far."

Mick replied, "I had a meeting with some work colleagues at 09:00; that meeting lasted maybe ninety minutes. I took a couple of calls before lunch before heading across the street for a sandwich. When I crossed the street, I noticed a man darting toward me. When he got closer, I saw it was Anthony McTiernay, a member of the union I represent. He informed me that he wasn't happy with the recent election results. He accused me of forcing him out of work for six months, which wasn't true. He then pulled out a knife from his belt. At that point, I raised my weapon, drawing down on him. I told him to stop, but he lunged at me instead, so I shot him."

Detective Kelly asked, "Had you drawn your weapon before seeing the knife?"

Mick responded, "Yes. I had it in my hand but hadn't drawn on him."

Detective Kelly asked, "Why did you feel the need to remove the weapon from your holster?"

Mick replied, "This guy has a reputation for being crazy. My brother called to warn me about a threat he was making just this morning."

Detective Fredricks asked, "Why'd you leave that out of the story?"

Mick said, "I'm sorry, I didn't think of it until Detective Kelly asked. Look, I'm trying to cooperate fully."

Detective Kelly said, "Appreciate that. Look, we need to run this by the DA."

Mick coldly said, "Then I've got nothing more to say. Also, none of you thought to Mirandize me. So now, I'd like to make my phone call."

Detective Fredricks said, "If that's how you want to handle it, so be it, but it becomes adversarial from here on out. Got to ask why you're turning this adversarial?"

Mick said, "I'd like to make my phone call."

With that, the detectives got up, leaving the interview room. Another plainclothes officer came in, escorting Mick to a phone. Mick called Jack.

Jack said, "Speak!"

Mick replied, "Jack, it's Mick. I've been arrested. You know the threat you warned me of this morning? Well, that idiot came here at lunchtime and attacked me with a knife. After our call, I took out my weapon to have on me for protection."

Jack said, "You've told all this to the police?"

Mick replied, "Yes. They said they got two statements. Sounded like it backed up my story. But one of the detectives thought it was interesting I had pulled my weapon as McTiernay walked toward me. Was I supposed to wait until he stabbed me? Also, let the lawyer know I was never Mirandized."

Jack replied, "Don't say another word. I'll send my lawyer down to help sort it out. I'll also make a couple of calls. Just don't do anything stupid."

Mick replied, "I won't, thanks."

Jack hung up, making the call to his lawyer, laying out the facts as he understood them, and then ordering him down to the police station. Jack's next call was to the Borough Commander's office. They were quiet friends, but friends nonetheless. The Borough Commander was a highly decorated cop, making his bones as part of the unit that brought in Son of Sam; his name was Joseph O'Shea. O'Shea was a tall man, 6'5", a former basketball player at St. John's University, a jovial guy who was a problem solver.

O'Shea answered, "Jack, what can I do for you?"

Jack replied, "Have you heard about what happened to Mick in the street today?"

O'Shea replied, "No, I haven't. The lieutenant from the detectives' squad asked to see me about a case, but I haven't been briefed."

Jack said, "Look, my brother shot a man attacking him with a knife. Seems to be cut-and-dry self-defense. Also, he mentioned he was never Mirandized."

O'Shea replied, "Jack, let me get with my lieutenant. We'll get this straightened out. Is his lawyer on the way?"

Jack responded, "On his way now."

O'Shea said, "Jack, thanks for the call. Let me get it sorted out."

Jack thanked him before hanging up the phone.

O'Shea called the lieutenant downstairs so he could run the case by him. The lieutenant was Lieutenant Arthur Wilson. Arthur was a tall Black man with a very muscular build, wearing a mustache. He had risen through the ranks quickly, making detective at twenty-seven, and got his gold shield at thirty-two. O'Shea was Arthur's first partner in the detectives' bureau.

Wilson arrived in O'Shea's office shortly after O'Shea's call with Jack.

Wilson said, "Morning, sir."

O'Shea responded, "Is this the Mick Quinn case?"

Wilson replied, "How'd you know that?"

O'Shea responded, "His brother called me and told me he wasn't Mirandized. Is that true?"

Wilson said, "We're checking with the squad car. The detective said the arresting officer had Mirandized him."

O'Shea replied, "Okay, let's get the facts on that. Run the case by me."

Wilson went through the story, the witness statements, and what happened when the detectives interviewed Mick. He laid out the sequence for O'Shea in ten minutes. As Wilson wrapped up, there was a knock on the door.

O'Shea said, "Come in."

It was the district attorney, Silvia Henderson, a seasoned DA with four years of experience. She was a feisty, pretty lady with short, dark brown hair and brown eyes, standing 5'6". She worked well with her colleagues. The detectives had a great deal of respect for her. She was fair in her dealings with other attorneys as well.

Silvia said, "Talking about the Quinn case?"

O'Shea said, "Yes. Sounds like clear self-defense. I appreciate a man's dead, but from what Wilson just ran down for me, it seems like he didn't have any other options. Have you heard he's claiming he wasn't Mirandized?"

Silvia said, "No. I hadn't heard that."

Wilson chimed in, "We're checking with the patrolmen; one swore he was."

Silvia said, "Perhaps it won't matter. Look, this lines up with self-defense. If I bring this to a grand jury, we'll get laughed out of court. I'm recommending we don't prosecute. Give him a fine for unlawful possession of a firearm."

Wilson said, "He said he had a permit for the weapon. He thought he had it in his wallet, but it wasn't. We sent a patrol car to his house to get it."

Another knock on the door.

O'Shea said, "Come in."

Detective Fredricks entered the room, "An update. We got the permit; it's legit. Also, the two patrolmen gave each other blank stares when we asked who Mirandized him. Apparently, one thought the other did it. So we've got nothing."

Silvia said, "Release him. Taking this to the grand jury is a waste of time."

O'Shea said, "Wilson, release him."

Detective Fredricks said, "I'll take care of it."

With that, everyone left O'Shea's office. O'Shea reached for his phone to call Jack.

Jack answered, "Joseph, what can I do for you?"

O'Shea replied, "He's being released. Self-defense. The DA won't bring it to the grand jury."

Jack replied, "Thanks for the call. Best to you and the family."

Jack then hung up. Detective Fredricks went into the interview room, finding Mick staring out the caged window. When the door opened, it seemed to startle Mick a little.

Detective Fredricks said, "You're being released. The DA won't bring this to the grand jury either, so you're free to go."

Mick grabbed his jacket, then said, "Thanks. Look, I'm sorry about earlier; it felt like your partner thought I planned this."

Detective Fredricks said, "We've got a job to do: follow the facts. You get that."

Mick nodded as the detective held open the door. Mick headed downstairs, where he saw Jack's lawyer talking with the DA. Mick stopped to listen to what was being said. The lawyers exchanged pleasantries.

The assistant district attorney said, "This was clearly self-defense, so we're choosing not to waste the court's time with it."

Jack's lawyer and Mick nodded but said nothing. Both headed to the exit of the police station, going their separate ways, but not before Mick thanked him for coming down. It was 17:30, so Mick decided to head home.

When Mick arrived home, Bridie was sitting on the porch waiting for him.

Bridie asked, "Mick, what happened?"

Mick explained what happened during the day. When he finished, she stood up and hugged her husband.

Then Bridie finally said, "I knew Jack had to be involved in this."

Mick replied, "Jack had nothing to do with this other than the lawyer."

Bridie said, "You're blind if you think he's not trying to gain control over the union. Why else would those two go to visit him? He's got his hooks in them."

Mick stood in front of his wife, amazed by what she was saying, but then, thinking through it, he thought perhaps she had a point. Jack was chummy with Lefty and Mack. What was the angle Jack was playing? Then he thought about Jack's suggestion to bring Mack in to oversee the finances. That's got to be key in this, but what?

Chapter 20
September 1980

Mick had set up a meeting with Lefty and Mack on a Tuesday morning. Mick had been reviewing the finances, noticing some irregularities. Perhaps the accounts were fine, but Mick noticed a large uptick in loans since Mack took on his new responsibilities.

When the meeting started, Mick went right to work.

Mick asked, "Why have we been issuing many more loans over the past few months?"

Mack replied, "The returns were attractive."

Mick shot back, "We are up tenfold from a year ago. Who are we issuing the loans to?"

Mack, sensing Mick's frustration, said, "Several local businesses are willing to work with us on projects as well. For example, the project in Bay Ridge. We provided seventy-five percent through a loan; returns are eight and a half percent, plus we're getting fifteen jobs. It was a good deal."

Mick came back, "That business is affiliated with my brother, no? Isn't that a conflict of interest, doing legitimate business with a known felon? Look, he's my brother, but we've got a responsibility to our membership to be aboveboard."

Mack said, "Known felon?"

Mick said, "Yes, he did time in Ireland fighting for the cause. Also, he had a scrape not long after he arrived. Mr. Carmody got the whole thing squashed, but he's been known as a felon since that event."

Mack said, "Peter Carmody?"

Mick nodded, "This is why I don't like having Jack being part of or knowing our business. Too much exposure. No more loans to businesses he's affiliated with, got it?"

Both men nodded, stunned that the very man who helped get Mick this appointment was essentially turning his back on him. When Jack heard the party was over, he was quite angry, angrier than many had ever seen him. Jack thought this would improve community relations, create more jobs, and benefit many in the community. Again, Mick's pious streak was shining through. Jack would have to talk to him. Jack drove to Mick's office.

When Jack arrived, Mick's secretary asked him to wait for a minute, informing him that Mick was wrapping up a call.

As Mick wrapped up the call, he went to his office door to ask the secretary for something when he noticed his visitor.

Mick said, "Jack, what are you doing up here?"

Jack replied, "Got a minute for your big brother?"

Mick smirked, "Come in."

Jack sat down, going straight into it, "Mick, why are you boxing me out of the loans?"

Mick said, "Appearance. I can't have the rank and file think we're doing business with the underworld."

Jack, stunned, said, "Underworld, what the fuck's that?"

Mick replied, "Look, you travel in lots of circles; some are unsavory types. I'm sorry, but I didn't know a better word to use."

Jack said, "Look, these loans are for legitimate businesses and causes in the community. I can assure you of that."

Mick replied, "But it doesn't address the appearance. It looks like a hooked-up boss is controlling this union. I won't have that."

Jack was stunned. "I can't believe you."

Mick sat stone-faced, feeling like he was in the right. Jack sat shaking his head, thinking his own brother was turning his back on him. Jack was so angry that he stood up and left Mick's office. Jack closed Mick's door, then went out the front door, never saying a word to Mick's secretary.

Mick called Mack first to let him know that he had broken the bad news to Jack.

When Mick told him the news, McDermott said, "Okay."

Mick's next call was to Lefty, where Mick told him the same news.

Lefty said, "I understand the appearance of it, but these causes are good causes."

Mick responded, "If it goes bad, who's got to explain it to the rank and file? We're constantly fighting off elements of organized crime; how do I let Jack in and no one else? It's a slippery slope. If you guys choose to do that when I'm gone, that's your call. But this call is *my* call."

Lefty said, "Okay, Mick, if that's what you want."

Mick hung up the phone, not saying another word. Mick was getting fed up with both men defending his brother. Mick had his secretary draft a memo to both, wanting a full listing of each loan, terms, conditions, and investors. Mick wasn't going to be put upon; it was a matter of honor to honor his commitments to the membership.

After Mick had dictated the memo, his secretary left the room to type it up for Mick's approval and signature. The memo was short and sweet, so she figured she'd knock it out right away.

When she finished, she went to Mick's door, knocking; however, there was no answer. She knocked a little harder—perhaps he hadn't heard her at the door—again, no answer. The secretary walked into the office and found Mick had passed out on the floor.

The secretary screamed, prompting another secretary to come to the door.

The secretary yelled, "He's still breathing. Call an ambulance!"

The second secretary raced to the phone, calling for an ambulance. Within five minutes, Mick was moaning incoherently on the floor, grabbing at his chest with almost every heartbeat. When the paramedics arrived, it was clear to them Mick had had a cardiac event. They placed him on the gurney before taking him to the hospital.

Before arriving at the hospital, Mick's heart stopped—Code Blue—where paramedics used the paddles to revive his heart. Upon arriving at the hospital, he was rushed to the ICU, where doctors made assessments. The doctors ordered all sorts of blood work while a nurse set up the heart monitor, placing the leads on his chest. Mick was still incoherent when the doctors asked him a couple of questions.

The nurse called out, "190 over 110."

The doctor called out, "Get the CCBs ready; we'll do an IV push, stat."

The second nurse brought the doctor what he asked for. Within ten seconds, Mick's blood pressure went to 125 over 90. While this was unfolding, a third nurse, for some reason, ran a blood glucose test, seeing Mick's legs seemed very dark, like bruising.

The third nurse said, "Doctor, his blood glucose is 700. Could it be a diabetic episode?"

The doctor called out, "200 mg of insulin; we need to bring the blood sugar down, too."

The third nurse called out, "Here, doctor."

The doctor nodded as he pushed the insulin syringe into Mick's stomach. With his heart rate down to 120 over 85, the nurse took another glucose test, noting the sugar levels were at 125. Slowly, Mick started to come around in the ICU.

After two hours, Mick tried to sit up, pulling the leads from his chest, and a nurse came running as the heart monitor was on full-blown alarm. The nurses told Mick where he was and what had happened.

Mick asked softly, "Did anyone call my wife?"

The nurse replied, "What's her number? I'll ring her now."

With that, Bridie came to the ICU desk and asked for Mick. The secretary who found Mick on the ground called Bridie to let her know what happened, as well as what hospital Mick was being brought to. The nurse at the desk escorted Bridie to the room.

When Bridie entered the room, Mick perked up, not wanting her to worry more.

Bridie asked, "What happened?"

Mick softly said, "I don't know. The last thing I remember was telling Jack no more loans. Everything after that is a complete blur."

The nurse was checking Mick's vitals when he asked, "Do you know what happened to me?"

The nurse replied, "I'll let the doctor know you're up. He'll tell you."

With that, the nurse left the room, found the doctor, then reemerged with him.

The doctor said, "In layman's terms, you had a severe heart attack, which we think may have been associated with your extremely high glucose levels. That's blood sugar. Your level was seven times what it should be."

Bridie said, "Seven times? Mick, you've got to start taking better care of yourself. All the desserts and the drink, look where you ended up."

Mick said, "Doc, was it that bad?"

The doctor, sensing the tension in the room, said, "Honestly, the worst case I've seen. You should see your regular doctor as soon as possible; he'll need to put you on blood pressure medication, as well as something to regulate your diabetes. Does diabetes run in your family?"

Mick shrugged his shoulders, "I don't know. My father died at an early age; my mother passed a couple of years ago from cancer. She was a heavy smoker."

Bridie replied, "I'll call the doctor when I'm home."

Mick said, "Looks like I'll finally have to grow up."

Bridie started to cry, knowing that she was finally reaching him.

Three days later, the doctors agreed to release him, having been given proof of an appointment with his personal doctor. During his three days in the hospital, Mick noticed one absence: Jack. Jack never came to see him in the hospital despite having been told about what happened. When Mick got home, three days went by, still no Jack, not a call or a visit. As it turns out, they wouldn't speak again for many years. Mick's slight toward Jack kept him away.

Chapter 21
December 1985

After Mick's heart condition in September 1980, Bridie was up his ass constantly about taking care of himself. She made his breakfast each morning, monitoring his intake of caffeine and sugar. She sent him to work each day with a lunch she prepared. Bridie was even in contact with Mick's secretary, who was acting as a spy for her each day, calling Bridie each evening after Mick left to provide a status update. Bridie knew about any infraction. Mick, on the other hand, found this constant monitoring not offensive but amusing, making a joke out of any infraction he was caught in, perhaps having a cocktail before arriving home. Bridie was determined to keep him around for much longer; however, Mick joked she was nagging him to death.

In December 1985, Mick decided to retire. After the loan debacle in 1980, he felt obligated to stay on longer, giving McMullen and McDermott the boot and replacing them with two other young lads that better fit Mick's mold. Today was retirement day.

Mick's son, Bill, decided to go into the office with Mick to clean out his desk. So they drove over to Mick's office. When they got upstairs, Bill realized this was the one and only time he'd see his dad at work. Mick was in a jovial mood, which took everyone by surprise, as Mick was anything but jovial, ever. Mick introduced Bill to the office staff. Curiously, other than hello, they said very little.

With the first box, Bill went toward the front door and overheard one secretary say, "Good riddance; he's one angry man. I thought he'd never retire."

The second secretary saw Bill and then motioned to the first secretary to shut up. Bill ignored them from that moment on. He felt they didn't know his dad the way he knew his dad. As Bill brought the first box to the car, Uncle Jack appeared on the sidewalk.

Bill said, "Uncle Jack? Surprised to see you here."

Uncle Jack said, "Billy boy, how's tricks?"

Bill replied, "Just helping Dad move out."

Uncle Jack said, "Old fuck's upstairs?"

Bill laughed, "Yes."

With that, both made their way to Mick's office. Jack and Mick had only reconciled a few months ago—July 4th, to be exact. Mick had decided he would retire. Also, Mick wanted to bury the hatchet with his brother. So Mick called to invite the family for a barbecue on the 4th. Initially, Jack declined, but Aunt Kick called a couple of hours later to say they'd love to come. It was the one and only time Bill could remember the old family beefs being left in the car.

As they arrived on the third floor, Mick saw Jack coming in the big glass doors.

Jack said, "You old fuck, finally getting out of here?"

Mick smiled, "Retirement Day. Finally."

Jack smiled, "I'm sure the staff's thrilled too."

Mick laughed, "Probably."

Jack asked, "Got a minute?"

Mick said, "Sure, Bill, here's the next two boxes. Can you give us a minute?"

Bill said, "Okay."

As Bill grabbed the boxes, Mick and Jack went into Mick's office one last time.

Jack said, "If these walls could talk."

Mick nodded but said nothing.

Jack continued, "Thanks for approving that loan for the new recreation center."

Mick said, "I was happy to do it. Good cause."

Jack replied, "I didn't appreciate being excluded for so many years. Why now?"

Mick said, "Why now did I approve the loan?"

Jack said, "Yes."

Mick said, "I spoke about it with Martin; he said all the due diligence was appropriate, regardless of your involvement. He saw no conflicts; besides, he knew I was retiring. Also, it was a small loan."

Jack smiled, "Well, I'm glad we finally got to do business together."

Mick smiled, "Anything else?"

Jack said, "When are you heading home?"

Mick said, "Once the last box is packed. All my business has been transferred to Martin now. He's got the keys to the store."

Jack replied, "Happy retirement."

Mick smiled as Jack headed out the door; however, he missed Bill in the elevator. When Bill arrived back at Mick's office, Mick had boxes three and four ready to go.

Bill asked, "Where'd Uncle Jack go?"

Mick replied, "He left while you were packing up box two."

Bill replied, "I didn't get to ask about Joseph."

Mick responded, "You'll see them Saturday at the retirement party. Your mother thinks I don't know, so let's keep that secret between us."

Bill smiled, knowing how much his mother wanted this to be a surprise, but it was impossible to keep a secret in the Quinn household.

On Saturday, family and friends gathered at the Three Aces Pub. Bridie asked Jack to host, figuring they could use it as an excuse to go to Mass in the old neighborhood, then surprise Mick afterward with a party. Jack agreed.

When Mick walked in, he acted surprised enough to fool Bridie; however, when he saw Jack, they hugged one another.

Jack whispered in his ear, "You knew the whole time."

Mick smiled, "I knew nothing."

Following behind Mick was Bill.

Bill said, "Hey, Uncle Jack."

Jack said, "Hey, Billy boy. Tell me what you want to do when you're done with high school and college?"

Bill said, "Not sure yet. I was thinking of joining the Marines, using the GI Bill to pay for college after my tour is up."

Jack smiled, "Keeping the family tradition going, huh? The blood of patriots flows through your veins, that's for sure. You know, your grandfather was in the IRA, killed by a traitor. I was in the IRA, too, and did prison time during World War II. Did you know that?"

Bill smiled, "My dad spoke about that a few times with us. My dad's a patriot, too, fighting for this country during World War II."

Jack smiled, "A real hero he was. Did he ever tell you about getting the Silver Star for his service on Guadalcanal? He also received a Bronze Star, along with a Meritorious Unit Award for his actions in Okinawa."

Bill looked confused, "Dad never spoke of those things. The only thing he told us was to never forget the sacrifices of those who laid down their lives on the altar of freedom. We owed it to them to live our best life, in peace and prosperity."

Jack smirked softly, "Typical Mick, only focus on the lessons, not the actions. When are you deciding about the military?"

Bill replied, "Soon. I need to graduate first. My dad won't sign the papers for me to go in early. He said I need to finish high school."

Jack responded, "He's right about that."

About three hours later, the party broke up. When they headed home, Bill knew enough not to ask about Mick's service medals. Bill started to think that he needed to do his part to keep the family legacy. He decided that evening that he'd finish up school, then join the USMC, and when he returned, he'd use the GI Bill to go to college.

First, he needed to finish high school. Bill wasn't a great student—he wasn't failing, but his grades weren't good for colleges. He figured this was why the GI Bill would be best. It shows dedication to country, which might impress the admissions board, essentially turning a boy into a man.

Chapter 22
April 1988 – Belfast, NIR

It was a clear night in Belfast, with cool, crisp air and a strong wind. The family was heading to the theater for a musical at the Grand Opera House. *The family hadn't done this in a long while,* Maura kept thinking. Maura, Daddy, Mother, and her brother were in the car, heading down to the theater. Owen, Daddy's friend's son, didn't enjoy musicals, so he remained at home. Owen was staying at a family friend's house for the evening after coming to live with them two years ago.

Maura McTiernay was dressed in an emerald green dress, with her beautiful auburn hair tied up in a ponytail, keeping her long, flowing hair up for this special occasion. Maura was slender, approximately 5'7", 135 pounds, with a soft smile that lit up the room. She had freckles on her face, softly covered with her makeup. Maura was a smart, sensitive young woman, a woman whose opinions were shaped very much by her father, a controlling sort. In contrast, Maura loved her father very much, understanding he was always looking out for her best interests.

As they made their way through the busy streets, her father asked the driver to pull over and stop at the corner. They were only two blocks from the theater; Daddy was out of smokes.

As the car stopped, Maura asked, "Daddy, can I go with you to get some chocolates?"

Mother, a stern woman with graying hair, dark brown eyes, and milky white skin, rolled her eyes, as Daddy never said no to his Maura.

As Maura got out of the car, Daddy told the driver, "We'll be a minute."

Times had been rough in Ireland; warring factions of the IRA were fighting for legitimacy, and the divide between the Catholics and the Protestants was continuing to intensify. Maura's father was a local brigade commander, but the fighting was taking a toll on him. Maura's father was a tall, slender Irishman, standing 6' tall, with red hair, hazel eyes, and a chalky complexion. Having been a heavy smoker, combined with the stress of the fighting, Maura's father looked ashen most of the time, a controlling fellow with an outwardly stern demeanor, never seemingly with a smile on his face.

The second thing that was bothering Maura's father was Owen's interest in his daughter. Maura and her father would go fifteen rounds a time or two over his interest in her. *Owen was a devious little shite,* her father thought. *Good for the IRA, not for my daughter.* Also, Owen had a possessive streak—possessive over whatever he thought was his. Nothing would stand in his way of having it once he thought he needed it. Also, he'd go to any lengths to make it happen. Again, great for the IRA, just not good enough for his only daughter. Her father was once told that Owen tortured a schoolmate, tying him to a chair, burning him with cigarettes, and beating on him until another mate interceded. Owen was a wicked child, growing up to be a sinister man.

However, this would be the first night out for the family in two years, so Daddy wanted to put down his rugged cross for the evening. Daddy and Maura stepped out of the car and onto the sidewalk, heading into the local grocery store for a pack of smokes and candy for the show. Maura loved sweets chocolate especially. After leaving the grocery store, Maura and Daddy headed down to the theater. Daddy was on Maura's left, holding her hand. He was closest to the vehicle they had just gotten out of.

BOOM, BOOM! A massive explosion. The car Maura's mother and brother were in was now engulfed in flames. Daddy lay on the sidewalk motionless, bleeding from his arms and torso. Maura's dad had heard the click of the detonator, so he shielded Maura from the explosion. The scene quickly became pandemonium; the Garda were screaming down the street almost instantly, and fire engines were racing to the scene.

A few meters from where Maura was standing, a shadow emerged from the vacant store doorway. Maura could tell it was a young man through the smoke-filled haze. The young man had dark brown hair, dark brown eyes, a sullen expression on his face, and wore a beard that made him look much older than he was. Owen was a smart, cunning fellow, always looking for some angle that improved things only for himself. Owen was very much in love with Maura, but Maura's father had been against the relationship. Owen was obsessed with Maura, wanting to make Maura his own at any cost. As the young man approached Maura, he took Maura's hand. Maura recognized the young man named Owen DeValera.

Owen said, "Maura, love, you all right? It's going to be okay. I'm here to protect you, keep you safe."

Maura replied, "Owen, what are you doing here?"

Owen replied, "I needed to protect you. I've got some friends in America. We'll be safe there. Besides, we're now the only family we've got left."

Maura started to sob, letting the events start to sink in. She turned to Owen, "Why did this happen? When are we leaving? I don't feel safe here."

Owen replied, "Right now. Around the corner, I've got a car parked, waiting for us. We'll drive to Dublin tonight and fly to America tomorrow."

Maura was still in shock as the events started to sink in. Memories of Daddy, Mother, and her brother began to flood over her.

Owen grabbed Maura by the arm, "Maura, my love, we need to go now."

Still in the fog of the moment, she began to understand this was an attack. Maura began to calm herself, instantly realizing she needed to have a clear head about her.

Finally, Maura said to Owen, "Let's go. Promise me you'll always keep me safe."

Owen nodded, taking Maura's hand and escorting her to the waiting car. Somehow, Owen and Maura managed to move down the street without being stopped by the Garda. As they turned the corner, Owen pointed to the car. When they got into the car, a big, burly man emerged, standing in front of the car.

Owen got out while Maura heard Owen say, "We're heading to Dublin now, Uncle Jack. We'll see you in New York?"

The big, burly man was Jack Quinn, also known as Uncle Jack, a mountain of a man, standing 6'4", with light red hair with gray streaks in it. He wore a beard that was more gray than red, and he had blue eyes. He was a large, imposing man, but for all his girth, Uncle Jack had a welcoming presence, an easy smile, and was considerate, always looking to help or support. However, in business, he was tough. He always seemed to be compassionate for folks down on their luck, but conversely, in matters of business, Uncle Jack was harsh, even ruthless at times. The bottom line is that you never crossed Uncle Jack. If you did, you never got a second chance at redemption with him.

Jack replied, "Come to Brooklyn so we can figure out the next steps."

Owen asked Jack, "When will the merchandise arrive from the Colonel?"

Jack responded, "Aye, soon. We'll talk about it in Brooklyn. Get moving."

Owen nodded, getting back into the car, while Jack walked down to his waiting car. In a few seconds, Jack's car drove past Owen and Maura toward the theater.

Maura was sitting in the passenger seat, still in shock, saying nothing when Owen returned, sobbing softly, mourning the death of her family. Owen waited a few minutes before starting the car as he let Maura compose herself. Owen then started the car, starting off for the M1, south to Dublin. As Maura and Owen made their way to the M1, a young man came around the corner as Owen raced by, nearly striking him down in the street.

That young man was Bill Quinn, Jack's nephew, visiting from America. Bill was 6'2", with auburn red hair, blue eyes, and light freckles on his face, weighing approximately two hundred pounds, with an exceptional physique. Bill was eighteen, visiting Northern Ireland for the first time, in Belfast for two days, seeing the sights. He had been in Ireland, taking in the family sights in County Clare and County Kerry, as well. Uncle Jack helped in planning this visit.

Bill was a serious fellow, curious about things he didn't understand, bright, funny, loyal, and standoffish at times. He was measured in his demeanor, private, and self-determined. He was awaiting his assignment date for boot camp in the USMC. One thing Bill hated was bullying; he wouldn't tolerate it in any form. Bill was the guy others went to for help. Usually, Bill's size was a deterrent. Point in case, in his junior year in high school, a male student was bullying a freshman boy, pinning him up against a locker, embarrassing him for his own amusement. When Bill saw this happening, he intervened, prompting a fight with the assailant, who stood 6'4" tall probably 215 pounds. However, the dispute ended in seconds, as Bill pulled the assailant off the younger boy, throwing him into a locker. When the assailant attempted to strike back, Bill blocked his punch, landing a right cross to the assailant's jaw, knocking him out instantly. By the time teachers arrived to deal with the situation, Bill had ended it with one punch.

Before almost being run down in the street, Bill was stopped by his Uncle Jack. Uncle Jack had driven down to the corner by the theater when he saw Bill looking dazed.

Uncle Jack rolled down his window, "Billy boy, what are you doing here? You okay?"

Bill replied, "I'm fine. Moving away from the blast site."

Uncle Jack replied, "Are you hurt?"

Bill showed his left arm, "A little shrapnel; walked away so I couldn't be questioned."

Uncle Jack said, "Good, smart. You did well this evening. I appreciate you helping the family out. There's a hospital three blocks from here, straight down this road; you can't miss it. Remember, when you're at the hospital, you were an innocent bystander."

Bill nodded, starting toward the hospital, while Uncle Jack rolled up his window, sitting in the car, watching the activity near the theater. It had been thirty minutes since the explosions, and the scene remained in total pandemonium.

As Bill made his way to the hospital, he went over what happened, not knowing about any bombs. Uncle Jack had told Bill there was a threat against the family. He needed Bill to spot a specific car when it arrived at the theater, then provide the agreed-upon signal: removing his cap from across the street, like a curtain call after a big home run. Bill had no idea how this would help the family, but it was a blood code of the family; when Uncle Jack said there was a threat and asked for help, you did it.

Chapter 23
April 1988 – Belfast, NIR – Dublin, IRE – Brooklyn, NY

Bill arrived at the hospital three blocks from the scene. When Bill entered the emergency room, he was greeted by a nurse, who sat Bill down and looked at his wounded arm.

The nurse said, "Doesn't look too bad. Were you down near the bombing?"

Bill replied, "Yes, across the street when it went off."

The nurse said, "Terrible thing. Goddamn the IRA for this."

Bill didn't respond, politely nodding while the nurse tended to his injuries. What was there to say? Bill knew Uncle Jack was wrapped up in the IRA. Bill began to realize he played a part in tonight's events. Bill's father told stories of Uncle Jack's dealings all the time. Bill started to think of his dad at the moment, pondering what the threat against the family was.

Bill's father was Michael Anthony Quinn, better known as Mick, a World War II veteran who fought in the Pacific, a proud Irish American who abhorred armed conflict. After his service, Mick was a carpenter working as a union laborer, moving all the way up to union president before retiring. During his military service, Mick fought on every Pacific island, clearly earning the right to his opinions on armed conflict, seeing both the best and worst of humanity. He rarely talked about his time in the war, only telling one story from Okinawa when his unit found out the Japanese had surrendered.

Living through such an experience impacted how Mick lived his life when he returned home. Mick had been wounded several times, carrying scars over his cheek from the wound he received in the Battle of Guadalcanal. Mick only spoke of the lessons of war, how one must remember and honor the blood of patriots by leading a better future that is free of war.

Mick was a hardened man from the war. He had a silent toughness but could be indifferent to the suffering around him. Many called Mick pious. Bill recalled when his grandmother was ill with cancer, and Mick would go once a week for an hour to visit with her. When they came from Ireland, Bill's grandmother was a heavy smoker. Bill's father thought his mother got what she asked for—a lack of compassion brought on by the evils of war, anesthetized to suffering. As a returning veteran, Mick took to getting to work, as well as drinking each night. Bill thought the drinking was to help him sleep, but it was to forget the night terrors. Mick was affable with friends and could be very kind, but he had a streak in him that was self-righteous. With family, he was different: irritable, judgmental, and unkind. No matter what was happening in your life, it was never as bad as what happened to him. He could be very selfish in that regard.

As Bill thought about his dad, the nurse continued examining him and then escorted Bill to a room where a doctor could examine him more closely. She removed one piece of shrapnel from Bill's upper arm. However, Bill waited for almost an hour before the doctor arrived to remove the final piece.

The doctor finally arrived, "How are we, lad?"

Bill replied, "A little shrapnel in this arm. The nurse was great but said you needed to look at this piece."

The doctor said, "Let's have a look. Doesn't look too bad. Was this from the theater?"

Bill became guarded, saying nothing, just nodding affirmatively.

The doctor took out his instruments and then loosened the last piece of shrapnel. In less than two minutes, the doctor removed it, stapling the wound and placing sterile gauze over it. Finally, Bill was patched up.

The doctor said, "All done. You may have some discomfort for a couple of days."

Bill replied, "Thanks. Am I free to go?"

The doctor replied, "Yes, just see the nurse outside so you can pay your tab."

Bill smiled, putting on his white, bloodstained dress shirt, then headed to the front desk and paid his bill, thankful to be on his way back to his hotel.

Bill walked from the hospital to the hotel, stunned that nobody questioned him. The hotel was eight blocks from the hospital. As he exited, it started to drizzle, with the wind picking up. As Bill walked through the streets, there was an ominous silence, and people on the street seemed to be going about their business like the bombing hadn't happened. By the time Bill got to his hotel, he was soaked and freezing cold. The rain had picked up steadily on the walk back to the hotel. Bill entered the hotel, clearly looking like a victim of this evening's bombing.

The hotel clerk asked, "Are you okay, lad?"

Bill replied, "Yes, I've been to the hospital; it looks worse than it appears."

The hotel clerk smiled as Bill headed to the elevators. When Bill reached his room, he decided to shower and remove his bloodstained clothes, placing them in a plastic bag. When Bill finished his shower, he heard a knock on his door. Bill went to the peephole to see who was at the door. It was Uncle Jack, as well as a man Bill didn't recognize.

Bill opened the door, "Uncle Jack, what's up?"

Uncle Jack replied, "I wanted to see how you made out at the hospital. Any problems?"

Bill said, "No, no questions either."

Uncle Jack responded, "Good. This is Martinez, a business associate."

Bill nodded in Martinez's direction as if to acknowledge his presence. Martinez reciprocated.

Uncle Jack continued, "Billy boy, I need to dispose of some things. Where are your bloody clothes? We'll dump them somewhere safe."

Bill replied, "In this bag."

Uncle Jack continued, "Billy boy, you're on the 12:00 flight from Dublin home tomorrow. I talked with your dad; your orders came through. This time next week, you'll be in basic. Camp Pendleton."

Bill smiled, "Great."

Uncle Jack replied, "Here's your ticket. A car will be downstairs at 06:00 to get you to Dublin Airport. Remember, not a word about what happened here. Got it?"

Bill simply replied, "Got it."

Uncle Jack said, "Billy boy, I know this is what you want, but be safe. If we don't see each other before you ship out, all the luck in the world to you."

Bill replied, "Thanks, see you soon."

With that, Uncle Jack and Martinez left the room.

Martinez said nothing the entire time. He was a portly man, about 5'7", with a large beer gut, reeking of alcohol. By the look of his tan skin and the tattoos on his neck, Bill suspected he was in the Mexican cartel. What Bill didn't understand was his connection to Uncle Jack. Martinez was never mentioned in any conversation with Uncle Jack. It was the first time Bill had met Martinez, but it wouldn't be the last.

Bill lay down on the bed, not giving Uncle Jack's visit much more thought, thinking it was Uncle Jack's business, nothing more. It was 22:00 when he drifted off to sleep. 06:00 would come quickly. Within a few minutes, Bill was sound asleep, as all the earlier excitement had worn off. Bill had set his alarm clock to go off at 05:00; this would give him time to shower and pack before heading downstairs to get the car.

At 05:00, Bill woke up and headed for a shower, then took his dirty laundry to put it in his bag. At 05:55, Bill headed downstairs and outside the hotel, finding his livery car. The driver popped open the trunk so Bill could put his bag in it. Bill placed his bag in the trunk and got into the car, using the passenger-side rear door. When Bill clicked his seatbelt, the driver, without saying a word, took off toward the M1. Over the next two hours, Bill rode to Dublin in silence, as his driver never said a word.

It was 08:00 when they arrived at Dublin Airport. Traffic was light on the M1, so Bill was able to get breakfast before the flight home. Inside the terminal was a pub serving breakfast. Bill was escorted by the hostess to his table, where she placed the menu in front of him.

The waitress came over, "Can I get you some coffee?"

Bill replied, "Black, please."

The waitress replied, "Grand, anything else?"

Bill responded, "Yes. I'll have the Irish breakfast with no beans. Also, a glass of orange juice if you have it."

The waitress said, "Grand."

Bill was now staring at this beautiful waitress—slender, with black hair and dark brown eyes. The dress she wore was light blue and tight-fitting, clearly showing she had the body to pull it off. Bill felt like she was flirting a little with him as the waitress left to place his order, returning with Bill's coffee and orange juice.

Bill sat quietly, taking in the sights of the airport, as well as his waitress. Within fifteen minutes, the waitress returned with Bill's breakfast. As he ate, he continued to take in the sights. The waitress looked over a couple of times with a bright, sweet smile.

The waitress saw Bill was finished. She came over to the table, "Anything else, love?"

Bill smiled at the waitress, "No, thanks."

As Bill got up from the table, he saw a couple walking into the pub. The man had dark brown hair and dark brown eyes. The woman had a beautiful head of auburn hair with slight freckles on her face. He recognized them but couldn't think of where he'd seen them.

As they got closer, the woman said, "Owen, can we sit by the window?"

Owen replied, "Sure thing, Maura, my love."

As Bill walked past the couple, heading for the terminal, he thought this might be the last time he'd be in Ireland. As Bill put aside those thoughts, he made his way over to the gate and then waited for his flight to be called. About an hour later, Bill, sitting near the terminal desk, noticed the same couple from the pub coming over to the gate. They sat down a few rows behind Bill while Bill went back to reading his magazine.

At 11:15, preboarding was called. They boarded the flight as they went through their preflight checks. By 11:45, the cabin door was closed, and by 12:00, they were taxiing down the runway. At 12:05, wheels up. Six hours before landing at JFK International Airport in New York.

The flight was uneventful. Bill spent the first hour thinking about Uncle Jack, as well as the events from the previous day. He recalled his dad telling him about how Jack got involved with the IRA. Bill's grandfather was killed in a gunfight after a traitor had given him up to the British, or so the family legend went. Uncle Jack was recruited by Paddy, Bill's grandfather's best friend, over the objections of Bill's grandmother. Uncle Jack fought for the IRA after the revolution, even serving a five-year jail term at Limerick Jail before immigrating to the US.

After an hour, Bill fell asleep, hoping the jet lag wouldn't be too bad after landing. Thankfully, the flight landed on time. Bill grabbed his bag from the overhead compartment, disembarked the plane, and headed to the customs counter. Fortunately, the customs line was light, so Bill was able to make it through quickly. From customs, Bill headed down to baggage claim to meet his dad. Anytime anyone flew, baggage claim was where you met. Bill made it to the baggage carousel, seeing his dad in the distance.

When they met, Mick said, "Safe trip?"

Bill replied, "Aye, it was grand."

They shared a laugh as Mick found Bill's attempt at an Irish brogue amusing. Mick and Bill bantered as they made their way to their car.

When both were in the car, Mick asked, "Can't believe what happened in Belfast."

Bill replied, "It was crazy, huh?"

Mick asked, "Did you see Uncle Jack yesterday?"

Bill responded, "Yes, he brought me the tickets for the flight home."

Mick said, "Strange, Uncle Jack was in Ireland when this happened. Please tell me that you weren't involved."

Bill lied, saying, "Nope. Got the tickets from Uncle Jack as planned."

Mick then asked, "When did you meet up with him?"

Bill replied, "Yesterday evening, just after supper."

What Bill didn't share was that Uncle Jack had asked Bill for a favor that night in Belfast. Bill was a lookout, signaling when the car was at the theater. Unbeknownst to Bill, Owen had informed Uncle Jack when the family left for the theater. All Bill was asked to do was signal when the car arrived.

As they made their way home from JFK, the traffic was terrible getting back to Brooklyn. It was a parking lot. Mick attempted to take the surface streets, but the traffic was just as bad. Finally, when they made it home, nobody else was home. Bill went straight upstairs to his room, feeling the need to start packing for basic training. He'd be leaving in three days for Camp Pendleton, and he was very excited to be serving his country like his dad.

Chapter 24
April 1988 – Brooklyn, NY, USA

Owen and Maura disembarked from the plane and headed down to the baggage carousel to retrieve their luggage. As they made their way downstairs, Maura was sad but captivated by the size of New York through the windows at JFK, still in shock over what had happened. Conversely, Owen was in a great mood as they made their way through the airport, feeling a sense of satisfaction with his role the night before, as well as now having Maura all to himself. He expected they'd marry now that Daddy was out of the picture, playing on her sense of insecurity about being alone. Owen was a possessively manipulative man, having plotted to get to this very moment where Maura was solely dependent upon him. Maura was still somewhat innocent as a young woman, but Owen knew he could manipulate the situation to solidify his hold on her. As Owen escorted Maura through the terminal, they waited for their luggage for what seemed a long time.

Maura asked, "So, tell me about Brooklyn?"

Owen replied, "We've got an apartment to stay in. It's a nice place, close to work."

Maura replied, "Will I have my own bed?"

Owen smiled, "I was hoping we'd share one."

Maura was taken aback by Owen, blushing at his forwardness, but she didn't respond to Owen's comment either, thinking she might have to consider it. *What choice did she have?* When Owen sets his mind to things, he usually gets his way.

Finally, the baggage carousel started to turn, with bags coming up quickly. Owen found his bags while Maura grabbed her only bag. Owen had packed the bag after the family left for the theater, planning all along to take Maura with him. Other than her purse and $50, she had a lifetime in one suitcase. Still trying to understand why she was alone in this world. Once the bags were collected, Owen motioned his head toward the door marked *Ground Transportation*. With Maura following, Owen hailed a yellow cab.

When the cab pulled up, the driver asked, "Where to, Mac?"

Owen replied, "Brooklyn, 3rd Avenue, and 86th Street."

The driver nodded as he pulled on the meter, proceeding out of the terminal. The ride from JFK to Brooklyn was filled with first-time sights for Maura; the New York City skyline looked beautiful against the bright, sun-filled day. The traffic was terrible getting to the apartment, taking nearly two hours to arrive.

Owen sat holding her hand, appearing to comfort her, but he was plotting his next move with her. Owen felt he had the best intentions toward Maura, and he had already proven it in Ireland. Owen openly professed his affection for her to Maura's father at the pub. Maura's father wasn't very impressed with him speaking of his daughter at the pub.

Maura's father told Owen, in front of several witnesses, "Owen, I'll never give you my daughter's hand. Never. I promised your father and mother that if anything happened to them, I'd look after you. My daughter is off-limits to you."

Owen had been through some adversity over his young life. His father was killed during the Troubles in the 1970s in Belfast. His mother did the best she could, getting him through school, being a single mother, and working in a shop. Owen's mother worked long hours, having little time to tend to her children. When Owen was fourteen, his older brother was killed at the local Sinn Féin building in Belfast. His brother was a runner for the local brigade commander, getting caught in the crossfire during a shootout. At sixteen, Owen was getting into trouble with the Garda also starting his own affiliation with the IRA. Owen's mother died two days before Owen's sixteenth birthday, which is why Maura's father took him in.

While Maura's father didn't want him for a son-in-law, Owen was good at bloody mischief, moving him along quickly. Owen was smart, sharp, and cunning, always looking for an angle to score or support his cause. At this moment, his cause was Maura, whatever the cost.

Upon arriving at the apartment, Owen escorted Maura to the front door like she was a new bride.

Owen said, "Follow me, love; we're on the third floor."

Maura took it all in, following Owen's lead. What happened in Belfast weighed on her mind, and she wanted to talk more about it with Owen. But first, she wanted to get settled.

Owen reached the apartment door, unlocking it, "Maura, my love, this is our new home."

Maura started through the door, but Owen said, "Wait. Let me carry you over the threshold."

Maura smiled awkwardly, "We're not married; that's bad luck."

Owen looked over at her, "We can fix that tomorrow. Do you want to get married tomorrow?"

Maura was taken aback, replying, "We just got here; perhaps it could wait a little? I'd rather talk about what happened to my dad."

Owen said, "Your dad was caught in the crossfire between rival factions of the IRA. You did know he was in the IRA?"

Maura replied, "I did, but he never spoke about it. He only talked with my mum about it. Why was he killed?"

Sitting down at the kitchen table, Owen formulated an answer in his head, taking several seconds before responding. *Do I tell Maura the truth or what she needs to hear?*

Maura's father was killed mainly because of conflicts over the drug trade, an increasingly unpopular position. Her dad was a traditionalist whose time had passed, one of the older brigade commanders, more pragmatic, having grown up before the Troubles. The up-and-comers were full of piss and vinegar, wanting to escalate things, always doing it for the glory of a unified Ireland.

Also, Owen, with Maura's dad being eliminated, could convince Maura to be with him without any parental interference. Essentially, he killed two birds with one bomb.

Owen finally replied, "Your dad was mixed up in something I never understood. I think that's what got him killed."

Sitting down next to Owen, crying, Maura asked, "What was he into?"

Owen lyingly replied, "I don't know for sure. I heard it had something to do with drugs. I've heard some of the younger brigade commanders thought your dad was getting too soft."

Maura sat for a moment, trying to take it all in. While Owen lied to her, she had no reason not to believe him. Owen tried to return to the earlier marriage conversation, but Maura kept him at bay.

Maura sensed something wasn't adding up, but what? Owen was part of the team Uncle Jack assembled to kill Maura's father. Owen was with Uncle Jack, which made him enemies with her dad. There was no getting around that fact. Given Owen's love for Maura, he couldn't bring himself to tell her the truth. Owen wanted Maura to be his wife terribly, but she never would've married him, knowing Owen was part of the plot to kill her dad.

Owen ended the conversation, "Maura, I love you. I will protect you if you'll be mine."

Maura was stone-faced as she stood up and headed down the hallway. She noticed the apartment had two bedrooms, so she started for the one on the left.

As Maura made her way to the bedrooms, Owen said suggestively, "The room on the right has a double bed."

As Maura headed into her room, she said nothing. Owen sat at the kitchen table, contriving his next move, needing to press her further on a future, to seal the deal, so to speak.

Maura opened the door on the left. Once inside, Maura sat on the bed, sobbing. After a minute, she opened her suitcase and hung up the handful of clothes she brought. After unpacking, she changed into pajamas and lay down on the bed, sobbing softly, trying to understand what had happened over the past forty-eight hours. Before long, Maura cried herself to sleep.

Chapter 25
May 1988

Owen and Maura had been living together for a month. Owen pressed on the marriage issue, while Maura said she was considering it, but she recalled her father's efforts to not let it happen. Maura was in a predicament, navigating living in peace while fending off Owen's advances. She would come to understand the business Owen was involved with. Also, she would come to understand how violent Owen could be.

From the outset, Owen lived at the Three Aces Pub, always wanting to fit in and be one of the fellas. However, many didn't care for him, as Owen's cunning approach didn't sit well with the rank and file of the outfit. Owen made it clear he was in this for himself.

Many refused to work with him on assignments. Even Uncle Jack had to rein Owen in, as he got carried away, mostly with violence. This was most evident when Uncle Jack asked Owen to pay a visit to Francis Murray. Francis owed Jack a decent sum of money; Francis was a degenerative gambler, usually on the losing end of the bet.

Owen paid him a visit at work one afternoon, but Francis had gone home early. Owen then paid him a visit at his home. Francis had gone home to tend to a sick child whose mother was working as a nurse.

When Owen knocked on the door, the little boy answered. Instead of asking to speak to Francis, Owen pushed into the house, grabbed the child, and yelled for Francis. Owen had a knife in his hand, threatening to kill the boy unless Francis paid Owen $5,000, which was $1,000 higher than Francis owed. With him holding a knife to his son's throat, what could Francis do? He agreed to pay the money, $3,000 now, followed by $2,000 tomorrow.

Owen replied, "Not good enough."

Francis said, "$3,000 is all I've got right here. I need to get the other from the bank in the morning; it's closed."

Owen said, "Which bank?"

Francis replied, "The one on the corner near Jack's pub."

Owen replied, "Meet me there at 08:00 tomorrow morning. I'll take the $3,000 now. Stand me up tomorrow morning. The boy pays your debt. Get it."

Francis nodded as Owen released his son. Nothing was out of bounds for Owen, including extorting money someone didn't owe. Again, he was in it for himself. What Owen didn't realize was that Francis had called Uncle Jack after Owen left.

Francis regaled Uncle Jack with the story, and Jack grew angrier by the minute. Jack understood that Francis owed the money and that Owen was there to collect, not to threaten his child in the process.

When Owen returned to the pub, Jack shouted, "Owen, my office now!"

As they entered the office, Jack slammed the door behind them.

Owen asked, "Something wrong?"

Uncle Jack shouted, "You were supposed to see Francis to get the money, not threaten to kill his son. Also, where do you get off demanding more than what he owes?"

Owen sat stone-faced. "Jack, he owed us; what difference does it make with my methods?"

Uncle Jack became irate. "Listen, you little shit, when I ask you to do something, do it to the letter, no exceptions. This was extreme; it better never happen again."

Owen replied, "So you still want me to meet this guy in the morning to get the money?"

Uncle Jack said, "He's going to bring $2,000 by tomorrow to me. I want you to pay him $1,000 for the pain you've caused. Again, this isn't what I wanted."

Owen nodded, then got up from the chair and left the office. He headed to the pub, sitting with a pint, contemplating his next move. Instead of listening to Uncle Jack, Owen decided he'd meet Francis, steal the money from him, and pocket the $2,000. But first, he needed a plan.

Owen decided to use one of the vans from Jack's business, park it outside the bank, and then abduct Francis in the street after he came out of the bank. Since the bank was close to the pub, it wouldn't be suspicious to have the van parked there.

Owen parked the van in front of the bank at 06:45, waiting for Francis to appear. At 08:00, Francis walked toward the bank, which had just opened. Owen watched from the front seat as Francis headed to the teller for the withdrawal. When Francis started toward the bank exit, Owen jumped out of the van and stood close to the bank door. Francis didn't notice him at first, but it was too late.

Owen said, "Get in the van; we've got some unfinished business."

Francis replied, "Jack told me to drop the money this morning."

Owen said, "Change of plans. Get in the van."

Francis complied, getting into the van with Owen. Owen opened the door, pushed Francis in, and then jumped into the driver's seat, speeding off to a spot he had picked the evening before, someplace private. Owen drove to Ward's Island, down to the abandoned textile buildings, the private spot Owen had chosen.

As they drove over, Francis asked, "Where are we going?"

Owen didn't answer, continuing to drive. When they arrived at the abandoned building, Owen ordered Francis out of the vehicle, pushing him with a gun to his back into the structure. Once inside, Owen pistol-whipped Francis, knocking him unconscious. With Francis passed out, Owen took the $2,000 from his pocket. However, rather than leave Francis to fend for himself, Owen had other ideas.

Owen had brought some rope with him, having tied a noose on one end of the rope. He placed the rope around Francis' neck, then hoisted it over one of the beams. Owen pulled on the rope until Francis was upright, then dangling off the floor. Francis started to come to as his feet left the floor. Within five minutes, Francis was dead.

Instead of cutting him down or burying him, Owen left Francis dangling in the air while he made his way back to the van, then returned to Brooklyn. When Owen arrived back in Brooklyn, he walked into Jack's office, offering him $1,000 as requested, and pocketed the other $1,000.

Jack said, "You're paying a tax for your extreme behavior."

Owen replied, "Did the guy show up?"

Jack responded, "Not yet. But when he arrives, leave him be. You've put him through enough. Understand?"

Owen nodded. "What are you going to do with the $1,000 I gave you?"

Jack coldly said, "None of your business. We're done here."

Three months later, the police were called to the scene where Francis was found rotting in the abandoned building. Owen had left Francis' ID on him so he could be identified. The police contacted his family, stating that it appeared to be a suicide, with no signs of a real struggle.

When Jack found out, he immediately questioned Owen.

Jack asked, "Did you have anything to do with this? My cop's telling me this looks suspicious."

Owen simply said, "I had nothing to do with this. After you reamed me out, why would I do that?"

Jack had no proof but always suspected Francis died at the hands of Owen. This was one of a dozen stories related to Owen. For several years, Uncle Jack wondered if his partnership was worth it all.

Chapter 26
July 1988 – Camp Pendleton, CA

Before Bill Quinn enlisted, he was an affable guy, somewhat irresponsible and carefree. When he arrived for boot camp, that changed quickly; he learned there was a right way to do things and a wrong way to do things. Each Marine needed a plan every day. It felt, for the first two months, like he was just surviving in this new environment, not realizing how it would shape his future.

However, on this day, many of the fellas were up at 05:00, getting ready for graduation day.

Bill said to Tommy, "Tommy, we made it."

Tommy replied, "We did, Skipper. Thanks to you."

Tommy was Thomas Francis O'Donnell, standing 5'10", with dark brown hair and blue eyes, a handsome young buck from Houston, Texas. As Bill got to know him, Tommy was one of the smartest people Bill had ever been around. Loyal, tough, great at reading situations, always could be counted on—he was smart *and* instinctual.

The other fellas in Bill's squad were Michael Aloysius Connors (or Big Mike) as well as Fredrico Rodriquez (or Freddie).

Big Mike was a huge guy with blond hair and a large, imposing head, which was very intimidating before getting to know him. Mike was really a pussycat underneath all that guff, a real Chesty Puller Marine, tough, disciplined, the type of guy you always want on your side. He was from Galveston, Texas. His family owned a construction business, so he planned on doing his bit and then heading back to work in the family business.

Freddie was a proud Mexican American whose parents immigrated to the US when he was ten. Freddie was a very fit man, standing 5'9", with six-pack abs. As a young Marine, he had a jet-black crew cut; however, he was a lot bigger than his 5'9" frame would suggest. He took Big Mike down a few times during close-order drills—not many men could claim that, even once. Fred was reserved and thoughtful, and he always seemed to have a quiet smile on his face, as if he had just told himself a joke. His parents immigrated to Cleveland, Ohio, from central Mexico, where his dad had a job waiting for him in the Ohio shipyards.

They quickly became great friends, remaining as close after their service. However, Tommy and Bill's relationship was a bit different—they became brothers, reading each other's minds before either could speak. They were always the first to call each other with news, supporting one another through everything. While all four were close, the bond between Bill and Tommy was uniquely special.

The four Marines bonded not only because of the rigors of boot camp but also over one unforgettable evening. It was the night Tommy finally talked to Amanda. He had tried a couple of times before, but Amanda hadn't shown interest. All four went into town, just off the base, to blow off some steam.

On this particular Saturday night, Tommy pointed out a real beauty to his comrades. Amanda Wilson was a petite young lady with brown hair and hazel green eyes, working as a bar waitress in a very raucous bar. By all accounts, she seemed bright and funny, not taking much guff from the patrons. Simply put, you always knew where you stood with her. She wasn't unkind, just direct.

The bar patrons she dealt with weren't only anxious marines but also unsavory locals who thought she owed them some loyalty because they were locals. This bar even had a biker gang hang out. Fortunately, the bikers respected the servicemen, so the Marines never had a problem with them. It was rare to have an altercation between those two groups.

Tommy tried to talk to Amanda several times during the evening, even trying to weasel his way into her section. After an hour of standing at the bar, Tommy managed to secure a table in her section. Amanda came over to take their order while Tommy flirted with her. Amanda was wise to Tommy's game, but she didn't shy away from him either. Bill sensed she was as interested as Tommy was, especially after his repeated attempts.

Two hours after securing the table, Bill went to the restroom in the back of the bar. When he got to the back, he noticed a man hassling Amanda. Amanda had a bar tray full of pitchers of beer, along with frozen beer mugs. One local harassed her and then touched her right breast as her hands were full carrying the tray. Amanda yelled at the local, putting the tray down on the table, took one of the pitchers, and then poured it over the idiot's head. Bill laughed out loud, thinking, "Good for you, sweetheart."

However, the local decided he wouldn't be outdone. He picked up one of the other pitchers of beer and swung it at Amanda. Bill saw what was happening. As he moved toward Amanda, he managed to catch a piece of the pitcher with his hand. Unfortunately, he couldn't catch it all, and Amanda was struck on her right cheek by the glass pitcher, leaving a mark. Bill at least cushioned the blow. Now, standing in front of Amanda, he protected her.

Bill said to the local, "You want to hit something, hit me. I dare you! Who the fuck do you think you are, hitting a hard-working woman?"

The local yelled back, "Shove it jarhead!"

The locals at the table were now trying to surround Bill, standing with their friend. One was a woman. The first local lunged at Bill, but Bill stiff-armed him, putting his left hand around his throat and squeezing his trachea, quickly subduing him. His other friends initially attempted to come to his rescue.

Bill warned, "One step closer, and I'll serve his throat for breakfast."

Amanda went to get Tommy, Fred, and Mike. When Tommy saw Amanda's face, he was irate. The owner came to the back after hearing the commotion at the bar.

Upon arriving and seeing the locals at the table, the owner commanded, "Throw them the hell out of here."

Bill said to Tommy, "Look after Amanda; we've got the rest of this."

Tommy asked Amanda, "Which one hit you?"

Amanda replied, "Please, this is bad enough."

Tommy yelled, "Who fucking hit you?"

Amanda pointed at the local Bill had already subdued. Tommy then stepped in front of Bill while Bill removed his hand from the man's throat. Tommy grabbed him by the throat, dragging him to the back door. When the back door didn't open as planned, Tommy used the man's head to force it open. After the door opened, Tommy dragged him through it into the parking lot. The other friends at the table, standing with their hands on their hips, talked tough but were unwilling to make a move on Bill, Fred, or Mike.

Bill looked at the woman in their group and asked, "You let them treat you like that?"

The woman softly replied, "No, look, we don't want any more trouble."

Bill was sympathetic, but this idiot had hit Tommy's woman. Tommy wasn't going to let that go.

Bill responded, "You and your friends, out the back door. Where are you parked?"

The woman said, "We're the first white car in the parking lot."

Bill replied, "Come with me."

Outside, Tommy was in the parking lot, unleashing a beating on the assailant—a beating he wouldn't soon forget. The woman in their party started to cry when she saw the condition he was in.

The woman screamed, crying, "Please. Stop."

Tommy turned toward the woman, his fists covered in blood.

Tommy yelled, "He hit a woman. Nobody puts their hands on her, especially this piece of shit. If we were in West Texas, he'd be hanging from a tall oak tree."

Seeing that Tommy had made his point, Bill said, "Tommy, he's had enough. Go check on Amanda. We'll clean this up."

Tommy looked at Bill, sensing it was more an order from his squad commander than a request. Unbeknownst to Bill, Amanda was standing in the doorway, watching the events outside unfold. When Tommy looked at Amanda, she began to cry, then took him inside to help clean him up, as blood was dripping off both of his fists and face.

As she led Tommy into the door, Amanda said, "Nobody's ever stood up for me like that."

Tommy stoically replied, "I'll protect you from now on."

Amanda started to cry as she brought Tommy into the kitchen to get him cleaned up.

After ensuring the unruly group had left, Bill, Fred, and Mike returned inside the bar to a hero's welcome. The patrons cheered them on, and the bartender brought over two free pitchers of beer. Once Tommy was cleaned up, he and Amanda joined them at the table, and they began to recount the evening's events. Amanda, feeling grateful, even kissed Bill on the lips playfully to thank him for coming to her rescue. Bill winked at Tommy, signaling that he'd be her prince charming.

Bill said, "Amanda, I can't believe that idiot groped you like that. It was brilliant, dumping the pitcher over his head. All I did was hold him so Killer here could do the hard part."

This generated a fair amount of laughter at the table. Tommy winked at Bill, acknowledging not only his role in protecting Amanda but also Bill's way of deflecting credit to make Amanda think more highly of him.

It was 2:00 AM, closing time. The four Marines, Amanda, and the proprietor, were the only ones left in the bar.

The proprietor called out, "Last call, grunts."

They all gave a complimentary salute and then started for the door.

Amanda asked Tommy, "Walk me to my car, please."

Without saying a word, Tommy obliged. However, Bill had a sixth sense feeling that something else might happen, so he followed them outside, intending to cover their six without intruding. Mike and Fred noticed the apprehension on Bill's face.

Tommy walked Amanda to her car, holding her hand and putting his arm around her. Bill stayed close enough to intervene if necessary but far enough not to intrude. His instincts were correct; the idiots were foolish enough to return, including the female friend. The same local Amanda had doused with beer was waiting to ambush her from behind her car.

Bill yelled, "Tommy, 3 o'clock!"

Bill charged toward the car as two more of the troublemakers appeared from the passenger side of Amanda's car, banging on the hood.

Tommy yelled, "Skipper, go 12 o'clock!"

Tommy wanted Bill to protect Amanda from any further harm while he went after the main aggressor. This guy was foolish, and Tommy was angrier than before.

Tommy yelled at him, "A real man you are, hiding in the shadows like a bitch, ambushing her on her way home. Why? All because you were an asshole to her. You're lucky she didn't break the pitcher over your head."

The local, quite drunk, slurred his words incomprehensibly and lunged at Tommy, who then threw him against a tall oak tree next to where Amanda was parked. When Bill reached Amanda, he stepped in front of her while Mike and Fred came up, covering their six.

The woman with the troublemakers cried out repeatedly, "Please, he's drunk."

Tommy continued his confrontation with the main aggressor.

Bill said to the other two troublemakers, "Let them resolve this. Nobody else needs to get hurt unless you really want to."

One of the men then yelled, "Phil, enough. Get in the car." Bill looked over at Tommy, saying, "He's had enough. Let them get in the car." Tommy walked back to Amanda, who was bawling her eyes out. He put his arms around her, hugging her tightly, trying to console her. At this juncture, the three troublemakers and their female companion made it back to their car, with the woman taking the wheel to drive them home.

As she got into the car, she said, "I'm sorry for all this." Bill's group didn't say another word, watching them pull out of the parking lot.

Bill said, "Tommy, why don't you ride home with Amanda? We'll follow you to make sure these idiots don't come around again." Tommy, now the gentleman, asked, "Amanda, is that okay? I'd like to see you home if you'll let me."

Amanda still had tears streaming down her face but smiled when Tommy asked her respectfully about taking her home, knowing he wasn't expecting anything. As Amanda would later reveal, she didn't have anyone in her family who respected her or treated her as Tommy did. She felt like she was there to do chores, be seen, and not heard.

Amanda asked Bill, "You're following us?" Bill replied, "Yep, we'll follow you. We'll wait until you're situated, then we'll head back to base. I know this sounds forward, but consider having Tommy spend the night on your couch. Who knows if these idiots have another round in mind? Don't worry about the killer; I'd trust Tommy with my sister."

Amanda saw that Bill was concerned for her safety, not Tommy's love life. She hugged Bill before Tommy escorted her to the passenger side door.

Bill said, "Okay, we've got a plan." Tommy smiled while helping Amanda into the car, insisting on driving because she was too upset. That night, they saw not only Tommy's tough side but also the softer side he reserved only for Amanda.

After Tommy got Amanda into the car, he said to Bill, "I could've killed that guy."

Bill replied, "She's safe now. That idiot wasn't worth it. Take her home; we're right behind you."

With that, Tommy got into Amanda's car and quickly started for her place. Bill, Fred, and Mike went to Bill's car, following Tommy to Amanda's house. Amanda lived in a small bungalow just off base. The homes were nice, mostly filled with military families. She had a roommate named Tammy, but they weren't close, as she had told Tommy. When they arrived, Tommy gave them a thumbs up from the front door to head back to base. The next morning, Tommy returned at 06:30.

Bill asked, "Go okay last night, Killer? I call you 'Killer' because you slay me."

Tommy laughed, sensing the joke, "Fine, thanks for your help. We stayed up most of the night talking about what happened, but she told me about her life, too. Some of it was ugly. Her parents were drug addicts and didn't have a nickel. She made breakfast for us, French toast—she's a dynamite cook. If she said it once, she said it two hundred times, 'Thank God Bill was walking into the back room.' Thanks for protecting her."

Bill replied, "That's what we do, brother!"

Tommy smiled before sitting on his bunk, then laid down, falling asleep almost instantly with a terrific smile on his face. Mike and Fred came over to Bill's bunk as they were heading for breakfast. They noticed the smile on Tommy's face. Bill thought to himself, oh yeah, he's whipped.

Mike laughed, saying, "Take it things went well?"

Bill said, "Let Sleeping Beauty get some winks. All he said was that they were up most of the night talking. I'll leave it at that."

The three Marines headed over for breakfast, replaying the events from the previous evening—a habit that would soon carry over to the battlefield. This was the period before the Gulf War escalated before Saddam Hussein dared President George H. W. Bush to invade Iraq. Although this confrontation was still three years away, their instructors had repeatedly warned that they would likely find themselves in a Middle Eastern skirmish sooner rather than later. Consequently, much of their training was focused on desert warfare.

However, today was a day for celebration: graduation. They would finally have the chance to head into town, hit the beach, and scope out the girls. Tommy was particularly looking forward to spending more time with Amanda. They were all eager to leave the base, having not had leave for a while. Unfortunately, the previous night's events at the bar caught up with them. One of the locals had driven to the main gate to complain, prompting the MPs to investigate. Bill explained what happened at the bar, laying out the sequence of events for the entire evening. The MPs made Bill recount the story to Captain Michaels and Sergeant Fischer. Neither was happy about the situation, but both understood.

Captain Michaels told the MPs, "This is a platoon matter. I'll handle it."

After the MPs left, he said, "Son, I've decided to do nothing, provided it doesn't happen again. I appreciate the gallantry, as well as having a buddy's back in a bad situation."

It was 05:30, as many were starting to wake up.

Sergeant Fischer marched into the barracks at 05:30 on the dot, hollering, "Drop your cocks and grab your socks, boys. It may be graduation day, but we've got PT."

Sergeant Fischer was the stereotypical Marine drill sergeant— loud, crass, always yelling, no-nonsense. Standing at 5'10" and weighing 175 pounds of solid muscle, he was a man of imposing presence, notably large hands for his size. However, his leadership qualities were indisputable. He had combat experience in Grenada and Panama. The men respected him more than most non-commissioned officers because he didn't just talk about combat—he lived it.

The whole platoon groaned at the thought of PT, known simply as physical training to those outside the military.

Sergeant Fischer yelled, "Ladies, knock off the pissing, moaning, and whining. Five minutes out to the line."

The platoon had been mulling about before Sergeant Fischer burst in, not expecting PT on the morning of their graduation. Bill had a deep respect for Sergeant Fischer. Despite his penchant for yelling, Fischer was always approachable and willing to answer questions. Bill often took the opportunity to pull the sergeant aside to inquire about the importance of a particular skill being taught, which helped him really connect the dots. Sergeant Fischer created an environment where no one felt out of place. It was all about teamwork. He never let anyone fall behind. If someone was off track, unlike other sergeants, he wouldn't embarrass them. Instead, he'd take them aside, away from the group, to explain what went wrong and how to correct it, ensuring the mistake wasn't repeated. Their platoon seemed to be the one that truly learned from its mistakes.

When they participated in field drills against other squads, Bill's squad almost always won. They weren't necessarily better than the other squads, but they had learned to improvise, adapt, and overcome—a philosophy Bill believed was crucial to his success as the Skipper of the squad. Sergeant Fischer had a system of appointing one man from each class to be a leader in the unit, acting as a liaison to him, a bridge between the men and the sergeant. It was a brilliant strategy. The term "Skipper," usually associated with baseball managers, fits well in this military setting where the appointed leader would decipher complaints or concerns, distill the issues, and determine whether they could be resolved within the squad or needed the sergeant's intervention.

Sergeant Fischer assigned the role of Skipper in every class that came through Camp Pendleton. In this class, Bill was named Skipper after just the second week of basic training, recognizing his innate leadership abilities. The men naturally gravitated towards him, and it was noted that his ascension to this post was the fastest since the role was introduced.

Sergeant Fischer met with his Skipper daily, usually before the evening meal, to discuss anything that might require his attention. The Skipper was also granted the right to speak freely without fear of reprisal. These were the rules set by Sergeant Fischer, and Bill adhered to them faithfully. To his credit, Fischer always stuck to his own rules. For that, his men respected him immensely. When Sergeant Fischer asked you to do something, you did it. Aside from his stern demeanor, he was akin to Uncle Jack—meticulous, keen on learning from mistakes, and staunchly dedicated to the creed of never leaving a comrade behind.

The "never leave a man behind" lesson was reinforced the hard way one afternoon after a long 20-mile morning hike. Sgt. Fischer had the platoon do four-man drills, essentially small squad patrols, getting units used to be separated in the field, forcing them to communicate over comms. During the afternoon exercise, one of the men in the third squad twisted his ankle badly, unable to walk. By sheer coincidence, a medic was present, telling the third squad leader he'd bring him back to base.

When squad three showed up, one man down, Sgt. Fischer hit the roof. It was the one and only time during basic they saw Sgt. Fischer loses his composure in front of the whole platoon. One of the men attempted to explain what had happened.

Sgt. Fischer screamed in his face, "Do you think that's how it happens in a combat zone? Are medics joyriding the battlefield? How many times have you been told nobody gets left behind, EVER!"

All the men were now standing in formation while Sgt. Fischer chewed them out, repeating himself five or six times.

When he finally wrapped up, Sgt. Fischer said, "Skipper. My quarters, immediately."

Bill replied, "Yes, Sgt."

Tommy looked at Bill, "You're in for it now."

Bill shook his head but also refused to dress down the third squad after the sergeant left.

Bill walked over to Squad 3, "Notwithstanding the tongue-lashing, what did you learn?"

The squad leader said, "Skipper, we thought we did the right thing. He couldn't walk with us, with the medic right there?"

Bill replied, "Heard, but Sgt. Fischer's been abundantly clear. No one gets left behind."

The squad leader said, "We didn't leave him behind."

Bill shot the squad leader a disapproving look, saying, "Not according to the sergeant. You could've carried him, radioed for help. He's right. A medic isn't going to be joyriding on the battlefield. Regardless, what did you learn from this?"

All three men in the squad replied, "No one gets left behind. EVER."

Suffice it to say, the tone of the conversation between the sergeant and Bill was very different.

When Bill walked into his quarters, the sergeant asked, "Did they get the message?"

Bill replied, "Yes, Sgt., they did. I reinforced it after you left."

The sergeant said, "Appreciate he was hurt, the medic right there. Just not how it happens on the battlefield. I know you get it. Make sure they do."

Bill responded, "Yes, Sgt. Anything else, Sgt.?"

The sergeant replied, "Bill, I appreciate what you've done for the class. I know it's a hard situation for you. Being the platoon's ambassador isn't easy, but you've handled it well. Dismissed."

Bill returned with, "Yes, Sgt."

That was Sgt. Fischer. Decent leader and teacher. Many of the men in the platoon owe him their lives for what he did to prepare them. He was unparalleled by any other non-com.

As we made our way to the line, Sgt. Fischer hollered, "Ten huts!"

The platoon came to attention.

Sgt. Fischer addressed the platoon, "Men, your basic training is over. It was my pleasure to be your instructor. You've all come a long way, both as a unit and as individuals. I hope that all this training prepares you for what comes next. No PT on graduation day. I'm not that big a hard ass."

Bill asked, "Sgt. Fischer, can I say something?"

A little surprised by Bill's request, Sgt. Fischer nodded affirmatively.

Bill began to speak, "Platoon—Three cheers for Sgt. Fischer! Hip, Hip, Hooray!"

The platoon chanted "Hip, Hip, Hooray!" three times. At the end, Sgt. Fischer saluted his platoon, while the platoon reciprocated.

The platoon would be assigned to an undisclosed region in the Mediterranean Sea. Their training was intense in desert warfare; they would train for two long years before being deployed into an active combat situation.

Chapter 27
February 1991 - Kuwait

Tommy came up to Bill in the chow line, "Hey Skipper, Captain Michaels is looking for you. Just swung by the barracks."

Bill said, "Ok, I'll head over to the CP, save me some chow."

Bill was lucky; his captain was a good man. In private, you could say just about anything to him. He was a career man, a great officer, one who cared for his men. Captain Alan Michaels stood 5'9", 180 pounds, with a dark crew cut and sunburnt face. Bill headed to the CP, finding the captain.

He said, "Colonel Hernandez wants us to attend a briefing at 18:00, a mission tonight."

Bill said, "Another weapons capture that'll get many men killed, only to have the weapons disappear after the mission."

The captain looked at Bill, "Gunny, change your tone. Remember, Colonel Hernandez likes you; you get the job done."

Bill said, "Great, but I'm not looking to get every swinging 'Johnson' shot off for his amusement! Been hearing a lot of talk about what happens to those seized weapons."

The captain shook his head, "Be there with bells on."

The captain made his point; ours wasn't to reason why, just to do or die.

Bill left, heading back to the chow hall. It was burger night. It's one of the meals everyone looks forward to all week. The cooks make a show of it. The chow here is pretty good. The lead cook was an executive chef at the InterContinental hotel in KC, who really cared for his troops. They're luckier than most units.

As Bill made his way back, Tommy grabbed him two burgers, no onions, with tater tots. They'd been together so long; Tommy knew Bill's preferences. Bill went over, sitting down on the bench across from Tommy, pulling his tray toward him.

Tommy looked at him, "Whiskey Tango Foxtrot, what was that about?"

Bill said, "I'll know more at 18:00."

At 18:00, Bill made his way over to Colonel Hernandez's CP. The colonel was a large man, weighing 250 pounds, standing 6' tall, with a round face, dark brown eyes, and an almond complexion. He had marks over his eyes made by wearing sunglasses in the desert. The colonel greeted him as if they were long-lost friends.

The colonel said, "Billy boy, how's tricks? Or would you rather I say 'Skipper'? Your Uncle Jack's a good friend. Told me you're a good man!"

Bill, surprised, said, "Thank you, sir. What's the mission?"

The colonel said, "Right to business, just like Uncle Jack. The mission is a sweep and clear one. We've got intelligence this area isn't secure, with a substantial weapons cache. Your squad will infiltrate the area, clear any enemies, and secure the weapons."

Bill responded, "Yes, sir. Size of the enemy force? Any movement from our northern or eastern flank to support us?"

The colonel said, "Intelligence says no. Force estimate is 25 men."

Bill said, "Yes, sir. I'd like to take the second squad along with my squad."

The colonel replied, "Sounds like a plan. When you get the weapons secured, radio in. We'll have a unit come out to remove them."

Bill replied, "Yes, sir. Anything else?"

The colonel said, "A lot like your uncle Jack. All business. That'll be all, Gunny."

Bill nodded, making his way back to his squad. As the colonel was talking, he was taking in his CP. Pictures in the background—he was surprised to see so many personal effects in a CP. This seemed odd, given where they were. If the CP was ever overrun, the enemy would have all sorts of proof of the existence of his family.

He had a picture on his desk of a beautiful young woman, maybe 18, with olive-brown skin, very slender, with a great big smile and light brown hair. She had her arms wrapped around the colonel in the picture, which looked recent, as he looked very much like the man in front of Bill. Bill was taken aback by her beauty. She had an embroidered spot on her dress—Eva, it appeared.

When Bill returned, Tommy was waiting for the squad's briefing. Bill briefed the squad.

When Bill finished, Tommy said, "Skipper, the third squad, did this same mission a week ago. After the weapons were secured, some non-military personnel showed up to collect the weapons. Irish and Mexicans dressed as soldiers. One of the boys in the third squad said those weapons were heading to Mexico. How much of that's true, I don't know."

Bill said, "Keep that under your hat for now. What's strange was that the colonel told me he knew my Uncle Jack and was going on about what great friends they were. Blew a lot of sunshine up my ass, how I was a lot like him. I know Uncle Jack runs with a different crowd, but I never thought he'd be involved with that guy!"

Tommy rolled his eyes, "Isn't that same Uncle Jack fronting for the Irish cause in Brooklyn?"

Bill glared at Tommy, clearly a look that he wasn't engaging in stories about Uncle Jack or his family—not now. Tommy decided to back off the topic. As they began to outline the mission for the squads, Colonel Hernandez came into our briefing. He nodded at Bill to continue, and within two minutes, Bill wrapped up.

Bill asked, "Any questions?"

The colonel waited to see if anyone had any questions, sensing quickly nobody was going to say anything in front of him.

The colonel said, "Need to get this done, boys. Safe travels."

Everyone answered with their best "Yes, sir!" heading for the door.

At this point, the colonel stopped Bill as he headed for the door.

The colonel said, "Good luck. Remember Uncle Jack's counting on you."

Bill looked at him a little puzzled but decided not to comment. It was GO time to focus on the mission. Leaders lead the way, undistracted by useless information.

As they got to the front gate, Bill said, "Ok, boys, saddle up, lock and load!"

The squads were four clicks from the target zone. Bill issued the squad leader's night vision gear. The squads did the four miles in 45 minutes—not bad considering the gear and 50-pound packs.

As they were 500 yards from town, Bill split up the first squad, sending Mike and Fred down the left side of the main street while Tommy and Bill went up the right side. Intelligence reported no activity west of the village. Bill sent squad two up the east side to cover their flank.

As they got within a hundred yards, Tommy said on comms, "Skipper, you on comms?"

Bill replied, "Yes, status?"

Tommy responded, "100 yards from the cache. No movement. The place looks abandoned."

Bill responded, "Stand fast. Mike, Freddie, status?"

Mike responded, "No resistance. Seems like an ambush."

Tommy said, "Skipper, standing fast."

Bill inquired over comms, "Squad two, come in, status."

Squad two replied, "Squad two. Same status, no unfriendlies. Nothing's moving here other than the sandstorm."

Bill said, "Squad two, hold position, calling in trucks. Nobody's out here but us. Tommy, you hearing this? Is there anything there?"

Tommy came back on comms, "Skipper, you're not going to believe this, but the entire weapons cache is larger than our weapons cache. I've counted at least 50 RPGs, enough assault rifles to arm a division."

Bill responded, "Keep alert, calling in the trucks."

Bill radioed back to the CP, and they seemed to be at the weapons cache within two minutes like they followed them. There were 15 trucks with men jumping out with the dexterity of paratroopers. In 30 minutes, the trucks were loaded, heading back to camp.

Bill asked the commander of the unit loading the truck, "Need help?"

He muttered words in Spanish, going back to pushing the other men to get the trucks loaded. Bill tried to stay focused, but he couldn't stop wondering if what Tommy shared after the briefing was true. What would a bunch of Spanish-speaking personnel be doing here in Kuwait? Were they even part of the coalition? Why are US military personnel being sent out to support this? Bill wanted to chat with the colonel about what this mission was about. As the last truck left, both squads pulled back, the timing of which was perfect, as the wind picked up, making it harder to see. Both squads double-timed it back to the base.

Upon returning to base, Colonel Hernandez was waiting at the entrance to Bill's barracks.

The colonel was holding a box of cigars, "Thanks, boys, some cigars with my compliments."

Bill asked, "Did you want a briefing, sir?"

The colonel said, "No, monitored from the CP. I got the picture. Good job, Skipper."

Bill asked the colonel, "A moment, sir?"

The colonel said, "Sure, make it quick. Must plan for the disposition."

Bill started, "Sir, this mission was odd, to say the least. No resistance, but why'd we have ten times the resources to move the weapons? None of the men on the trucks spoke English."

The colonel paused for a moment, collecting his thoughts.

The colonel said, "Not your concern. Uncle Jack would be proud of you."

Bill asked the fateful question, "Where is the cache going?"

At this point, the colonel glared at Bill, "That'll be all, Gunny."

Bill was dumbfounded, but what could he do?

Tommy approached, seeing the look on Bill's face, "What was that about?"

Bill said, "You're right about the caches. Who was talking about it?"

Tommy replied, "Angel Martinez was drunk the other night, shooting his mouth off about how the weapons were disappearing into friendly hands. If you're thinking about talking to him, he shipped stateside last week. Heard he was going home to get married. Rumor has it, he's Hernandez's nephew."

Bill replied, "How's it he got shipped stateside? Wasn't he here only a month? How the hell did he rotate stateside after one month?"

Tommy shrugged his shoulders with a devilish smile, "You know the military, Skipper. Someone's always making a buck."

Tommy's words hung in the air as they walked back to the barracks. When they got back, they each lit a Cuban cigar, the only treat of the evening. They both stood quiet, looking out over the horizon, puffing away on a newfound love.

Chapter 28
Late February 1991 – Kuwait

Bill was a squad leader in Lt. John C. McGuire's platoon. McGuire was a rookie officer straight out of ROTC, standing 5'9", weighing 175 pounds, with a blond crew cut, as well as a massively sunburned face. *Man, was he green,* Bill thought. He'd trip over the front line if he ever found it. For his first three months, the platoon didn't know if McGuire was in charge or if Bill was.

Lt. McGuire told Bill, "We're to clear the village, despite intelligence reports."

At the briefing, Bill didn't ask many questions, focusing on what the mission was, where it was taking them, getting the job done, and getting back alive. No heroes in our unit. Do your job. Everyone makes it home after each mission. Sgt. Fischer's lessons were still deeply rooted in this squad.

Tommy couldn't make the briefing; he was on the phone with Amanda. She was with Tommy's father, who was fighting colon cancer. They were able to schedule a call for him, Amanda, and his dad so Tommy could say goodbye. The prognosis was terminal—an inoperable tumor, stage 4 cancer.

Tommy was a great Marine, picking up what was needed while they moved out. Bill wasn't worried about Tommy focusing on the mission; he understood the score with his dad. At the briefing, nobody knew Tommy was missing, getting the lowdown on the village. It had been a stronghold for the 2nd Brigade of the Republican Guard Corps, but no activity had been witnessed in the village for three weeks. In Bill's mind, that meant nothing. Intelligence was as accurate as the weather, so he became concerned immediately.

Bill's squad was to work with another squad on their western flank, pushing north of the village, while Bill's squad came up from the south, covering the right flank. Bill's squad was to provide a block from the east, while the last squad was held in slow-rolling reserve. When they got to the objective, they swung west, entering the industrial area.

As they mounted the AAV-7, Major Franks gave them a wink, "Expect light resistance, but get it done."

Famous last words, Bill thought. As the squad pulled out, they had to move three clicks to get into position, which gave Bill time to get Tommy up to speed. Also, it gave Bill and Tommy time to talk about his dad. Unfortunately, Bill couldn't leave Tommy behind; he wouldn't have allowed that to happen even if Bill suggested it.

As the platoon got one click outside of town, Bill told the team, "Saddle up, lock and load."

Bill wanted things quiet on their approach. In the two squads, there were eight men. As they were within half a click from the village, Bill decided to split the squad, four moving north into the village while four flanked east to provide cover from a potential northeastern assault, also ensuring they were covered from the east if the village was being watched by anyone looking to ambush any unit entering from the south. The second squad was coming in from the northwest and would cover the northern flank.

As the squad moved toward the opening of the village, they wouldn't have cover, so they moved toward the main road, taking up positions near the buildings on each side of the street. Fred and Mike were on the west side of the main street. Tommy and Bill were on the east side of the main street. As the squad started to sweep and clear each building, Bill raised his fist to indicate, "All stop."

Then, BOOM, BOOM, BOOM, with a hail of gunfire coming from the northeast flank. They were in one hell of a street fight, heading past the objective, ordered to sweep and clear a small village nearby, which intelligence told them was abandoned for months by the enemy. *Great God almighty, what a surprise;* intelligence was wrong.

At this point, Bill heard men yelling in Arabic. They'd been in-country for a few months, but no one really understood Arabic—a few words, maybe. They were here to kill the enemy, not converse with them.

As the squad held up, the enemy soldiers began to yell frantically. Fred and Mike went into an abandoned building on the west side of the street, taking an elevated position near an open window. Tommy and Bill were about to do the same, but Bill noticed a window in the back bedroom providing a better view into the enemy's encampment. Bill saw a commander's tent, a central fire for cooking, as well as three cages, each holding a soldier. At first, Bill didn't get a great look at them, until the enemy pulled one of the soldiers from the cage. It was a British officer, based on his insignia, who looked wounded and filthy, with bruises on his face and arms. He was clearly weak from a lack of food and water.

Tommy looked at Bill, "What do you want to do, Skipper?"

Bill replied, "Get Fred and Mike over here to formulate a plan. I don't want us getting hung out trying to be heroes. Mike has the strongest radio; have him radio back our findings. We'll need some Whiskey support, too."

Bill recalled a briefing two days prior about missing British soldiers, presumed killed in action, or KIA. The British officers were very animated during the briefing but wouldn't say why. Bill was surprised the "Yanks" were invited. Bill asked the captain why they were invited.

The captain said, "Honestly, don't know."

Bill kept his eye on the enemy while Tommy drew Fred and Mike's attention to move into Bill's area. Bill wasn't keen on doing this, as this could get all of them killed quickly, but Fred had the best radio. Bill wasn't getting any signal, nor was Tommy. Their AAV-7 was no help either, as it would wake up every jihadi within a click of their position. The enemy didn't know they were there, so they needed to use that to their advantage.

The squad huddled to come up with a game plan. Mike would signal back to the east flank, outline what was going on, and radio back to HQ. Freddie would get into the God spot, having a broader field of targets in the building on the west side of Main Street.

Suddenly, Mike said, "Can't connect with the second squad coming in from the south."

Bill told him, "Get with HQ to see if they can reach them ASAP."

As the words hung in the air, a tremendous amount of screaming started in front of the wall where they were positioned. The second squad was starting to come in from the north, and the insurgents began to take a position to defend the village.

At this point, the enemy had no idea Bill's unit was in the village. Mike frantically tried to reach the second squad but had no luck. They reached their eastern flank, continuing south by east to avoid detection. Bill's rationale was if the enemy was focused on the second squad coming in from the south, the first squad could surprise the enemy from inside the village, protect their second squad, and perhaps even recover the British prisoners.

As the second squad entered the village, the enemy started to engage them.

At this point, Bill called out, "Fred, suppressing fire, get that saw going."

Fred made it to the God spot, which made him a difficult target. Also, he'd be able to switch to sniper from that position if needed.

Fred radioed, "Skipper, got three vantage points, protecting our six. Got 300 rounds."

Bill had Mike stay with him to protect him and also be a runner if needed.

Bill barked, "Try to get that radio up, or we won't be getting any Whiskey support!"

Tommy and Bill maneuvered from behind the back bedroom through a back exit, advancing from the rear surrounding the enemy garrison. The second squad came up to assist on their flank. What Bill didn't know was that the second squad was taking fire from an enemy unit moving south by east into the village to reinforce the garrison.

The next thing they knew, two units were surrounded. The original garrison was surrounded by a second squad, while Tommy and Bill were now in the middle of the original garrison, as well as the new oncoming garrison.

Tommy looked at Bill and yelled, "Skipper, not good."

Bill calmly replied, "FUBAR."

Bill must have said it in a funny manner because Tommy started laughing—a big belly laugh. Here they were, in the middle of a battle. Tommy starts laughing, bullets flying, mortar shells raining down—a real Fourth of July BBQ.

Bill said, "Tommy, suppressing fire, here's my weapon, so you won't have to change mags. It's topped off. I've got my 9mm, and I'm going in. That's the rallying point. Keep it secure. Be ready to pull out quickly."

As Bill pushed off, Tommy yelled, "Are you fucking nuts?"

At this point, Fred was chattering with Tommy on comms, "Second squad is split up, but they've got our western flank covered. We can start to move west while we circle the wagons."

Bill heard this over the comms and sarcastically said, "Love it when a plan comes together."

With that, Bill exited his position, sprinting to the cages. Within seconds, the British soldiers were yelling.

As Bill approached, he told them, "Back up. Need to shoot out the locks."

Bill pointed at the rally point and opened the first cage.

However, the commanding officer said, "I'm not leaving my men."

Bill said, "We'll leave no one behind. Now move it, sir!"

Bill thought for a second this was noble, but it was time to get all four of them to the rally point. They could talk about nobility later. However, instead of doing what Bill asked, the commander followed him to the next cage. The soldier in the second cage had been badly wounded and beaten. In the end, his commander picked him up, threw him over his left shoulder, and started for the rally point.

The third soldier was probably the best physically but mentally shattered, just mumbling under his breath, tears streaming down his face. Bill holstered his weapon, threw him over his left shoulder, and moved toward the rally point. All the while, bullets were hailing down upon them from both the north and west.

As Bill got to the rally point, Tommy said to Bill, "Skipper, how the fuck are you still here? You almost bought it three times."

Bill looked at Tommy, saying, "FOCUS, rendezvous point."

Tommy nodded his head, "You got it. Time to get out of Dodge."

At this point, Bill began to signal to Fred and Mike that they needed to start for the rendezvous point, providing covering fire while moving southwest. Tommy and Bill needed covering fire, pulling back with the unarmed British soldiers.

The squad made leapfrogs of 250-yard increments until making it to the rendezvous point, which took them an hour, given the hail of gunfire. The fighting was fierce, hand-to-hand combat for what seemed an eternity. They didn't have an eastern flank, as those men were pinned down, now cut off from moving west. The western flank was now north of their position, continuing to move west until Fred reoriented them so they could help the eastern squad pull back.

Fred and Mike laid down an ungodly amount of suppressing fire while Tommy and Bill continued to defend themselves and the wounded. The British commander was able to tend to his men, which helped. While he was the best of the three, he was wounded himself.

In addition, the northern flank moved past them, mistaking them for the enemy, so they took some friendly fire before Fred got them to realize they were on the same team.

Not long after the enemy body count was upward of 50, the battle was done, without any air support. Tommy killed ten enemy soldiers, while Bill eliminated 15 enemy soldiers, ten during hand-to-hand combat. It was brutal and ugly, still haunting Bill's dreams to this very day. How Tommy and Bill escaped unharmed is a miracle.

Tommy said, "I'm glad you're on my side."

Bill replied, "No one is left behind, EVER."

Suffice it to say, it was a long morning. The mission was accomplished—they retrieved three wounded MIA British soldiers and didn't get their squad's asses shot off. Amazingly, their casualties were light, mostly minor flesh wounds. However, Bill caught a bullet in his arm and right thigh, never feeling it nor noticing it until Tommy said something.

Tommy looked down, "Skipper, are you bleeding?"

Bill shrugged his shoulders but acknowledged the blood.

Tommy, Fred, and Mike were unharmed. From the rendezvous point, both squads were flown out on a UH-1 to the nearest base. The three British soldiers, as well as Bill, were treated for their wounds. The British soldier Bill carried to the rendezvous point was being looked at for battle fatigue as he got worse on the chopper ride, attempting to jump out of the helicopter during one turn. Thankfully, Bill strapped him into the seat, where the medic was quick to give him a sedative to calm the soldier down.

After a debriefing—useless as the day was long—the British commander came by the Yanks' tent to thank them. Not sure how he got it, but he brought a fine bottle of Johnnie Walker Blue with him. They each grabbed a mug, toasting to good health.

After the British officer left, Fred said, "He look familiar to you?"

Bill replied, "No, he doesn't."

About an hour later, with a pretty good load on, Bill was summoned to see his commanding officer. Usually, this was never a good thing, usually a reprimand or your team volunteering for a mission of strategic importance. For Bill, neither excuse was a good reason; it was clear he'd been in-country too long.

When Bill got to the CO's tent, he was greeted by Major General Clifton, who was with an admiral of the Royal British Navy. Major General Clifton was a living legend and a recipient of the Naval Cross. He stood 6'0", 200 pounds, all muscle for a man of 40, with gray hair, a traditional Marine haircut, and a steely jaw. He had blue eyes that went off like fireworks when he talked. He was a career man, seeing combat in several campaigns, with a tough demeanor but a reputation for being good to his men. The admiral was a portly man who looked 50 years of age, 5'8", around 200 pounds. He was bald, with a large, round face, flushed from being in the desert sun. To be honest, he looked like Winston Churchill.

As Bill settled in, he said to himself, *Better mind your Ps and Qs.* His CO was present, greeting him at the door.

He whispered to Bill, "This is no joke, best behavior."

Bill quietly said, "Yes, sir."

Clifton asked, "Gunny, do you know why you're here?"

Bill replied, "No, sir. Was there something you wanted to discuss about the mission?"

Clifton politely said, "No. This is Admiral Smythe of the British Royal Navy."

Bill looked at the admiral, saying, "Yes, sir. Nice to meet you both."

Clifton said, "Gunny, your squad did a terrific job today."

Clifton went on to recap his version of events, as Bill, standing at ease, thought to himself, *What bullshit. Where's this going?* Listening to Clifton fall in love with the melodic tone of his own voice.

After ten minutes, he said, "The British commander was rescued today. Do you know who he is?"

Bill responded, "No, sir. If memory serves, his tags read 'Johnson.'"

The admiral then chimed in, refusing to be outdone by his American counterpart, speaking for ten minutes in long soliloquies. Finally, after the English literature lesson, Bill was informed that the commander was a senior member of the Royal Family. The admiral came to pay his respects to the men assisting the monarchy.

For many folks, this would be a great honor, but to be honest, Bill was too drunk to really care. Not because Bill had anything against the Royal Family, which some would find strange, knowing his grandfather fought in the Irish Revolution.

For Bill, it was simple: the commander did his duty, protected his men, looked after them, and got them back safely. The commander didn't act "royal," coming to the barracks with a lovely bottle of scotch, never pretending to be someone with a golden spoon in his mouth. Bill's thought, *He's a soldier.* Bill respected that. As Bill stood, taking in more pomp and circumstance, he thought back to the commander's appearance. He had blondish hair, somewhat balding on top, even for a young man, and stood 6'2" with a pale complexion.

After the soliloquies, Bill looked at the major general, then the admiral, saying, "Thank you for letting me know. He was kind enough to swing by with some scotch, which we've already indulged in. Admiral, please tell the commander I hope his men recover."

Thinking this was done, the admiral said, "Son, I've spoken with Her Majesty. She'd like you to pay a visit to Buckingham Palace when your service is up. She'd like to thank you in person."

Bill was stunned, "I appreciate the invitation, but that's not necessary. Also, I'm not sure she'd want my Irish mug visiting. My grandfather was in the IRA."

The major general was appalled, but the admiral laughed, "I'm sure she won't hold it against you if you don't hold it against her."

Bill replied, "Very well. My tour won't be up for a few months."

The admiral said, "We'll coordinate it with your return home."

With that, the major general dismissed the CO and Bill.

As they emerged outside, Bill's CO looked over at him, saying, "Well handled, until that IRA thing. Are you nuts?"

Bill said, "Thanks. I'm heading back to the barracks to check on my men. That's all that matters to me right now."

As Bill walked back, he replayed the battle in his mind. *Was there something I should have done that I didn't? Was there something we did that we wished we hadn't?*

Then, he pictured the faces of each man during the fight. As Bill got back to the tents, he was alone, laying down on his bunk, figuring he'd get some rest. As Bill closed his eyes, the hand-to-hand fighting was as vivid as if it was happening, weighing on his mind. Being attacked at the same time, one from behind with a knife and another coming at him with a pistol. Bill pulled at least two enemy soldiers off Tommy while he fended off two others. Mike and Fred were also pulling back, picking off the enemy as they made it to the rendezvous point.

Bill's thoughts ranged from shock to telling himself, at those moments, *It's kill or be killed.* His breathing was hard. Adrenaline was pumping hours after the siege, recalling the smell of the attackers looking to impose their will. In those situations, they were doing everything in their power to defend themselves. Hand-to-hand combat is murderous rage; anything that gets in the way gets eliminated.

Before long, the first squad would be heading home.

Chapter 29
Early March 1991 – Kuwait

At the morning briefing, Bill's squad was deployed to work with a village on the northeast outskirts of Kuwait International Airport. One of the local elders was working with the USMC to remove Saddam Hussein. When Bill's unit deployed to the area, he met with the tribal elder, as well as his eldest daughter, Fatima.

Fatima's family lived in the village for hundreds of years. Her grandfather was the tribal elder in the village, a highly respected man who hated Saddam Hussein. Just the very mention of Saddam's name would send him into a frenzy. Fatima seemed to be the only one who could calm him down after his tirades. Upon meeting her, one could sense Fatima was a natural at easing others' pain—soft-spoken, considerate, and appreciative. Bill appreciated her, as she had a wealth of intelligence in the area. Fatima was a petite woman, but it was very hard to get a sense of her features, given the *abaya* she wore. She had hypnotic, deep, dark brown eyes, and she was gentle and kind despite the environment she lived in.

One early morning, the squad was deployed in Fatima's northeastern village. Their orders were to push out of the village north, then east, and engage the enemy if necessary. Fatima's father assigned her to the squad, asking Bill to protect her like she was family. Bill agreed. On this morning, the squad pulled out just as dawn broke, pushing north two clicks and then east one click. A small village appeared on the horizon. Bill put up his fist for an all-stop.

Bill said, "Fatima, there's no village on the map."

Fatima said, "It's not a village. It's an encampment. Built up over the past three days. These people had nowhere to go after their villages were destroyed. They create a new village."

Bill looked at Tommy, gauging his reaction. *Setup, or was she telling the truth?* Bill had no reason to think she was lying, but he also needed to consider the possibilities.

Tommy said, "Skipper, makes sense. What do you want to do?"

Bill said, "Tommy, come with me, we'll take Fatima. Mike and Fred set up some firing lanes about 200 yards outside the camp. We'll go in to see if they're friendlies."

Fred pointed at his map, "It's probably best if we're here. Might be a bit of a run if you need to hightail it out, but we'll have a better line of sight."

Bill responded, "Good, let's execute. Fatima, on my left hip."

Fatima looked confused, "On your left hip?"

Bill smiled, then positioned her where he wanted her, saying, "Just like this, stay as close to me as you can. I promised your father I'd protect you. Tommy, let's move out."

Tommy and Bill started forward while Fatima remained on Bill's left hip. As they got about 100 yards away, they heard hollering in Arabic.

Bill asked Fatima, "Can you hear what they're saying?"

Fatima said, "They know you're coming."

Bill asked, "Is that a good thing or a bad thing? Can you tell?"

Fatima replied, "I think so."

They moved forward, entering the encampment. Fatima talked with two men she knew, informing her their village was destroyed by

Iraqi forces, who burned the buildings. They'd been at this encampment for two days. The other settlers were fascinated with Tommy and Bill, especially the children. None spoke English, but they all knew the word "candy." Tommy and Bill dispensed the chocolate to one of the mothers so that she could dole out. Seeing the children playing and enjoying the candy brought smiles to Bill and Tommy.

As the woman doled out the candy, BOOM! A round from an RPG rained down.

Bill yelled, "Take cover!"

Unfortunately, the only cover was the pushcarts in the encampment, the apparent target. It was bad enough that these people had their villages destroyed, and now their encampment was under attack.

After the RPG came in, over comms, Fred yelled, "Skipper— status!"

Bill replied, "RPG, direct hit on one of the carts, civilian casualties."

As Bill was replying, the gunfire started. Three men came out of one of the tents with AK-47s, hailing bullets down. Bill hit the dirt, bringing Fatima to the ground, then laid down almost entirely on top of her while she covered her head, curling up in a ball. Bullets were flying. Tommy was hit and took a bullet in the arm, but over comms, informed them he was ok.

Tommy said, "Just a flesh wound."

Bill laughed at his comment. Fatima was screaming underneath Bill.

From Bill's position, he could see the three-man unit attempting to outflank them from the east. Bill turned in their direction.

Over comms, Bill said, "Freddie, you see my firing lane?"

Freddie said, "I got your six. I'll stay down the main street. You stay to my left, Tommy; you go left outside, Skipper."

Bill said, "Bingo, draw them in a little. When I start, you lay down the saw hard, got it?"

Freddie came back, "Copy that."

With the gunfire over for the moment, Fatima seemed to calm down a bit.

Bill joked with Fatima, "Never thought you'd be in this position, huh?"

Fatima nervously laughed, not sure what Bill meant. She knew he was trying to protect her, make her feel secure, and attempt to lighten the mood.

The three-man team started toward Bill and Tommy. Bill let them get within 25 yards of their position.

Bill whispered, "Fatima, don't move."

Fatima whispered back, "I won't."

Bill pointed his finger in Tommy's direction, indicating it was time to move northwest so Freddie had clear firing lanes. Tommy obliged, but Bill didn't move. When laying out the plan, he never considered protecting Fatima. He couldn't leave her unprotected.

Bill whispered on comms, "Freddie, Tommy's in position, but I need to stay here. Alter your firing lines by ten yards. I'll stay with Fatima to cover her."

Freddie was yelling, "Skipper, you got to move! They're on top of you!"

Bill didn't respond. The three-man team was now 15 yards from Bill's position but, for some reason, didn't engage. Fatima was underneath Bill, crying, as a strange silence fell over them. The three-man team signaled as if they heard something. They heard Fatima crying.

Bill said to Fatima, "I'm going to lift up. I want you to slide out behind me. I'll spread my legs so you can nestle between them. Hurry, they're coming."

Without saying a word, Fatima did exactly what Bill wanted. Bill figured he was wearing his vest, which would shield them both. The three-man team was on top of them but still hadn't fired, yammering a mile a minute, but Bill didn't understand what they were saying. Suddenly, the leader of the three-man team saw Bill. Bill had been in a firing position all along, waiting to draw them in.

BANG! Bill took out their leader, a clean headshot. BANG! The second man down, another headshot. Freddie opened fire when he heard Bill's first shot, taking out the final assailant. Bill was down, shot in the left shoulder. Tommy ran to him while Fatima was already putting pressure on his wound, crying.

Fatima said, "Please don't die on me now."

Tommy radioed in, "Skipper's hit, shoulder wound. Extracting."

Bill was losing some blood, but he felt he could walk back to camp with his unit. However, when Bill stood up, he fell back down, lightheaded. Tommy called for a bus to come pick them up.

When they got on the helicopter for the return to base, Fatima curled up on Bill's right shoulder, rubbing his hand, trying to comfort him.

Fatima said, "Thank you for keeping me safe."

Bill smiled softly, looking at her, "I made a promise to your father."

Fatima sank into Bill's right shoulder, crying.

Bill was brought to the field hospital. Luckily, it was a clean shot through. Other than some stitches, he thought he'd be ready to return to his squad. Bill didn't think he was wounded badly, but Tommy noticed how much more animated Bill was in the hospital barracks. Bill wasn't being shipped out, as he was told by the doctors the wound wasn't serious enough.

However, Tommy noticed that Bill is jumpy and very agitated with everyone. Tommy asked Bill to stay in the field hospital to recuperate. He needed to redress the wound twice a day anyway, what with the desert sand getting through any bandage worn, making it almost impossible to maintain. This was the only way to get Bill to remain in the hospital.

It was Fatima who comforted Bill after being wounded. Three days after Bill was wounded, Tommy snuck Fatima not only into camp but to Bill's hospital bed. Bill spiked a fever the night he was wounded, so doctors gave him something to address it. It was before dawn when Fatima arrived, where she sat with Bill, even before the nursing staff realized Fatima was there.

When Fatima joined Bill's bedside, Bill was up, unable to sleep. The fever broke, so Bill felt more like himself, anxious to get out of bed. When Fatima arrived, he felt much better, perking up, so much so the nurses even noticed.

They talked about the future of her country and how she wanted to go live in the United States. She also expressed concerns over Bill's wounds, sitting, holding his hand, and comforting him. Bill thought it strange, given her culture, to touch a man. Before deploying, each squad went through etiquette school. The one thing they stressed a lot was: don't even look at the women, let alone touch them. He was surprised she held his hand. Then Fatima got even more brazen. When no one was looking, she removed her headwrap, leaned over, and kissed Bill, exposing her light brown skin—warm, inviting—with beautiful dark brown hair. Without the *abaya*, she seemed more real, revealing the subtle contours of her beautiful face, accentuating those wonderful eyes. Fatima moved closer to Bill.

Fatima said, "You're the first man I've ever kissed. It was wonderful."

Bill smiled, replying, "You do it well. While you started it, I was happy to finish it."

Fatima smirked as she became a little embarrassed. Being her first kiss, even at the age of 18, she didn't know what to expect or how it would feel.

Fatima said, "While my family supports you against Saddam, I don't know how they're going to feel about us."

Bill replied, "Copy that. *Us*, huh? You're their only daughter. Why would he want you mixed up with a bum like me?"

Fatima nervously laughed, "Bum? What's that?"

Bill said, "It's a person that doesn't have any real meaning in life. They live off the kindness of others. Does that make sense?"

Fatima replied, "I think so. Have you ever been in love before?"

Of course, being 20 years old himself, Bill was clearly an expert on love.

Bill said, "Yes, once. Mary Ellen Moffatt in high school. She broke my heart."

Fatima seriously asked, "How did she do that?"

Bill replied, "After two years of dating, she secretly started to see another boy in our class, one with whom I'd been best friends since grammar school. When I found out about it, it hurt, knowing they betrayed me. That was four years ago. You know, I've never spoken to either of them since. Don't want people in my life I can't trust."

Fatima said, "If she loved you, why would she do that?"

Bill said, "Honestly, I don't know. Perhaps we were never really in love. Or maybe I cared more for her than she did for me."

Fatima replied, "In our culture, that never happens. Usually, marriages are arranged, and families are known your whole life. I'm lucky. My parents wouldn't accept an arranged marriage. I'm one of two girls in my village, and I am free to marry who I want. Do you have this custom in the US?"

Bill said, "I've heard of them, but it's not common in America."

Fatima asked, "When do you get out of here?"

Bill replied, "Tomorrow morning, I'm being told. Why?"

Fatima replied, "I want to make you dinner, be alone, just the two of us. I know a quiet place nearby that's safe. Can you meet me there?"

Bill said, "I'm not sure. Where's this place?"

Fatima said, "It's in your patrol area. Please, it's important. I see you with your men. See how you look after them. Even my father said you're a good man and trustworthy. Over the last month, I've fallen in love with you."

Bill was out of his depth. He admitted he noticed her as well but never thought she could be with him. Now, she wanted a night alone together. Fatima waited in anticipation of his response.

Bill said, "I'd love to, but are you sure? I don't want you getting into trouble with your family."

Fatima said, "I love you; I know that. Besides, I don't care about getting into trouble, not for this."

Bill replied, "Okay then. We'll try to work it out once I'm out of here."

Fatima smiled, "I've got to go. I'll get things arranged for tomorrow night."

Fatima left the hospital. Bill was released early the next morning.

As fate would have it, his squad was ordered to head to the exact village where Fatima wanted to be together. As they made their way onto the field, the squad headed northwest into the small village, arriving at 20:00 to begin clearing it. For the most part, the village was abandoned, except for three families. The men from each family greeted Bill's squad like liberators, offering food and drink. Despite the genuine offer, they didn't take anything, as these villagers barely had enough food for themselves.

The squad got situated, settling in at one of the houses on the southwest side of the village.

Tommy asked Bill, "How was your girlfriend's visit?"

Bill glared at Tommy, "'Girlfriend?'"

Tommy said, "Fatima. She's nice. Hard to tell if she's pretty, though."

Bill replied, "She's beautiful. She took off her *abaya* when she visited. Believe me, she's stunning underneath that getup. It's funny we're in this village."

Tommy replied, "Why?"

Bill responded, "When she visited me in the hospital, she asked about meeting in this village tonight so we could be together."

Tommy said, "Can't make that up. Wait, is that her in the window?"

Bill replied, "Yes, it is."

Tommy responded, "Then why are you here? Go take the night off. We got this."

Bill said, "How can I? If anyone ever found out, they'd kill her. I promised her father I'd protect her. You remember all those etiquette lessons about not looking at the women. No?"

Tommy said, "Copy that, but she told me she loved you, did from the moment she saw you. Talking to her, I could tell immediately it was the same as what I've got with Amanda. Make sure, or you'll never forgive yourself for missing this chance."

Bill was stunned by Tommy's support.

Fred and Mike had been overhearing the conversation, both saying, "Skipper, go be with Fatima. Tommy's right, we got this."

Bill reluctantly grabbed his gear, heading toward the building Fatima was in. Bill had his guys covering his six, so he only had to worry about crossing the road. Fortunately, the desert sun was setting, making it darker by the second. To the west, the horizon was a sea of deep orange. Considering where they were, it was quite beautiful at that moment.

Bill made his way across the main road, then upstairs to Fatima. When Bill arrived on the second floor, he noticed some open windows. With the scope on his weapon, Bill surveilled the area before going into the room where Fatima was. After a proper recon, Bill entered the room. When he got inside, she was cooking over an open flame in a makeshift kitchen. The room had concrete walls, with a few holes from RPG fire. Fortunately, it was downwind, so there wasn't a haze in the air. When Bill called her name, she turned, smiling.

She wore a different outfit, looking more like a ballroom gown, but it had a hood that covered her hair, but not her beautiful face. The outfit was dark green, with a dark green veil over the top of her head. When she unwrapped the veil, she smiled so beautifully. Fatima was a thin woman, 5'4", 100 pounds, maybe, with dark brown hair, rich brown eyes, and silky tan skin. Like many women of her culture, she hid her beauty with her attire.

Fatima said, "I wanted to make a special effort. What do you think?"

Bill replied, "You look beautiful."

Fatima smiled, replying, "Thank you. Can I kiss you?"

Bill said, "You don't need to ask. I'd like that very much."

As Fatima approached, Bill put down his gear. When she got to Bill, Fatima planted a soft, wonderful kiss on him. Bill had to admit that it was a pretty good kiss for her second kiss.

Fatima asked, "Was that all right?"

Bill softly said, "Very nice. What's next on your agenda?"

Fatima replied, "Dinner's ready. Grab a plate. I'll show you how we do it."

Bill smiled, saying, "Show me the way."

Fatima walked over, grabbed a plate, handed it to Bill, then placed a variety of things on his plate. Bill didn't recognize any of the food, but it did smell good. She made sure his plate was ready before getting something for herself. Bill guessed it was a cultural thing but didn't feel the need to inquire. Also, she had glasses of water out, but Bill grabbed his canteen, as they were told on day one to be very careful drinking any water off base.

Fatima sat down at the table, "Eat. I can't wait to see if you like it."

Bill took out his fork while she laughed, "No, silly. Let me show you."

Fatima began picking things up with her hands or the naan bread she made. The meal was different than anything Bill had ever had before, but the food was terrific. He was thankful for a home-cooked meal.

They bantered the whole evening, talking about their hopes, their dreams for the future, and what it was like living in America. They promised each other that they'd be together in America someday soon. They talked all night. Suffice it to say, it was the best first date they'd been on.

The following morning, with Fatima's head fast asleep on Bill's chest, Bill woke up to Tommy calling out.

Tommy said, "Skipper?"

Bill replied, "In here. We're pulling out?"

Tommy said, "No, look out your front window."

Fatima sleepily asked, "What's happening?"

Bill didn't answer, picking up his weapon and moving toward the open window. Panning from the northeast to the northern flank, Bill saw a platoon of Iraqi Guardsmen approaching.

Bill said, "Guardsmen patrol. Get Fred in the God spot, 10:00 on my bearing. He'll have a great look at them up there."

Tommy replied on comms, "Affirmative. Freddie, get the 'Kate' in the God spot, 10:00 from our position."

Fred responded, "Affirmative, moving into position now."

Fatima repeated her question, "What's happening?"

Bill replied, "Not sure yet. Guardsmen patrol, but I'm not sure if they've seen us. Get your stuff together, love. Come with me, now."

Fatima smiled at being called "love," then hurriedly said, "Okay."

She grabbed her backpack, collecting what she had brought for their evening together as quietly as she could. Then they headed down the stairs.

Bill said, "Fatima, stick close to me. Understand? Right on my hip. Got it?"

Fatima nodded her head, exiting the front door with Bill. Tommy was in the lead position. Bill was covering their six, with Fatima right on Bill's left hip.

Suddenly, BOOM, BOOM, BOOM!

Bill yelled, "Incoming, take cover!"

Instead of staying on Bill's hip, Fatima dove to her right while Tommy and Bill continued to their left, heading to the rally point. In the haze of the mortar strikes, Fatima and Bill were separated. When Bill saw Fatima wasn't with him, he panned around, noticing her position—exposed, alone, unarmed. Bill started toward her while the enemy fire rained down on them.

As they got closer to the platoon's original position, Mike had the saw rolling, laying down an ungodly amount of suppressing fire. Fred was picking off guardsmen with his 'Kate' from the top of the building. The firepower was unrelenting.

Bill ran toward Fatima, yelling, "Fatima, get down! I'm coming to get you!"

BOOM, BOOM! Two mortar shells dropped where Fatima was running to. Bill was blown back to the ground. Bill saw Fatima lying motionless after the mortar hit. Bill continued to make attempts toward her, but the return fire made it impossible.

Tommy yelled at Bill twice, "Are you fucking insane, trying to get out there?"

Bill yelled back at Tommy, "We need to get her! She'll be safer with us."

Tommy shouted, "Copy that, Skipper, but eliminate the threat first, then assess."

The attack lasted three hours before they neutralized the enemy garrison. Several of the survivors fled the village, heading for the open desert terrain. After the attack, the squad had 25 confirmed kills, all enemy casualties.

However, when Bill made it to Fatima's last position, she was gone. Bill spent the next hour retracing their steps, going back to the building where they'd spent the evening together, but nothing. It was as if she vanished.

Upon arriving back at the barracks, Bill walked right past the captain, saying, "Sir. Need a minute before I brief you."

The captain replied, "Gunny, come see me when you're ready. The squad did a great job."

Bill didn't say anything, returning to his barracks. Tommy was the only one who followed. When Bill got to his bunk, he pulled off his helmet, sat at the foot of his bunk, put his hands over his face, and quietly sobbed, mourning the loss of Fatima.

Tommy made his way over, saying, "Skipper, I know you cared about her. We all did. All I can say is I'm sorry. Wrong place, wrong time. It's not your fault."

Bill looked at Tommy, with tears rolling down his face, "I loved her. I failed to protect her. I need to go to her village and tell her family what happened."

Tommy replied, "The captain told me we're being redeployed, so we'll not be anywhere near her village. Skipper, I know you don't want to hear this, but you need to let it go."

Bill said nothing back, continuing to sit on the foot of his bunk, mourning the loss of sweet Fatima.

Tommy and Bill never spoke of that day or Fatima again. For years after the war, unbeknownst to the members of his squad, Bill paid for an annual inquiry about Fatima, paying contractors to locate her.

However, after each inquiry, nobody could locate her or give Bill the closure he wanted.

Chapter 30
April 1991 – Balmoral, Scotland

Bill had been released from Ramstein Air Base and out of the hospital. Captain Michaels and Lt. McGuire paid Bill a visit before Bill shipped out. He had recovered from his wounds; fortunately, nothing serious, only a slight complication. For some reason, when he got to Ramstein, he spiked a fever while convalescing.

The captain said, "Gunny, you've got your dress uniform?"

Bill replied, "They're getting me a new one; the sand ruined the uniform in-country. Why do you ask?"

The captain replied, "You're being sent to the UK for the meeting with Her Majesty."

Bill replied, "Seriously, that's actually going to happen?"

The captain said, "Not only do you get an audience with the Queen, but you've also been invited to dine with them and spend the night at Balmoral Castle."

Bill responded, "Get the hell out of here."

The captain replied, "You'll be leaving us tomorrow. Also, we've got something for you. By order of the President of the United States, for your act of bravery in the field, you've been selected to receive the Medal of Honor. Congratulations, Gunny."

Bill stood stunned, in silence, as the captain gave him the news of receiving the highest honor any soldier could receive.

The captain continued, "By order of the President, you are to proceed to Balmoral Castle this morning for an audience with the Queen of England. After spending the night with the Royal Family, you'll be sent to Washington, DC, for the official ceremony."

Bill had a lump in his throat, "Why me? What for?"

Lt. McGuire finally said something, "I put you in for it after the rescue of the three British soldiers. Tommy helped me with a lot of the details of the mission. But when I heard what you did that day, I was compelled to at least put you in."

Bill replied, "I don't know what to say. I'm no hero."

The captain said, "Son, yes, you are. Pack your bags; you've got a flight to catch."

Within the hour, Bill was presented with a new dress uniform, along with being newly promoted to Master Sergeant. Bill was still stunned by the day's events. He put on his new decorations and then headed to the airport for transport.

Everywhere he walked, everyone saluted him. A general stopped him to thank him, then saluted Bill. Bill was amazed at what that itty-bitty ribbon did to people.

Bill got a ride to the airstrip, where he boarded a Lockheed C-5 Galaxy, heading for London, then a connecting flight to Aberdeen, Scotland. Bill was told he would be picked up by the Queen's Secret Service in Aberdeen and then helicoptered to Balmoral Castle.

The trip with connections took a few hours. When Bill got to Aberdeen, it was cold, at least 25 degrees colder than Ramstein, far colder than Kuwait. As he got off the plane, a man and a woman were waiting for him on the tarmac. It was the British officer! As Bill got closer, he saw a large sapphire engagement ring on the woman's left hand.

When Bill got to the former British officer, Bill bowed his head, "Sir, good to see you."

The former officer reached out to him, hugging him.

He then introduced himself, "Please call me George; this is my wife, Margaret."

Margaret reached out to hug him, then kissed Bill on the cheek, "Thanks for sending him home to us."

Bill was taken aback by their hospitality. Finally, he said, "You don't look royal."

This, of course, prompted great laughter from them all.

Margaret said, "Our ride is waiting, boys."

As they walked to the helicopter, Bill noticed this was no ordinary bird. It had the royal insignia on it, maroon in color. As they approached the stairs, the helicopter rotors started. They quickly got seated.

George asked, "You'll get a nice view of the castle from that side. Granny loves that view."

Bill said, "This is where the Queen sits?"

Both thought this was hilarious.

Margaret asked, "Never been around royalty?"

Bill shook his head, "No. The only thing royal in my house growing up was the commode."

Again, this prompted more laughter.

Bill asked, "It's funny, nobody told me about protocols other than bowing my head when I meet your granny."

George said, "You'll need to do that with Granny, Pappa, and the Duke."

Bill said, "Okay, what happens if I hug your granny? Do I get slapped?"

George was pissing himself laughing, "I dare you to hug Granny."

Bill looked at Margaret, who provided a very reassuring look and nodded politely. Bill wasn't sure if she was playing along or if she was genuine. When they arrived about 20 minutes later, George was correct about the views of Balmoral Castle. Bill couldn't believe any of this was happening, let alone that the grandson of an IRA member would meet the Queen, as well as the next two future kings.

When they arrived, George escorted him to the room he would be staying in for the evening. George informed him that his stay was extended, as dinner would be late that evening. The Queen was detained on royal business.

George said, "You're welcome to join us for tea until Granny gets here. Why don't you get changed out of your uniform? You won't need it here."

Bill replied, "Thanks, let me get changed, and I'll be right down."

Bill went to his room, putting on casual clothes he had in his overnight bag. After changing, Bill went downstairs, back to the main entrance of the castle. As Bill reached the bottom of the stairs, a limousine pulled up to the front door. Bill stood silent as George and Margaret emerged from the library, where tea was served.

Within seconds, the Queen entered the castle. Much to Bill's surprise, she seemed shorter than he imagined, very polite to the staff as she came in, with the Duke of Edinburgh following closely behind.

Bill heard George say, "Granny, welcome home."

The Queen smiled, then noticed Bill standing by the stairs, dressed in jeans and a button-down dress shirt.

She asked, "Who's this?"

George whispered in her ear, unheard by anyone else. When he stepped back, she winked and smiled at her grandson.

She said, "So you're the soldier who helped get my grandson home to us."

Bill bowed his head, then answered, "Yes, Your Majesty."

She then asked, "So, when do I get this hug you so desperately wanted to give me?"

Bill smiled but was a little embarrassed. The others behind the Queen were hysterically laughing. The Queen noticed Bill's embarrassment at being set up. She walked over to him.

The Queen opened her arms, "Don't worry, sonny, I won't bite. Call me Granny. You've earned it."

This generated a fair amount of laughter from the group. Bill thought, *Hey, I get to spend the evening with the Queen of England, along with her family.*

Dinner was a humble affair, not full of pomp and circumstance, a simple family dinner, intimate, with lots of laughter, especially with the Queen's grandchildren. Bill was surprised at how loose and unguarded the group was in front of a stranger. The Queen doted on her grandchildren, showing them the way to eat their meals. Suffice it to say while this was fun, it wasn't what Bill envisioned.

The one formal thing that occurred at dinner was when the Queen said, "That's dinner."

Everyone immediately stood up and bowed in deference to the Queen. Then, all went back to the library at Balmoral Castle. The library, which they called a drawing room, was humbling. There seemed to be an endless sea of shelves and books on those shelves. It had a large fireplace, which a servant stoked as the crowd came in. There were several couches in the room, whereby the Queen and her husband sat on one, playing with their grandchildren. George and Margaret sat on the couch opposite the Queen, trying to balance between managing their grandchildren and letting Great Granny spoil them.

Bill sat on the same couch with George and Margaret. Margaret was a very pretty woman, standing 5'5", very thin, with shoulder-length brown hair and hazel eyes. By all accounts, she was a doting mother, but she had strength in her mannerisms. She wasn't afraid to speak her mind and offer her opinion on a particular topic, which Bill noted at dinner.

As Bill sat taking all this in—the Irish kid just hanging with the Queen—Margaret turned to Bill, asking, "Is everything okay?"

Bill replied, "Yes, ma'am."

Margaret responded, "Please, Margaret, always."

Bill nodded, then smiled, "Margaret, I'm fine."

Margaret asked, "How bad was George when you found him?"

Apparently, the whole room stopped as Margaret's question hung in the air.

Bill replied, "It's a little hard to recall every detail. Clearly, from my vantage point, it was clear he was wounded, even smacked around a little by his captors. What I recall was George cared more about his men than himself at that moment. When I told him to run to the rally point, he stayed to help carry one of his men to safety. All under gunfire."

George chimed in, "We don't need to talk about that anymore."

With that, the Queen suddenly announced, "I'm heading up. Good night, everyone. Bill, we'll see you for breakfast before you head back to the US. I've been told you're heading to the White House from here?"

Bill, a little embarrassed, said, "Yes, ma'am, I am heading to Washington, DC, from here. Thank you very much for your hospitality. I'm glad I got to meet George and his family."

The Queen smiled at Bill before leaving the drawing room.

George got up, saying, "I'll put the kids down for the night. Be back in 30 minutes."

Now Bill was alone with Margaret and a servant.

Margaret asked, "Bill, whiskey?"

Bill replied, "Sure, I'll join you if you're having one."

Margaret asked the servant, "Peter, three whiskeys, please. One for George when he returns."

The servant nodded, retrieving the three glasses of whiskey.

Margaret said, "I'm sorry if my question was awkward, but George won't talk about what happened. Any time I broach the subject, he gets very angry. I can tell tonight was the first time he relaxed since coming home."

Bill replied, "It's difficult to describe what we've seen in combat. He probably doesn't want to burden you with it. In the military, they teach techniques, discipline, and duty. I'm sure, being the future heir to the throne, he feels that more than anyone. What they don't teach is how to live with the scars inflicted or created by war."

Margaret responded, "But all I want to do is help him through it."

Bill said, "I can tell you are. He seems very much in love with you, not just the 'player in the firm' we so often hear about in the media. All soldiers compartmentalize what happened on the battlefield, rationalizing unspeakable horrors for the love of the country. But it's not really like that. In the field, you have your mission, but when you're in the thick of it, the only things that matter are protecting your team and leading them through the battle. They can drill you to death, but you're never sure what will happen once the shooting starts."

Margaret asked, "How did you find them?"

Bill said, "Honestly, by chance. I had been at a briefing with some British officers maybe two days before finding George. These officers were frantic, but nobody understood why. All they said was, 'Johnson is missing.' Two days later, my squad was ordered to clear this village north of the airport. When my squad came into the village, I saw George and two other soldiers caged up. My best friend, Tommy, and I saw the three of them in cages, knowing we had to do something."

Margaret asked, "Then what happened?"

Bill replied, "My squad covered me as I ran to the cages. I shot out the locks while my team kept the enemy occupied. George was in the first cage. He was wounded, but he was moving fine. We opened the other two cages. I carried one man to the rally point while George carried the other. All of this was happening through a hail of gunfire."

Margaret asked, "Then what happened?"

Bill thought for a moment. *Should I tell her the truth about the hand-to-hand combat that Tommy and I endured, bringing them to safety? How's this going to help George?*

Bill hedged, saying, "We got to the rally point, then waited for an extraction. Once we got on the bird, we were pretty much home-free. We tended to the wounded before we got back to base."

Margaret replied, "You're not telling me the whole story. I can tell you're holding back. Do you think I can't handle the details?"

Bill said, "Sure, there are details I'm omitting, but if George wants to talk about that with you, that's up to him. I'll say, about my own experience, I'm not comfortable talking about it now. You need to understand war is sheer bloody murder in its purest form. When your survival instincts kick in, you'll do anything to defend yourself or your men. I'm not trying to be evasive; I can see you're genuinely trying to understand and help."

Before Margaret replied, George came back to the study, asking, "What's going on?"

Bill quickly said, "Just chatting about this and that."

George said, "You're not a good liar, Bill. Margaret, if he doesn't want to talk about it, then I suggest we honor his wishes."

Bill replied, "I'm sorry, I'm just not prepared to say some of those things out loud yet."

Margaret said, "You told me enough for now. I hope someday you both tell me the whole story. With that, I'll say goodnight. Honey, I had them pour you a whiskey. Remember, we've got that early morning meeting."

George replied, "Thanks, love. Be up in 30 minutes."

Bill stood up, bowing his head to Margaret, who reached over to hug him.

She whispered in Bill's ear, "Thank you for bringing him home to me. That's all I ever cared about."

As Margaret pulled back, Bill smiled and nodded, saying, "Anything for a friend."

With that, Margaret made her way upstairs, leaving George alone with Bill to finish their nightcaps. Bill had finished his first whiskey, as did George. George asked the servant to pour two more.

George asked, "So, what was that all about?"

Bill replied, "She's concerned and wants to help if she can. Understandable; your wife wants to help you through this."

George replied, "I appreciate that, but all she wants to do is talk, talk, talk. I mean, what does she want to hear? How badly was I treated, and how did your team rescue my team? The hand-to-hand combat? It's hard enough to relive it in my mind, let alone tell the woman I love about it."

Bill said, "George, I get it. Those are tough images to process; I'm still dealing with it. Let me ask: are you having night terrors? Like reliving it in your sleep?"

George looked surprised, "How did you know that?"

Bill replied, "I've been having them myself. Assuming she's in bed with you when they're happening?"

George said, "Sometimes she is. Either way, I don't want to burden her with this."

Bill replied, "I get it, but would it help to get it out?"

George replied, "I'm tired of having to answer questions about it. No one in my family understands this. They think I'm a hero or something. I'm not; you're the hero."

Bill calmly said, "I'm not a hero; I did my duty. Now I've got to live with that, and so do you. I wanted to ask you for a favor if I might?"

George replied, "Sure."

Bill said, "When I was in-country, after our day, we had a girl named Fatima assigned to our group. About a week after our rescue effort, my squad was involved in a firefight, where we got separated. When I returned to where she was, she was gone, vanished."

George asked, "Was she a scout for you, or more? Based on your expression, it seems personal."

Bill replied, "It's personal. We were in love. Not sure how her family would react, but we spent a wonderful evening together, the day before she disappeared. To be honest, all I want to know is if she's alive and safe."

George inquired, "Do you have any information other than her name?"

Bill said, "I do. I wrote down everything I could remember: names, dates, places. Look, I don't want to interrupt her life. I just want to know she's okay."

George gulped his last bit of whiskey, then said, "I'll investigate. I'm going to head up; she's right. We've got an early morning. See you at breakfast."

Bill said, "I'll head up too."

The next morning came quickly: breakfast with the family, then a short helicopter ride to Aberdeen, then London Heathrow, then DC.

George and Margaret drove Bill to the helicopter.

Bill said, "Let's keep in touch. No matter what, you can always talk to me about this."

Margaret welled up while George said, "Thanks, you're a true friend. Safe travels. Enjoy the ceremony in DC. Wish I could be there."

Margaret said, "What ceremony?"

George replied, "Bill's been awarded the Medal of Honor."

Margaret asked, "As it relates to what happened to you both?"

George nodded, welling up himself. He said, "Can't thank you enough, Bill."

Bill smiled, "That's what friends do, sir!"

George smiled, "George, always."

Bill said, "Thanks for a wonderful evening. See you both in the funny papers."

All three laughed as Bill headed for the chopper. Within the next 24 hours, he landed in DC and was driven to the White House. Bill changed into his military dress uniform on the flight over. He took his seat quietly after changing.

When they landed in DC, Bill felt like he had his hand pinned to his forehead, saluting the entire world, it seemed. As he walked through the airport, people stopped, smiled, saluted. All they saw was the ribbon.

Bill hoped it would be easier wearing the medal than what it took to get it.

Bill and George would remain close friends, chatting usually every couple of weeks, checking in on each other, and catching up about their families. He'd help with one of the worst things that would ever happen to Bill, as well.

Chapter 31
May 1991 – Brooklyn, NY

Owen had woken up early this morning, needing to prepare for his meeting with Uncle Jack. He had several distribution ideas, along with ideas for getting weapons to Ireland. Owen sat in the kitchen, sipping tea as daylight emerged through the window.

About 30 minutes later, Maura came out of her bedroom, making her way to the kitchen before having to head to nursing school.

Owen noticed Maura, saying, "Morning, love. Sleep well?"

Maura replied, "Stop calling me that."

Owen coldly responded, "Why?"

Maura said, "You know why. We're not an item; all this IRA stuff is a nonstarter. I'm not interested in marrying my dad, a controlling unit."

Looking surprised, Owen replied, "We'll be rich someday, able to afford anything. Why can't you see that? You had no problem with it until last month's arrest!"

Maura shouted, "Dealing drugs and guns, that's your life's plan? Preying on the misery of others? I need to get ready for school."

Owen chuckled, "Hypocrite, how did you pay for school?"

Maura didn't answer, exiting the kitchen and heading back to her room. As she closed the bedroom door, she examined the exhausting task of dealing with Owen's last statement, as well as her living arrangements. The tension since her arrest had been palpable, seemingly having the same conversation every day over the past 30 days. She wrestled with her decision, as it was lucrative but also highly risky. Maura agreed to push drugs on college campuses in the area for a cut when she first arrived in America. It paid far more than the waitressing job at The Three Aces Pub. Maura rationalized she was only doing this for a while, providing a service to those who wanted to take drugs. Besides, she wasn't the first to push drugs for a piece of the action, especially to fund her college tuition.

Maura wanted to be a nurse. The drug-pushing was a means to an end in her mind. However, a long-term career in pushing drugs was not what she wanted out of life.

After sitting for a moment, composing herself, Maura got dressed, put up her beautiful auburn hair in a ponytail, and exited the bedroom. Maura made her way to the front door, leaving without saying goodbye to Owen. Maura then made her way to the street, but not before running into Uncle Jack and a man she didn't know. The two men were sitting at a table outside the pub, sipping coffee. Maura thought they looked alike, perhaps brothers.

It was Uncle Jack's brother, Mick, having stopped by for an early morning coffee to catch up. Their relationship had been strained since Uncle Jack married. Mick's wife, Bridie, didn't care for Jack's wife, Kick. Everyone knew about it. Bridie was quick to point out Kick's misgivings, leaving Mick with the added stress.

Anytime Jack and Mick were together, they would fondly remember the family farm and how Mick sponsored his mother, then Jack, to come to America. Both were hardened patriots, just with different causes.

When their father was killed, Jack became the man of the family at a very young age. In his early teens, he went to work to help his mother provide. Mick would tell Bill stories about his mother, especially how disappointed she was to know Jack was involved with the IRA. She was very angry at Paddy for getting him wrapped up in it. When Jack went to prison, his mother was devastated, as she had nothing left but the land, with no sons to work it.

Jack did his time in Limerick Jail, even enduring a 15-day hunger strike to protest English rule, as well as the treatment of IRA prisoners. While on strike, Jack would tell stories of having to lick the limestone cell walls to get some salt intake. Mick had it just as bad, not being able to help Jack, as well as leapfrogging from one shit island in the Pacific to another, facing death daily.

These experiences shaped their generation. Uncle Jack left Ireland in 1945, around the same time Mick was discharged from the service. The apartment Maura lived in was the apartment Jack, Mick, and their mother lived in when they got to the States.

When he opened the pub, it was a popular hangout for the local IRA. Jack got involved in raising funds, getting more involved as each year went by. Perhaps the best way to describe Jack was that he was like a Don in the Italian Mafia, always in the shadows, doing business but also giving back to his community. He recognized the opportunity that was America, so he tried to pay it forward while being unapologetic for his chosen profession.

Jack would always say, "I don't apologize for my life. Only God can judge if I'm worthy of heaven. I'll know that when it's my time."

Mick was the opposite, wanting no part of the IRA or its American factions. Jack tried several times to get Mick involved, promising a big payout. Mick didn't care about big payouts. He did his service and already wanted a better life for his family—a safer, more protected one. Mick worked six days a week, 50 weeks a year, leaving each morning at 05:00, usually not returning home until 18:00 each evening. Sunday was his only day off, reserved for church, then Sunday dinner with the family. However, his war experiences didn't make him appreciate the promise of America. They hardened him, keeping him bitter about life, scarred by battle, taking out his frustrations on his family, mostly Bill's mother. Mick continued to have night terrors throughout his life; they didn't fade at all. His son, Bill, recalled a night when he needed to separate his parents, as Mick had Bridie pinned to the wall, leaning into her with his arms over her head, screaming at the top of his lungs. Bridie endured this her entire life. Jack tried to intervene, but Mick wouldn't engage other than to say, "Mind your own business."

This morning, the topic was Bill, specifically how he was doing, hoping his service date was rapidly approaching. While the men were talking, Uncle Jack saw Maura emerge from the apartment building.

Maura said, "Good morning, how are you?"

Uncle Jack replied, "Morning, Maura, off to school?"

Maura responded, "Yes. Class in 90 minutes."

Uncle Jack smiled, "Owen told me yesterday you're no longer working with him."

Maura nervously replied, "Yes. Need to focus on my nursing studies."

Uncle Jack smiled, "Good for you. Best you stay clear of it. Lots of unsavory sorts."

Maura took a deep breath, "Owen's choice. I'm out."

Uncle Jack smiled again, "Aye, grand. Finish your nursing. Let me know if you need anything. Also, this is Mick, my brother."

Maura said, "It's nice to meet you."

Mick replied, "Same here."

Maura smiled, "Thanks for understanding, Uncle Jack. I'm sorry, but I need to run; I don't want to be late for class."

Uncle Jack nodded as Maura made her way to the subway, heading to school. Mick also decided to leave, as he needed to run to his next errand. Both brothers shook hands as Mick headed to his car. As Uncle Jack made his way into The Three Aces Pub, he went to his office in the back of the establishment. As he reached the office, his phone rang.

Uncle Jack answered the call, "Speak."

Jack's brother, Mick, was on the phone, "Jack, Mick. Just got word Bill's coming home. His deployment's up. But he's got a stopover at Balmoral Castle."

Uncle Jack replied, "Mick, great news! When? Wait, what?"

Mick replied, "He called this morning from Ramstein Air Base and spoke to Bridie. He's wounded, nothing but a scratch. He should be home within the next two weeks."

Uncle Jack asked, "It wasn't anything serious, was it?"

Mick replied, "No, not according to him."

Uncle Jack responded, "Okay. Balmoral Castle?"

Mick said, "He told Bridie it was a long story; he'll tell us when he's home."

Jack replied, "Need to run. Great news, thanks for the call."

With that, Jack hung up the phone, heading for his chair, thinking about his meeting with Owen. As much as Uncle Jack disliked Owen, he was good at this stuff, especially in Ireland. After reaching his chair, he grabbed his coffee, which the kitchen staff made each morning. Five minutes into his second coffee, Owen showed up for the meeting.

Owen knocked on the door, asking, "Ready for our chat?"

Uncle Jack said nothing but nodded yes, so Owen moved into his office.

Owen asked, "May I sit?"

Uncle Jack pointed, nodding toward the chair in front of the desk.

Owen sat down, "We have a couple of options to talk about."

Uncle Jack replied, "Go on."

Owen said, "Our first option is to bring the cache from Belfast, sailing them directly to Mexico through the Gulf. The exchange can be made offshore, with the drugs being sent to the US. We have multiple points of entry. If we had a second container, we could split the loads."

Uncle Jack, looking unimpressed, replied, "Option 2?"

Owen said, "This one's a little trickier. Sail the weapons into the Port of Houston from Belfast, offload the cargo to 18-wheelers, hauling them across the border into Mexico, returning with the cocaine in those same trucks. Lower cost option, but also riskier."

Uncle Jack thought for a minute, saying, "There's always a risk, lad. Option 2 is easier to execute and requires fewer men. Also, the DEA has been cracking down on offshore operations. Not sure anyone would suspect Option 2."

Owen replied, "Grand. I'll set it up."

Uncle Jack responded, "Yes, set it up. Use the primary contacts in Belfast and Mexico. Also, I have one last piece of business."

Looking curious, Owen asked, "Sure. What other business do we have?"

Uncle Jack replied, "Maura. I ran into her this morning as she was leaving. I know she's pushed for you on college campuses, funding nursing school. From now on, she's out, period."

Owen responded, "Of course, if that's what you want. It's been 30 days since the arrest."

Uncle Jack replied, "I understand that."

With that, Uncle Jack stood up, heading for the coffee pot. While Owen took this as his cue, the meeting was over. Owen got what he came for; Option 2 was the plan.

As Owen opened the door, Uncle Jack said, "Remember what I said about Maura. You don't want to be on the wrong side of this with me."

Owen nodded yes, exiting the office.

Uncle Jack picked up his phone, searching for his wife's number.

Kick answered, "Hello, love. Something wrong?"

Uncle Jack replied, "Nothing's wrong. Mick stopped by this morning, then called after he left. Bill's coming home. Was thinking we'd have a 'Welcome Home' party at the pub."

Kick responded, "Grand idea, you want me to call Bridget?"

Uncle Jack said, "No need, I'll have it taken care of here. Okay, got to run."

With that, Uncle Jack hung up the phone.

For some reason, the situation with Maura continued to bother Uncle Jack. He knew Owen and Maura had come over together after the deed in Belfast. Maura wasn't a babe in the woods; she knew what her father did. Clearly, she knew at least one thing Owen was up to. Owen had spoken to Uncle Jack numerous times about his affection for Maura, but Maura wasn't interested in Owen in that way. He was possessive, always trying to control every aspect of her life.

Owen would get on her if she wore something he felt was provocative. He would always need to know where she was going, who she'd be with, and what time she'd return home. When Maura went to a friend's house, Owen would call, needing to talk to her, only to inquire about when she'd be home. The attention was constant, relentless.

One morning, Uncle Jack noticed a slight bruise on Maura's face. When he asked, Maura told him she took a cabinet door to the cheek and said she didn't realize the cabinet door was open. As she told the story, Uncle Jack could tell it was bullshit, even going as far as to say he'd talk to Owen about this, but Maura said it might make things worse.

Uncle Jack recalled an evening several months prior, where Owen put a beating on a young man outside The Three Aces Pub. This young man was flirting with Maura, sending her a drink from the bar while Owen was sitting with her. All the while, Owen was paying more attention to the football game than Maura. However, Owen took offense, exchanging words with him. A fight ensued, spilling out onto the street. While the young man was clearly six inches taller than

Owen, Owen started out well in the fight. However, the young man was able to overpower him a little just before the police arrived.

Maura was an Irish immigrant, still attempting to find her place. She was practical about her situation, but her arrest two months ago was a turning point. Owen told Uncle Jack about the arrest just off the school grounds at New York University. Plainclothes police officers had been tipped off that she was pushing in that location. Maura was approached by the officers, soliciting cocaine. When Maura provided the female officer with the cocaine, the male officer arrested her.

In the grand scheme of things, it was a small amount of cocaine, her first offense. However, when Owen bailed her out, Maura made a scene at the 10th Precinct, visibly upset after being released, cursing at Owen as they left the station.

Uncle Jack received a call from his man at the 10th Precinct the next morning. When Uncle Jack ran into Owen, he inquired about the arrest, as well as what happened after Maura was bailed out. The contact told him Maura kept her mouth shut after the arrest but didn't provide any useful information. However, she flipped her lid when Owen bailed her out. When Owen told Uncle Jack the story, he said she was a little unhinged by the whole thing. Uncle Jack thought Owen was trying to protect himself rather than accept Maura wasn't interested in him or pushing for him anymore.

Later that afternoon, Uncle Jack was heading out for a meeting. He was meeting with Angel Martinez to talk about the last shipment from Kuwait. The profiteering from this war would conclude soon. The meeting was to discuss future strategies.

As Uncle Jack emerged from the pub, Maura was walking down the sidewalk with a pleasant smile on her face.

Uncle Jack asked, "Nice day. You look like you're in a good mood?"

Maura replied, "I just finished class. I'm graduating from my nursing program! I'm going to be an RN."

Uncle Jack smiled, "That's great. I've got to ask: how's your arrest thing going? Any word on that?"

Maura said, "The policeman said the charges would be dropped. Apparently, his sergeant felt there wasn't enough to pursue it further."

Uncle Jack replied, "That's a relief. When is graduation?"

Maura replied, "Next Thursday."

Uncle Jack said, "That's grand. I'm sorry, but I need to run to a meeting."

With that, Uncle Jack got into his car, where his driver was waiting. Maura waved as Uncle Jack drove off.

As Maura made her way upstairs to the apartment, she began to think, *Why did Uncle Jack ask about the arrest? How did he know?* She then turned her attention to her nursing license. She had overheard another student talking about her prior difficulties with the law. *Perhaps a name change was in order.* This student felt maybe it would help her with background checks. Maura started to think, *Would I want a new name? What would I want?* She wanted to honor her father's last name, but perhaps Jennifer or Jenn when working. *Jennifer Maura McTiernay,* she thought, had a nice ring to it. She took out the nursing application and filled it out with her new first name. Maura thought this would help her, too, if the arrest record ever came up.

Later that evening, Jenn—as she now was—was waitressing at the pub. Owen returned home to find the apartment empty, becoming very angry about coming home to an empty apartment. Owen headed to the pub.

When Owen arrived, he noticed Maura talking to one of the young line cooks, calling her Jenn. He became quite jealous as he headed to where she was standing. As Owen got closer, he heard Maura laughing at the line cook's joke.

Owen yelled, "Why are you not home making dinner for us?"

Jenn calmly said, "I'm working; make your own dinner. I'm not your maid."

Owen chirped back, "If you live with me, you'll do as I say."

Jenn, shocked, said, "Why don't you fuck off? I'll find my own place."

With the conversation getting louder, the line cook was smart enough to put his head down going back to work. Around this time, Uncle Jack emerged from his office, hearing the commotion by the kitchen door, getting angry that Owen was slowing down the delivery of food to customers.

Uncle Jack came up from behind Owen, placing his hand on his left shoulder and prompting Owen to turn around. Initially, his fist was drawn, but he quickly put it down when he saw it was Uncle Jack.

Uncle Jack said, "I don't know what's going on, but I don't want it in my pub. Either go outside to solve your problems or knock it off. Got it? Maura, one question: why does your name tag say 'Jenn'?"

Maura said, "From now on, I'm going by Jenn."

Owen said, "That's stupid."

Jenn said, "I don't care what you think."

Uncle Jack, sensing the next round, said, "Maura, Jenn, whatever your name is, take a break, take it outside, work it out. I won't tolerate this in my pub, period."

Owen grabbed Jenn by the arm, escorting her out the front door. When they got onto the street, Owen started to yell at Jenn about not being his domestic servant, essentially.

Jenn countered, saying, "I'm done being your slave. I appreciate you helped bring me here, but I'm not your possession."

Owen replied, "I've loved you all my life."

Jenn yelled, "We can't be together like this! You think you're my father, not my equal. I'm done being treated this way."

Owen became irate, reaching for her left arm, winding up his right arm, and getting ready to hit her. As fate would have it, a man was watching this unfold as he came up the street toward the pub. The man was Bill Quinn, freshly home from his service in the Gulf War.

As Owen swung his fist, Bill grabbed it from behind, twisting it, turning Owen's arm, almost rotating it from the elbow off Owen's body. Owen was quickly subdued.

Bill looked at Jenn while holding his grasp on Owen's arm, "Ma'am, are you okay?"

Owen screamed, "You're breaking my arm!"

Bill paid him no attention as Jenn stood in shock at what had happened. A stranger was willing to intercede on her behalf. She was amazed anyone would get involved, and she was thankful he did.

Bill repeated his question, "Ma'am, are you okay?"

Jenn said, "I'm fine. Please don't hurt him; he can't afford to be out of work."

Bill said, "Ma'am, that depends on him. Are you done, little man?"

Owen said, "Fuck you!"

Bill replied, "You're making it very difficult for me to do the right thing here. If I let you go, you'll stay away from this lady?"

Jenn said, "I'll make sure of that. Thank you for stepping in."

Owen yelled, "When I get loose, I'm going to kill you."

Bill smiled, "I'll give you this: you've got stones."

Bill started to pull down a little more while Owen screamed in pain. At this point, Uncle Jack emerged out the front door.

Uncle Jack said, "Enough! What's going on? Bill, what are you doing here?"

Bill continued to hold Owen and answered, "Uncle Jack, nice to see you. Got home this morning, so I wanted to pay you a visit. Dad told me how you're always asking for me. Also, I met one of your friends over there. When I got to the door, this idiot was about to punch this lady in the mouth."

Uncle Jack asked, "Maura, is that true?"

She replied, "Yes, but he never hit me. Your nephew stopped it, putting him in the spot he's in."

Uncle Jack said to Bill, "He's an associate."

Bill curtly replied, "Doesn't give him a right to hit a woman, does it?"

Uncle Jack looked at Owen, then Bill, finally saying, "You're right, but enough is enough. Let him go."

Bill reluctantly agreed while Owen was grateful Bill hadn't snapped his arm off at the elbow. As Bill stepped between Owen and Jenn, Uncle Jack walked up to Owen.

Uncle Jack said, "Lift your chin up."

Uncle Jack paused, then said, "Higher, you goddamn idiot."

Owen obliged. Then Uncle Jack hit his jaw with his right fist, instantly drawing blood from Owen's mouth and leaving him knocked out on the sidewalk. In a strange twist of fate, two beat cops happened upon the scene.

The lead cop asked, "What's going on? Oh, hey Jack, everything okay?"

Jack said, "Fine. A little trouble with this one inside. Sorry, it spilled out into the street."

The lead cop said, "Want us to run him in?"

Uncle Jack said, "That's up to you. Seems like a waste of paperwork to put him in the drunk tank."

The lead cop smiled. "Can you get him off the street at least?"

Uncle Jack said, "Yes, he lives right there. We'll hose him down, then get him out of here."

The lead cop replied, "Then you all have a nice evening."

Uncle Jack came up to Bill with a tear in his eye, seeing his nephew—essentially the prodigal son—had returned. Bill hugged his uncle while his uncle held him close for almost two minutes, appreciative of his sacrifice for his country, grateful he was home.

Jenn fled the scene as the cops approached, heading up to the apartment and locking the door behind her.

Uncle Jack and Bill went inside the bar, straight to his office, for the good Irish whiskey. He wanted to know about his deployment, as well as this friend Bill spoke of. When they went by the kitchen, Uncle Jack instructed one of the dishwashers to fill a bucket with cold water and then go outside to remove any trace of Owen or the blood.

Sitting down in the office, Uncle Jack poured two stiff Irish whiskeys, placing Bill's glass on the coaster on the table between them. Uncle Jack didn't sit behind his desk talking to Bill; this was a more intimate chat between the men. Uncle Jack sat to Bill's right, where they sipped whiskey, appreciating that Bill was home.

Uncle Jack asked, "Who's this friend of mine you met over there?"

Bill replied, "Colonel Hernandez. Each time we did a weapons cache recovery, he was involved, letting me know what great pals you were. Both of you counted on me for each mission. I must admit, it freaked me out, not just me, but my squad too."

Uncle Jack responded, "He's an idiot, Martinez's messenger boy. Plays it like he's important. The only reason he is is he's wearing the bird."

Bill replied, "He played it up like you two were weekend buddies. I didn't understand the attraction."

Uncle Jack said, "We're not buddies. We've had business together, that's all I'll say. Look, you just got home. Let's get something to eat and have a few pints. Why didn't you bring Mick with you?"

Bill replied, "You know, Dad, he's got to work in the morning. Although, I could eat."

Both got up from their chairs, heading into the restaurant for a bite to eat.

Chapter 32
September 1992 –
Westchester County, NY

After Bill's tour, his focus shifted to what was next in life. He worked with his father to understand more about the GI services he was eligible for, as well as any additional funds for college. This young Marine was going to study big business, making a fortune after college.

As Bill explored college options, he focused on schools with strong finance and business programs, while his dad focused on having Bill come out of school debt-free. They didn't see eye to eye on schools, entirely due to cost considerations, but his father's advice on this subject didn't fall on deaf ears either.

Mick came from a family quite poor in Ireland, a family farm not functioning well, even on its best day. Mick worked hard and saved his money, all so his children could have a better life. Of his three children, Bill would be the only one to attend college. Even Bill's Uncle Jack approached Mick about helping with the tuition. While Mick appreciated the gesture, his pride wouldn't allow him to accept it.

Ultimately, Pace University was selected for its strong accounting and finance department and its good connections for internships within the financial community. Proximity was important too—the school was two hours from home, just an hour's train ride to the city, making it ideal. It was far enough from home to provide independence, yet close enough to get back or reach the city when necessary. For Mick, it was also the most affordable option.

Initially, Bill took school very seriously, like a Marine on a mission. Academically, it paid off. Bill hadn't been the best student in high school; in fact, he hated it. The only reason he performed well enough in class was his love of sports: basketball, baseball, and football. In his parents' house, grades always came before sports.

Also, having been in the Marines, being in the thick of it, his perspective changed about many things, maturing him and making him appreciate the opportunities in front of him—very unlike his father's experiences. When in-country, one did their duty to protect their men, never leaving anyone behind. Once in the thick of it, bullets flying, the missions aren't meaningful, as survival instincts kick in, back to the lessons from basic training: Duty, honor, code, and leave no one behind. Bill was determined not to let his war experience embitter him like it did his father.

Similarly, Bill saw the best and the worst of humanity. Innocent civilians have their lives taken from them, losing their only possessions. In the first month, it was difficult to shake it off day to day, having hot chow nine out of ten days, clean beds to return to each night, and daily showers. Many casualties were innocent people, relegated to begging on the street or forced to choose a side to provide the bare necessities for their families. Unfortunately, seeing this each day, a soldier becomes anesthetized to the suffering, learning to shift their focus to the men, as they're the only ones that matter.

Also, he thought of Fatima, too, wondering what happened. Bill made several inquiries before being shipped out, but he couldn't get a straight answer as to what happened. Bill had a buddy from basic assigned to her sector when Bill left for Germany. He inquired, but it generated no leads. Bill was sad, thinking, "She's probably dead," wondering what would have happened if she had stayed on his left hip.

Now, Bill was home. This would be the first time in Bill's life the focus was solely on him. Bill maintained an orderly, proficient military manner regarding his life. Every Marine must have a game plan—it was drilled into him in basic training.

For the first year at college, he stayed clear of girls, partly to avoid distractions, partly feeling as though he was betraying Fatima by moving on.

That all changed when Bill met Jenn.

Jenn McTiernay was an RN student and a stunning young woman with auburn hair, hazel eyes, a few freckles on her face, an amazing smile, and an incredible body. She weighed about 120 pounds. When they met, she was a breath of fresh air—beautiful, fun, freer than this old Marine warhorse, an Irish immigrant who had immigrated to Brooklyn, NY, from Ireland.

Bill and Jenn passed each other, coming back from a lecture hall. Bill had forgotten this girl was the one from outside the pub the night he returned home from duty. As they moved toward each other on the sidewalk, their eyes locked, stopping each other in their tracks.

Bill said, "Bill. Nice to meet you."

Jenn said, "You don't remember me, do you?"

Bill replied, "I'm sorry, have we met?"

Jenn replied, "Uncle Jack's bar. You stopped Owen from striking me in the street."

Bill responded, "That was you? Sorry I didn't get a good look at you that night. It was dark in front of the pub."

Jenn replied, "By the way, I never got a chance to say thanks."

Bill came back, "What happened to that guy?"

Jenn responded, "He left not long after that evening. Where he went, I don't know. Honestly, I don't care either. He wasn't right for me."

Bill nodded at Jenn's response. Both hit it off spectacularly, talking for thirty minutes. Through the initial awkwardness, Bill got the sense it was like they had known each other for a lot longer. Bill never made it to his class. From that day, they were inseparable.

Jenn was captivating when she wanted to be but could be equally moody. They seemed to fall in love within the first month. Bill recalled that after three weeks, she told Bill she loved him. Within three months, they were talking about plans after graduation.

Bill had great plans to conquer Wall Street, while Jenn wanted to be an RN, working in the operating theater. She was dedicated to her studies, graduating third in her class. However, Bill wasn't the same student. He worked hard but was more street-smart than book-smart. After his first year in college, he felt college was keeping him from the Wall Street action. While he struggled with the degree being a means to an end, he felt he'd learn the business by doing.

At first, they provided great balance to one another. Jenn brought out his softer side, making him see perspectives that weren't just about making money, protecting his family, or providing. She brought out a sympathetic, compassionate side. At the time, Jenn was grateful for what she had, while Bill was always asking, "What's next?"

As for Jenn, Bill brought out an exterior toughness in her, as well as a silly side. Bill hated adults, hated being an adult. He was politically incorrect, with a weird, dry sense of humor. Bill could poke fun at anything or anybody, including himself, believing people are too full of themselves and unable to have a sense of humor about themselves. Bill didn't put down people for being reserved; rather, he was usually the one cutting through the BS quickly, telling it like it was.

Jenn was a peacemaker in any group. She wanted everyone to get along, no matter what. This was probably because of what happened to her parents and how they died.

Jenn once simply said, "They're gone. It's too hard to talk about."

Bill pushed Jenn on the guy from the bar, but she again informed Bill she had moved on, so there was no need to talk about it. Jenn was a great teammate, always able to be counted on to be a voice of reason. Bill helped her learn how to be a little tougher, to stand up for herself, and to be treated with respect all the time. They were a great pairing at the beginning.

On their one-year anniversary, they got engaged, marrying almost three years to the day after the engagement. In those early years, Bill couldn't have had a better companion in his life.

After six months of dating, Jenn informed Bill she was planning on hanging out with friends one evening. Bill didn't care, as he had to study. Having Jenn out with friends would give him the space to study in quiet.

Bill suggested, "Come back later to spend the night?"

Jenn smiled. "I'm staying at Christina's overnight."

Bill had been to this woman's apartment once before, which seemed like a safe area.

He told her, "Ring me if you change your mind."

After she left, Bill poured some coffee, loaded up some Skoal, and began studying. He was studying for a class called "The History of the American Presidency." This was one of the few electives Bill enjoyed.

The instructor was a short man, 5'5", 175 pounds, bald, always dressed like an old English professor. Despite his portly appearance, the professor was excellent, having a unique perspective on the presidency, ranging from FDR to George H.W. Bush. He had an advantage over others, as he was someone who was in the room, advising a president when many of their major decisions would be made and talking over any related consequences.

He told the class how Harry Truman agonized over the bombing of Japan, how he came to the decision, and what it meant to support the decision. The instructor lived in those moments; he talked about the personalities involved, the debates leading up to the ultimate decisions, and any subsequent actions. It was as if they were reliving history through his memory.

Bill had been studying for ninety minutes when his phone rang.

Bill picked up, saying, "Hello."

Bill heard an unfamiliar woman's voice on the phone.

She said, "Bill, it's Christina, Jenn's friend. Is she with you?"

Bill replied, "No, she told me she was heading over to hang with you to stay the night."

Christina said, "Yes, that's the plan. She rang me to let me know she was on her way, but she hadn't arrived yet. I was just getting a little worried, so I thought I'd call."

Bill replied, "Okay, let me get situated here, then I'll take a ride out to see if she just broke down somewhere. I'll have her ring you once I find her."

Christina said, "Thanks."

Bill put away his materials, locked up his laptop, and quickly changed clothes. He grabbed his keys, his Springfield XDA 45ACP, two extra magazines, and a windbreaker, then headed out the door.

As Bill got to his car, he noticed an unusual car parked 150 yards away. It was a black Oldsmobile Cutlass Supreme, a car that looked like an FBI vehicle. For the area, the car stuck out, not being a compact car specifically. In addition, from what Bill saw, two people were sitting inside the vehicle.

Bill pulled out, driving slowly down the street. It was a nice autumn night, so he rolled down the driver's side window, taking a better look as he passed the car. He placed his right hand on his weapon, slowly moving toward the vehicle. As he got closer, the occupants saw his car moving toward them, starting their car and turning on the lights. As Bill passed, he saw what appeared to be a young couple kissing, probably looking to fool around.

Bill headed toward Christina's place. As he drove around, he saw no evidence of Jenn's car or Jenn. Bill circled the area for twenty minutes, finding no trace of her. Bill stopped at Christina's, too, but she hadn't shown. Bill got more concerned by the minute. He decided to head downtown, checking out the local bars, restaurants, the diner, and the grocery store, asking for Jenn in each place. Still, Jenn was nowhere to be found.

While Bill was at the grocery store, he picked up a couple of odds and ends. He figured he was there, so why not? Perhaps Jenn changed her mind and showed up back at his place for the night. As Bill returned home, he noticed the black Cutlass Supreme was back. It was parked 200 yards down the street. However, after all the evening's excitement, Bill decided to head up to his apartment, put away the groceries, then take a late-evening walk. Bill didn't care for stalkers in the neighborhood.

Bill went into his apartment, turned on the light, and made his way to the kitchen. He put the groceries down on the counter, having a feeling he was being watched. His sixth sense—which his men never understood how instinctive it was on the battlefield—always let him know when his unit was being watched; he felt the eyes on them.

Bill opened the refrigerator and bent down to put the groceries in the lower part. The refrigerator door was hiding his hands, so he was able to draw his weapon. As Bill stood up, he shut the door and moved toward the living room. Bill saw a figure in his living room standing near the lamp by the couch.

With his weapon drawn, Bill ordered the man, "Turn on the light, show me your hands."

Bill could tell the man hadn't drawn on him as both of his hands were at his side. However, Bill didn't know if this intruder was alone or had a weapon. The man turned on the lamp. Bill moved back toward the kitchen, which gave him a line of sight into the hallway, ensuring he had an exit path where he could fight his way out if necessary. It also provided a line of sight to the bedroom, so if anyone was coming out, Bill would see them.

With his weapon drawn, Bill asked, "Who are you? What do you want?"

The man replied, "I'm sorry about busting in."

Bill blurted back, "That's not what I asked. Answer my questions, or I'll be cleaning your brains off my wall."

The man replied with a bit of an Irish brogue, "Okay, let's calm down."

Bill broke in, "Calm down? You're trespassing. Still don't know who you are or why you're here. So, let's start there. Who are you?"

He said, "I'm Owen DeValera, Jenn's stepbrother. I'm looking for…"

Bill interrupted, "Wait, you're that guy from the Three Aces that night! About a year or so ago, you were outside attempting to hit Jenn!"

Owen said, "Yes, but that's not why I'm here. I need to find her, talk to her."

Bill replied, "A knock on the door wouldn't work? Perhaps a note that you're looking for her? Break in instead. Brilliant!"

Owen said, "Jenn and I have been on the run from some bad people over the past twenty-four months, the kind of people that can really hurt you if they even think you've crossed them. About two years ago, we took possession of some merchandise from a distributor, the kind of merchandise that's, well, recreational, but law enforcement frowns upon."

Bill interrupted, "What's this got to do with Jenn?"

Owen said, "Well, let's just say this merchandise, she'd help me move it."

Bill shot back, "Jenn was selling drugs for you? Impossible."

Owen said, "Believe what you want, but she helped me move this merchandise when in downtown Manhattan. She never mentioned how she paid for Pace College?"

Bill replied, "No, I would have remembered that. When I asked about her family, she said she was an orphan—both her parents and brother were dead. A car crash, where she was the only survivor."

Owen replied, "Our parents are deceased, but it was a car bombing in Belfast in 1988. Jenn wasn't in the car but was next to the vehicle when it exploded. Our parents were deeply involved with *Sinn Féin*, a target in Belfast. Tragic situation."

Bill said, "The Belfast bombing at The Grand Opera? Hang on. She was involved in killing her own father, a drug peddler, and running drugs for the IRA. Seems a little far-fetched."

Owen said, "Yes, in its simplest form. About two years ago, after some major arrests of the top leaders, she tried to pull out of the business, went into hiding, changed her identity, and studied nursing. You know her as Jenn, but her real name is Maura McTiernay. She took the name Jennifer around the time she left. Before you ask more questions, she's in trouble."

Bill asked, "What kind of trouble?"

Owen replied, "This is why I came out of hiding. Some folks know she's been dating you. Now, from what I'm told, they've got no beef with you. However, Maura needs to answer for her departure. The issue is the new folks managing the merchandise are more cautious, wanting no loose ends."

Bill broke in, saying, "I can't believe this! Are you involved with the car down the street?"

Owen said, "Yes, associates of mine. I came to see if Maura was here. It's none of my business, but is she moving in here?"

Bill replied, "You're right. It's none of your business. Where is she?"

Owen jumped in, "She's nowhere to be found. Earlier today, she saw me from a distance over by her college, where we made eye contact. This evening, when she left your flat, she saw me watching from a distance. She must have figured it was time to get out of town. We've got some friends in Boston. I'll bet she's there."

Bill stated, "Then let's get her. What does she need to do to unwind this?"

Owen said, "I'm brokering a meeting, ensuring everyone's safety. I'm close, but this didn't help."

Bill replied, "Wait, she's alone, petrified, running, now this is a problem for you? Not sure I get that. Regardless, where is she? I'll take her to the police if need be."

Owen, shaking his head side to side, said, "Huge mistake. Will hurt you both. Be patient; she'll be back. I've already talked to our friends in Boston to deliver her a message. If all goes well, she'll be back tomorrow."

Bill replied, "That doesn't work. She's not doing this alone; I won't let that happen. Look, I was prepared to kill you. What makes you think I won't now?"

Owen coolly said, "Well, that's an option, but it involves you deeper. Also, when my friends down the street see something's happened to me, they'll be coming for you."

Bill retorted, "Bring it on. I only care about her. Why not go tonight? This way, we get her, ensure her safety, and bring her back to unwind this."

Owen thought for a minute. "Might work, but not until tomorrow morning. I'll be here at 7:30 tomorrow. We'll go to Boston together."

Bill said, "No. I don't want to wait."

Owen then turned, making his way to the door, saying nothing else.

What Owen didn't know—or Bill suspected he didn't know—was that Uncle Jack was Bill's uncle. Uncle Jack had contacts in the IRA dozens of contacts in the US and overseas. Bill thought it was time to take a ride to Brooklyn. The drive down was a mess due to the traffic, but overall, it could have been worse. Bill pulled up in front of The Three Aces Pub. Straight away, Bill saw Uncle Jack's presence by the door. When Bill walked in purposefully, his cousin Joseph greeted him.

Joseph shouted, "Billy boy, what the hell are you doing here? It's been a while."

Bill said, "Hey, Joey boy, yes, it's been a while. That party was unreal when I got back. Sorry I've been so distant, been focused on school. Look, I've got a situation. Where's Uncle Jack?"

With that, Uncle Jack came up from behind, turned Bill around, and gave him one of his great big bear hugs. Uncle Jack was the oldest of his father's brothers but clearly the black sheep due to his business dealings. It was strange; with all the negativity thrust upon Uncle Jack, he never refused a favor for a family member, doing it without expecting anything in return—usually. His soul was as good as gold, but his path wasn't pretty. Unlike Bill's father, who was a surly bastard who was getting worse in retirement,

Uncle Jack looked at Bill. "Seems serious."

Bill asked, "Can we talk privately?"

Uncle Jack nodded as they started toward his office for a whiskey and a chat. Uncle Jack kept the good whiskey in the office; it was always a treat to have such terrific Irish whiskey, having what you couldn't get in the US without a connection.

As he shut the door behind them, he asked, "Whiskey? Looks like you could use a belt. What's got you so wound up?"

Bill jumped into what happened earlier, stepping through the facts. Uncle Jack sat listening intently, sipping his whiskey. When Bill told him Owen came to visit him, as well as that Bill was dating Jenn, his eyes popped wide open.

Uncle Jack jumped out of the chair, animated. "What the fuck are you doing hanging around with that piece of shit?"

Bill said, "I'm not. He says I'm dating his sister. I had no idea about any of this until Owen's visit. I only recognized him after he spoke, you know, the night I got home."

Uncle Jack looked at him. "Okay, Billy boy, she's a sweet girl with a bit of a past. As it relates to this Owen thing, she's small potatoes. Owen had her selling nickel bags on college campuses to fund her schooling a few years back. I respected that."

Bill replied, "So, she was selling drugs for him?"

Uncle Jack continued, "Once she made enough, she was done; when she disappeared, none of my associates cared. Look, I'm not telling you what to do. It's your life. She was smart but never completely innocent. She goes by Jenn now, I think. Changed her name when she went into nursing school."

Bill replied, "I met her on my campus a few months ago. We've been spending a lot of time together since. She's not like that."

Uncle Jack said, "Billy boy, focus. She's not the problem, but this Owen character is bad news. I'm a pussycat compared to this prick. He screwed over a whole lot of people two years ago and took down some major operators. He was the one who took out those Colombians and made a play to be the top guy in the US. Guns, drugs, you name it."

Bill responded, "What can I do to help? I just want her to be safe."

Uncle Jack replied, "Don't get involved. After Belfast, I swore you'd be out."

Bill's jaw hit the floor. *What the hell is he into now?*

Uncle Jack looked at Bill. "Hey, you never knew about her. Her father was the target in Belfast."

Bill said, "I was part of the plot to kill my girlfriend's father?"

Uncle Jack said, "Forget that. Owen's been in here trying to sell her out to save his own ass two days ago, saying what happened twenty-four months ago was her doing. He tried to tell me she had gone to the police station. It's all bullshit, my source in the NYPD told me."

After draining the four fingers of whiskey, Bill said, "Jenn's father was the target in Belfast? I never knew that."

Uncle Jack answered, "Not going to lie, he was. You had no way of knowing until now."

Bill replied, "I understand, but I'm culpable for something in her eyes, no?"

Uncle Jack said, "Only if you tell her."

Bill transitioned to another topic, saying, "Owen's meeting me at 7:30. Driving to Boston to get her. As you can see, I'm already involved. I can't go to Boston without him!"

Uncle Jack smiled. "Boston, you say? I know where she is. Have it right here. Drive up tonight. Don't worry about Owen, I'll deal with him."

Bill replied, "Not sure I want to know more. Does Owen know we're related?"

Uncle Jack replied, "No. Nothing to worry about. He's a real liability if you know what I mean."

Bill replied, "If I see him, I won't hesitate to take him out."

Uncle Jack smiled, reached into his desk drawer, and pulled out a weapon. "Well, let's hope *I* get to him first, but if not, use this."

Uncle Jack pushed a Smith & Wesson .38 snub nose across his desk, continuing, "A piece you won't have to worry about. If you use it, ditch it after, okay?"

Bill said, "Done. Look, I'll do a better job coming to visit without all this drama."

Uncle Jack got up, gave Bill a bear hug, and said, "Love you, nephew. Be safe."

As Bill left the pub, he made a point to say goodbye to Joseph. Bill told him to say hello to his mother. As Bill was heading back to his car, he noticed the black Oldsmobile again. *How'd they find him?* Bill thought he'd been careful driving down. *Perhaps it's a tracking device.*

When he got to the car, he began to look around it. First, under the hood, thinking this would buy him some time, making it look like engine trouble. Next, he slipped down low on the side closest to the street, a spot he'd be hard to see from their point of view. Bingo! The tracker in the front right passenger wheel well.

At this point, Joseph exited the pub, noticing Bill hadn't left.

Joseph came across the street. "Billy boy, what are you doing here? Thought you left."

Bill held up the tracking device, nodding down the street toward the Oldsmobile.

Joseph said, "Give me that. I'll get rid of them. Take my keys; my car's in the back. I'll take these guys for a ride later."

Bill smiled, hugged him, then made his way back through the bar, out to Joseph's car in the back alley. Quickly, he was off. Nobody could tell the direction he was headed from where Joseph's car was parked. He lost Owen's henchmen.

As Bill started the journey to Boston, he laid out a game plan while grabbing something quick to eat. Bill needed to counteract the Irish whiskey, as he didn't want to fall asleep behind the wheel.

Throughout the drive, Bill thought about what he'd say, what questions he had, why she would lie to him, why she would hide this. His mind was on overload as he tried to focus on the road, ensuring the whole way that nobody was following him.

PS Cleary

Ps Cleary is a first-time author who has explored a family's story over three books in his series. Had it not been for his desire to take some time away from his career, who knows if he would ever have endeavored in such a project?

Cleary has served in numerous Executive Leadership roles in the financial services sector spanning over 30 years. He has been married to his wife, Cheryl, for 30+ years, building a life of mutual respect and love. Together they have two adult children, one an aspiring chef and a second who is afflicted with Autism. They are strong advocates for special needs causes, active in their local communities.

He likes to play golf and re-finish furniture. In addition, he is an avid hockey and Red Sox fan.